EVOLVING LEXIE

AWAKENING

By JUST KRIS

Published by Should Be Writing, LLC, Ocean Isle Beach, NC

Cover Art by Christina Yoder, DracoArts Studio, www.artdragon.net

Copyright © 2024

First Edition

Hardcover ISBN: 978-1-966050-00-1
Paperback ISBN: 978-1-966050-01-8
eBook ISBN: 978-1-966050-02-5

Visit our website at www.KrisWritesBook.com

DEDICATION

To my children
for showing me the importance of dreams
and
To all the dreamers who helped me on my journey

With Special thanks to Danny Adams
for introducing me to Theo

PROLOGUE

THE BEGINNING

clink

Clink

CLINK

JUST KRIS

1

AN EMPTY FEELING

Some nightmares refuse to let dreamers wake. Andrew Mosby walked the narrow plains between ethereal and material so often that he knew the difference between dream and reality. Dreams he could control, but this nightmare refused to end. He couldn't wish away the empty casket strewn with red, white, and blue roses behind him. The casket and the interminable line of mourners that stretched around the chapel waiting to offer condolences and replay fond memories of his father, the great Admiral Samuel Mosby, was real.

The chapel swarmed with military personnel attired in uniforms from all four branches of the military as well as the Admiral's wealthy clients from the private sector dressed in respectful black. For the past hour, Andrew had greeted mourners he had never met—people he didn't even know existed—people Helen, his father's loyal administrative assistant, had invited.

"It's important for the clients to have closure and a strong sense of the man who will be assuming your father's position in the company," Helen had said.

With decisive efficiency, Helen whispered names as each stranger approached and Andrew went through the perfunctory duties of the bereaved. He took offered hands and thanked each person for coming, sparking connections he could use later. Despite his resolve to focus on the clients, his mind still wandered. The truth was that none of the clients knew exactly how Admiral Samuel Mosby got results—answered the unanswerable questions. Only a select few in the private sector—Helen, Andrew, and Andrew's sister Coretta—knew his father was a dream walker. He let out a sigh at the thought of his sister.

"Denial is just one of the stages of grief," Coretta had said. "The sooner you accept it, the sooner you can get on with your life." In a fury, Andrew had hung up on her—a fury that did absolutely no good because Coretta knew that Andrew would call her again, eventually. Andrew's only mooring since the Coast Guard found the Admiral's sailboat adrift in the Pacific and declared him lost at sea had been Helen. When searches had turned up nothing and Andrew announced that he intended to go ahead with a memorial service, Helen swallowed his words and, for his sake said, "Your father would want you to move on. It's the right thing to do."

It didn't feel right. It felt like failure—like he'd given up on the one person who had never given up on him. Still, Andrew had done everything he could, hadn't he? He'd searched the physical world as well as the dream realm and found nothing, no trace that would lead him to believe anything other than his father was dead.

Peace lilies lined the pulpit of the chapel and exuded a sweet stench that sickened Andrew. Never mind that he'd requested donations to his father's favorite charity, Disabled American Veterans, in lieu of flowers. Large arrangements arrived from the florists by the truckful to dredge up his worst childhood memory, the day he'd had to accept that his mother was never coming back. The white flowers mocked him, reminding him that he'd lost not one parent now, but two. The acrid smell carried Andrew back to the day when he stood beside his father greeting a long line of mourners.

Fourteen years ago, the perfume of the lilies had been just as nauseating, and the gorge cleft in his heart that day had been for his mother. Barely eight years old, he hadn't known what to do. He'd followed his father's example, standing in the receiving line, shaking hands, listening to useless words like, "So sorry little man" and "Your mother was a good woman" as if he didn't know.

Coretta spent that day behind the family privacy screen, crying and being comforted by Helen. Now Coretta's absence was just as conspicuously apparent, if to no one else but Andrew. When Andrew asked Coretta to come to the memorial service, she had replied, "I made my peace when he disappeared, Andrew. I have my students to think about now."

How was peace even possible? At twenty-two, Andrew still felt just as helpless as he had when his mother died, only this time, he didn't have his father to give him strength. He felt as if his entire world had suddenly dissipated like a dream, leaving nothing but questions.

As the next person approached, a man perhaps in his fifties with black hair and silver sideburns, Helen was silent. Andrew glanced at her, and she shrugged apologetically. Forcing a smile, Andrew shook the man's proffered hand.

"My name is Dr. Polk," the man said, his lips tightening into a smile. "Your father and I were colleagues back in the day."

"Nice to meet you, Dr. Polk. Thank you for coming." Andrew braced himself for the questions he knew must be coming. Everyone had questions—questions like, "How could this have happened?" or "How are you holding up?"—questions that were always followed by stories of the amazing Admiral Samuel Mosby.

"No open casket?" Dr. Polk asked. He spread his hands, indicating the casket behind Andrew.

"No," he said, surprised at the man's bluntness. Andrew had ordered the casket for the memorial service hoping it would make it feel more real. It didn't. It only reminded him that he had no closure. "How did you know my father?"

"Forgive me," Dr. Polk said. "You must think me rude. It's just so hard to believe he's dead. We used to joke that he was coated in Teflon. Trouble never stuck to your father, though he created his fair share of it. I rather thought Sam invincible."

Andrew nodded. From the hundreds of stories he'd heard that day, everyone did. "Dad disappeared while sailing off the Pacific coast. There was a storm. The Coast Guard believes he was swept overboard and drowned."

Dr. Polk rubbed his hands together thoughtfully. "Then are you sure he's dead?"

"I'm sure," Andrew said. The words were bitter in his mouth. "I've searched everywhere."

"Hmm." Dr. Polk scrutinized Andrew's face for a moment. "I'm sure you have. Searched everywhere, I mean. My deepest condolences to you." He nodded toward Helen, "and your family."

"Helen is my business associate. I'm the only family my father had to come," Andrew said bitterly, thinking of his sister tucked neatly in some university office far from the torture of the memorial service.

"Then I'm doubly sorry," Dr. Polk said. He took a business card from his wallet and handed it to Andrew. "Alone is a wretched place to be."

Mr. Polk gave a nod and walked away.

Helen leaned toward Andrew, a wisp of her graying hair escaping the tight bun she wore for the occasion. "I hope you know you're not alone." She took the business card from his hand and tucked it into her portfolio with the others.

"I'm sorry, Helen. I didn't mean it that way. You've been so good to me over the years…since Mom died. It's just I can't believe Coretta wouldn't come."

"Coretta has to process this in her own way." Helen smiled that same chiding smile she reserved for his biggest blunders, the one that said *straighten-up, but I love you anyway*. "You're as close to a son as I've ever had."

If they'd been back in his office at Dream Simply Enterprises, Andrew might have hugged her. Instead, he nodded his appreciation with a look that he hoped conveyed it. "I just hate being in the middle of all these strangers who think they understand my grief. I'm tired of meeting people I'll likely never see again and pretending it matters."

Helen nodded. "Not much longer and we'll wrap this up."

Closing his eyes, Andrew tried to will himself out of the nightmare; yet he couldn't wake up from something real. The mourners kept coming. Many introduced themselves as General or Captain or Corporal or Admiral or Chief or Sergeant. His father's position in

Sojourner often crossed all the military branches. The Admiral had pulled people into his confidence based on their qualifications, not the uniform they wore.

Helen touched Andrew's arm lightly, bringing his attention back to the room. He looked at her, and she shrugged. He braced himself to meet another someone his father had known from the military. Before Andrew stood a gangly man with coke-bottle glasses in a wrinkled grey suit. The lines of Andrew's face softened into a smile.

"Now this guy, I know." He took the man's offered hand and pulled him into a crushing hug. "Jon! How great to see you!"

"I'm sorry it isn't on better terms," Jon said, his hand lingering on Andrew's shoulder.

"Thank you for coming." Andrew leaned to whisper to Jon, "And you may be the only one here besides Helen that I can honestly say that to."

Jon pushed his glasses up on his nose. "Sorry I'm late. I'm proof anyone can get lost even with GPS and printed directions. I finally had to park the rental car and take a cab."

"Seriously?" Andrew asked. "Why didn't you just call when your plane landed. If I'd known you were coming, I would have had someone pick you up."

"You know me," Jon winced. "I forgot my cell phone and I couldn't remember your number."

"And I see you still haven't learned to dress yourself either."

"Give me a break." Jon blushed, but his smile was good-natured, like he was used to this kind of ribbing from Andrew. "I packed in a hurry, okay? It's not like you let your best friend know these things. If your sister hadn't called..."

Andrew glanced at Helen. Helen shrugged. "I guess I didn't think you'd have time to come with your new job, Jon."

"She said to tell you, and I quote, 'When you get over yourself, give me a call.' And "You can thank me for Jon later."

"When I get over myself?"

Helen cleared her throat. "At least she had the forethought to invite Jon to be here for you."

"I think that's called being perspicacious," Jon said.

Andrew chuckled. "I didn't realize just how much I've missed you until just now."

"It's good to see you, too. Life hasn't been the same since the party-boy graduated and left town."

"Yeah. I leave and you get a big promotion. How long can you stay?"

"My flight leaves tomorrow evening."

"Then we don't have a lot of time. Jon, this is Helen."

"Nice to meet you finally," Helen said.

"Helen? As in *the Helen*, queen of the care package?"

"The one and only," Andrew replied.

"I think I looked forward to your care packages more than Andrew did."

"You certainly ate the lion's share of the cookies," Andrew laughed. "We'd best get you settled in so we can catch up. Do you know where you left your rental car?"

"I wrote it down." Jon patted the pockets of his suit coat and pulled out a wrinkled napkin.

Helen took the napkin and motioned to a girl wearing a dark tweed suit on the other side of the room. The girl wove through the throng of people toward Helen, a leather organizer tucked under her arm. Helen always anticipated Andrew's needs, like Radar from his father's favorite military sitcom.

Helen cleared her throat and handed the girl the napkin. "Jon, this is Nancy, my administrative assistant."

"You need me, ma'am?" Nancy asked. She smiled at Andrew as she spoke.

"Yes, Nancy. This is Mr. Mosby's friend Jon. Jon, Nancy will make sure your rental car is retrieved and returned to the airport. She can escort you while you are in town."

Jon looked at Andrew with admiration. "Your assistant has an assistant?"

"My new Director of Internal Affairs," Andrew corrected. "And I'd give Helen a thousand administrative assistants if it kept her happy. She's the one who really runs Dream Simply Enterprises. The rest of us just stand around in awe of her presence."

Helen frowned at Andrew. "Don't let him tell you such nonsense."

"It's not nonsense, is it Nancy?" Andrew said, winking at Nancy.

Nancy blushed. "No, sir."

"After you arrange for the return of the rental car, take him to my tailor and get him some new clothes and a decent pair of shoes. And some clothes for the gym. Maybe we can get a racquetball game in before supper."

"Yes, sir," Nancy opened her organizer and started writing.

"Shopping?" Jon pushed his glasses up his nose. "I came to visit you, not to go shopping."

"I'm going to be tied up here for a little while longer. You may as well spend the time productively," Andrew said. "Besides, your shoes don't even match."

Jon looked down at his shoes. He wore one black dress shoe and one brown, neither of which seemed that new, especially beside Andrew's freshly polished Italian Oxfords. "Well maybe just a pair of shoes," Jon said sheepishly.

"Just go with Nancy and let her work her magic. You need to look like you're telling the truth when you tell me all about your new job at—what is the place called again?"

"The National Human Genome Research Institute," Jon said.

"See. It even sounds important." Andrew indicated the line behind Jon. "I shouldn't be here much longer—I hope. I'll meet you back at my office when you're done, and we can catch up."

"Andrew, really." Jon shook his head, throwing a lock of curly brown hair across his forehead.

"Give me some small satisfaction on this dismal day, Jon. Please?"

"Ok. I get it. Be your whipping boy." Jon bowed his head and waved his hands in submission. "Just like old times, eh?"

Andrew pulled his wallet from his back pocket and retrieved his business card. He wrote his personal cell number on the back of the card and handed it to Jon. "In case you get lost again."

As Jon left with Nancy, Andrew let a genuine smile grace his face for just a moment.

"A bit harsh, don't you think?" Helen asked.

"Really?" Andrew glanced at his watch, wishing the formality of the memorial service was over. "Which do you think is better: to know the honest truth or believe a polite lie?"

Helen grimaced and smoothed the edges of her dress. She nodded toward a gentleman approaching and whispered, "Mr. Warren. Client."

"Mr. Warren," Andrew said, taking the man's thick hand. "So good of you to come."

"I knew your father for forty-three years. It's a damn shame. A damn shame," Mr. Warren said, shaking his head. "I've sailed with your father countless times. He doesn't—didn't—make mistakes. He was the best." Mr. Warren shook his head again as if contemplating something far away. "I just can't believe it. My condolences." He shook Andrew's hand again and left, heading for the exit. The space in front of Andrew filled with more people.

When the crowd thinned a little, another man approached wearing civilian clothes but carrying himself like a serviceman; he walked with that unmistakable, perfect posture. "Andrew Mosby," the man said as he took Andrew's hand in a firm grip. "You and I have business to discuss. Your father protected you from a lot you don't even realize. Now that he's gone, that falls to me. I made him a promise."

"Protected me from what?" Andrew asked.

"I expect to hear from you soon." The man said and turned to go.

Not releasing his hand, Andrew said, "But I don't know your name."

The man turned back and looked Andrew in the eyes for a moment. Then he shook Andrew's hand meaningfully. "That never stopped your father." He nodded and Andrew released his hand. As the man pushed his way through the crowd toward the door, Andrew tracked him with is eyes. He wanted to go after him, question him, but instinct told him this wasn't the time. A grizzled woman stepped into the void and offered her white gloved hand. "Your father was a miracle worker," she said. "You have my sincerest condolences, dear." She moved on, and more guests pressed forward.

The Admiral had shared so little about his work for the military, and after the nameless man's visit, Andrew put aside his distaste for the funerary niceties and absorbed the stories with keen interest. Often, they involved some version of his father's famous *Cycle of the Stupids* speech, a speech Andrew had heard so many times from his father that he had it memorized. Everyone at the memorial service had stories of the invincible Admiral. The more they spoke, the more a thought tugged at Andrew's subconscious: surely accidents didn't happen to people like his father.

Helen cleared her throat as a new face approached. A balding man, perhaps in his forties and wearing a First Sergeant's uniform nodded to him.

"Andrew Mosby," the man said. "I'd recognize you anywhere. Spitting image of your father." In one hand he held his hat. The other hand he offered to Andrew.

"And you are?" Andrew asked.

"First Sergeant Joseph Faeder. But you can call me Faeder. Your father always did."

"Thank you for coming." Andrew braced himself for another story about his father's greatness. He felt cheated that his father had never shared those stories with him. They'd shared sailing and things fathers and sons normally share. Never his work for the military.

Faeder rubbed the back of his bald head thoughtfully. "Your father knew the importance of our work at Sojourner. Work that only people like your father could do. People like you."

"Like me?" Andrew asked. So Faeder was close enough to his father to know his real talents—and Andrew's.

"When your father disappeared, he was *researching* several projects for me, as well as a few of his own."

"Such as?" Andrew asked.

"Well, I can't go into that specifically here, but one of the philanthropic cases he had undertaken involved missing girls."

"Missing girls?"

"Yes. Your father…was a good man." Sergeant Faeder reached into the breast pocket of his uniform and pulled out a letter sized envelope. "And as I told him on many occasions, your talents shouldn't be wasted on civilian problems." He paused as if looking for a reaction from Andrew. When he gave none, Faeder continued. "With your father gone, Sojourner has a gaping hole in its program. Sojourner needs you."

"Perhaps," Andrew said. Despite his curiosity, the Admiral had sheltered him from programs like Sojourner for a reason. "But I don't see any reason why *I* would need *it*."

Faeder nodded as if he expected Andrew's response. He handed Andrew the envelope. Then he leaned close to him as if whispering his condolences and said, "Not even to help us catch your father's killer?"

And there it was. The answer to the nagging thoughts he had been having. After a while, even Andrew had had to accept that his father wasn't coming back, but he couldn't accept that someone like his father, someone who had been sailing all his life, would just fall overboard. If, as he'd had to concede, his father really was dead, then perhaps it hadn't been an accident.

"Don't read it now," Faeder whispered. "Pretend it's a donation to DAV and put it away."

Andrew's mind raced with the questions he wanted to ask, but he nodded and said, "Disabled American Veterans thanks you for your generous donation."

"I'll be in touch, Mr. Mosby." Faeder left before Andrew could say anything else and another mourner took his place.

When the memorial service concluded, Andrew returned to his office. As he waited for Jon to change into clothes for the racquetball court, he took the envelope from his breast pocket and opened it. He read the letter carefully, holding the paper as if the words might slide off the page into a pile, a thousand tiny, scrambled letters and numbers on his father's mahogany desk. At that moment Andrew wished the letters *would* cascade off the page, like so many tiny magnets that had suddenly lost their attraction to the paper they occupied. The letter wasn't a request. Faeder had given him a week to get his things in order and report to an underground base in Colorado.

JUST KRIS

2

THE NIGHTMARE

A scream tore itself from Lex's chest as she fought her way awake and away from the nightmares that plagued her sleep. She panted deep gulps of air as if she had been running. Sweat pasted her nightshirt to her skin. The clink of fingernails on glass syringes and the warning beeps and whistles of medical equipment punctuated by screams—were they hers or someone else's—echoed in her memory. The shadow backlit by the dim light of a doorway spoke in a low voice, both strange and familiar, and filled the air with words she could not remember.

When she awoke, always the sounds and images lingered in her mind until she wondered if they were real, or if they had been real, or if in the time before here and now, the time she could not remember, she had done something truly horrible, and this was her penance. A choked sob escaped in gasps, and she drew her knees up to her chest and hugged them tightly as the residual images and sounds that clouded her brain slowly faded into the darkness.

3

MONGRELS

In the bowels of an ancient mountain in Colorado, Andrew Mosby slammed from one side of the hardwood racquetball court to the other, diving for the ball and smacking it brutally with his racquet. Sweat formed on his brow and ran into his hazel-gray eyes as he fought Private Heathcliff Payne for every point. Unlike playing racquetball with Jon after the Admiral's memorial service, Payne made winning a challenge that Andrew accepted whenever his work allowed.

Whether back home in Las Vegas or in the underground base, Andrew whittled his tensions down on the court before dream walking whenever possible. Playing to the pinnacle of exhaustion made it easier to fall asleep; more than that, racquetball calmed Andrew's nerves and helped him focus. He needed that now. Since arriving on base to join Sojourner, thoughts of his father's death clouded his thinking. Andrew couldn't afford to be distracted when he dream walked.

"You're never going to beat me, Payne," Andrew said, a crooked grin showing his perfect teeth.

"In your dreams," Payne drawled, serving the ball with a hard backhand.

"Or yours," Andrew grunted as he lunged for the ball.

Payne stopped and pointed a long finger at Andrew. "Stay out of my head, pretty boy."

Andrew ricocheted the ball off the front and side walls so that it came back and slammed Payne in the back of the head. "I wouldn't want to see what's in your head. It's too twisted."

Grinning as if a gauntlet had been thrown before him, Payne said, "You know me so well already."

First Sergeant Faeder tapped on the small square window of the court. Opening the insulated door, Andrew stepped into the drab hall, grabbed his towel, and wiped the sweat from his face. "Do you have something for me?"

"Not sure I'll ever understand this part of your preparations," Faeder said as he handed Andrew a manila folder and an envelope. "Not sure I care either, as long as you get results."

Payne stuck his head outside the racquetball court. "You coming back or...?" He stopped when he saw Faeder and frowned.

Faeder's round face reddened. "I think you forgot to salute Private Payne."

Mechanically Payne brought his flattened hand up, and laying it on top of his close cut high and tight, stripped it downward, sending a spray of sweat in Faeder's direction. "Yes, sir!"

Faeder dodged backwards and swore.

Andrew pinched his lips together to hide his smile. "I'll catch up with you later. Keep practicing. Maybe one day you'll get lucky and beat me."

"When I do, it won't be luck." Payne bounced his head once, scowled at Faeder, and closed the door. The thunk of the ball hitting the wall and the squeak of his athletic shoes marked his solitary return to the game.

"Damn mongrels," Faeder muttered.

"You did try to break up their happy family," Andrew said, which was true. After the Admiral's death, Faeder had disbanded the group, reassigning them to the ends of the earth.

"Happy? Demented is more like it." Faeder growled indignantly. "If you hadn't refused to join sojourner without them... I don't know what your father saw in those military misfits," His face was a patchwork of angry splotches. "Or you for that matter. I could

18

find someone else to torture you on the racquetball court."

Andrew laughed. "No one would enjoy it as much as Payne."

"I'll never understand why your father would gather the dregs of the four branches of the military and make them a unit. They're disrespectful and reckless."

"I've found the Mongrels to be quite useful," Andrew said. Faeder, meaning it as an insult, had first called the men who now served Andrew *mongrels* when Andrew's father had put them together as a team. However, the men wore the name with pride, if for no other reason than it seemed to irritate Faeder. "They're good at what they do."

Faeder pulled a pill bottle from his pocket, took out an antacid and crunched it between his teeth. "I'd have to agree. They're quite good at upsetting my ulcer. At least you've done me the favor of not keeping the chief flunky on base."

"I'll talk to them," Andrew said, hoping to bring an end to the argument. He swallowed the remaining water from his water bottle and then opened the folder designated simply as Hector. The first article in the folder was an eight by ten photo of a man fully clothed in a gabardine suit with a wilted boutonniere pinned to the lapel. One hand grasped his chest as if keeping his heart from escaping; the other lay lifelessly by his side.

"You know I can't work with the dead, right?" Andrew asked, taking in the minute details of the twisted victim bathed in the gloom of the fluorescent lights.

"Hector's not dead. At least not yet," Faeder said, shoving his stubby fingers into the waist pockets of his battle dress uniform. "That's how we found him. We took him to the infirmary and sedated him. That won't mess things up for you, will it?"

"No. That's actually good." Andrew gathered the rest of his things off the bench outside the racquetball court and stuffed them into his duffel. In the private sector Andrew felt more like a dream stalker, having to wait until he could find his subjects asleep and dreaming. Here in the mountain, the doctors and scientists could just create the right conditions for a dream walk.

"You dream walkers all have your quirks."

Andrew threw his duffel over his shoulder and started walking toward the elevator that would take him to the infirmary. He needed to see Hector for himself. "So, what's wrong with him?"

Faeder scratched his bald head in search of the hair that long ago flourished there. "We don't know. It's like he's in some kind of trance. He's one of our top scientists. Good one, too. Specializes in genetics. Of all the people here at the base that could have been targeted, this one doesn't make sense. The doctor's running tests to see if he was drugged."

They halted at the elevator. Andrew flipped through the rest of the file. There was nothing out of the ordinary at first glance.

"The only thing he's said since they found him was, 'Killer' or 'Kill her' or something. God only knows what he meant by that."

"Killer?" Andrew mused as they boarded the elevator.

"That's it."

"Huh." Andrew looked at his reflection in the hazy elevator doors as they closed in front of him. He ran a hand through his black hair letting it fall in thick waves. Even though he spent a great deal of time working underground, his face was tanned from hiking in the Colorado Mountains, a habit that aggravated Faeder since it generally meant Andrew couldn't be located.

Silence settled around them as Andrew considered the possible meanings of Hector's words. In the photo, Hector's eyes stared into nothingness as if the fire that burned deep within him blocked all desire for the life that was here and now. What could so completely consume a man who just a few days prior worked as an otherwise happy, productive scientist?

Faeder shoved his thick fingers back into the front pockets of his BDU's. His fatigues fit him comfortably, as if simply an extension of his body. "I just need you to work your voodoo and give us what you can. Your father always came through for us when we needed him."

"I'm not my father. I never claimed to be."

"And I'm not asking you to be, although if he were here, God rest his soul, he'd be the first person I'd ask to do this," Faeder said. "Look. I know there's a lot your father didn't teach you yet—things I couldn't possibly. But if you've got half the talent your father had, then I know you can get more from one walk with Hector than all the other dream walkers in the program."

When Andrew arrived on base a few weeks earlier, Faeder briefed him in his office. Andrew spent most of the briefing staring at the plaque over Faeder's shoulder which listed the ten names of the original dream walkers in Sojourner, including his father, Admiral Samuel Mosby. He'd interrupted Faeder twice to ask about the plaque, at which point Faeder had said, "Yes, yes. That's your father's name. I realize you're not military, but could you at least pretend to have a little discipline so we can get through this?"

Andrew hadn't interrupted again, but he didn't stop looking at the plaque either. It wasn't his father's name, Samuel Mosby, but his mother's maiden name, Rebecca Longfellow, which captured his attention. The other names, some of which also sounded familiar, seemed to dim and fade into the background. Had his mother really been a part of Sojourner?

The elevator stopped and two men in white lab coats entered the elevator. Faeder twisted his head to look at the photo in Andrew's hand. "You know I've tried to impress on you, without great success I might add, that your position as a dream walker makes you a powerful and influential man."

"Things my father tried to impress on me as well, I assure you."

"Then I'm sure he also told you that with that power and influence comes...."

"Seriously? You're going to quote comic books?" Andrew said tersely.

"Wisdom is wisdom," Faeder said.

"I get it. I do." A world of responsibility had been thrust upon Andrew. Not only had he assumed his father's positions as president and dream walker at Dream Simply Enterprises when his father was declared lost at sea, he was here, wasn't he? Andrew had to accept his father's death, but he would never again accept that it was an accident.

He had come to find his father's killer, a responsibility he took seriously when he accepted Faeder's *invitation* to join Sojourner. For that reason, he swallowed the rest of what he wanted to say to Faeder and asked, "Is there anything you can tell me that this file can't?" Faeder supervised all the dream walkers in Sojourner, but as First Sergeant to the base commander, his knowledge extended beyond Andrew's unit.

The elevator stopped and the two men in lab coats debarked. As the doors closed again, Faeder's voice dropped to barely a whisper. "We think this might be the work of Omega Industries. We think they may have had something to do with your father's death."

Andrew's eyes focused on Faeder. "Here?"

Faeder shook his head. "Not here necessarily." He glanced at Andrew as if confirming that he'd been hooked. Then he looked back at the photo of Hector. "He had a few days R and R. We don't know where he's been, which is why we need you. He's obviously not talking or not able to talk, and with Omega's possible involvement, I thought you might be properly motivated. I need results, and I need them now."

"And if I get those results, you'll tell me more about Omega?"

Pulling a hand from his pocket, Faeder began rubbing his stubby fingers nervously on the back of his bald head. "I can't risk tainting your paradigm."

"Can you risk not finding anything at all?"

A vein in Faeder's temple throbbed faster and his voice became even more serious. "We need to know what he knows. And soon. Before this happens again. Sojourner can't afford to lose more dream walkers like your father and the government can't afford to have its top scientists FUBAR."

Andrew didn't have to ask what that military acronym meant, nor what the consequences would be if all their scientists ended up like this, mentally malfunctioning *beyond all recognition*.

The elevator doors opened, and they entered the infirmary. Hector lay in a hospital bed hooked to various monitors and tubes. He looked fragile, his face still anguished despite his sedation. Andrew took Hector's hand in his. He wished he could tell him it would be alright, that he would be there soon to help him find his way back. A stray shock of curly brown hair cascaded over Hector's forehead and into his eyes. He reminded Andrew of Jon.

"You really think what happened to Hector has something to do with my father's death?"

Faeder nodded. "I do. I believe Omega is responsible for both."

Andrew brushed the hair away from Hector's eyes, trying to imagine what he might find in his mind. He couldn't help wondering what the derangement of a scientist had to do with his father's death. If it truly was the work of someone in Omega, he was thankful Faeder had given him the opportunity to search Hector's dreams. "I'll do what I can. Is everything ready?"

"I believe so. You're sure moving and sedating him isn't going to make things more difficult?"

Andrew nodded and released Hector's hand. "Not a bit." While Faeder might oversee the dream walkers, it was clear he had no idea how they worked. However, having access to information and files, like the one on Hector, made him useful.

"I hope you're right," Faeder said nervously. "I'll be waiting."

As Andrew walked through the drab, gray corridors to his room, his thoughts drifted. He had never been able to keep secrets from his father. If the Admiral couldn't extract the truth from him in his dreams, he could always get it from Andrew's friends' dreams, though he rarely resorted to that. Eventually Andrew simply told his father everything about his misadventures, sometimes even before he did things. It was easier that way, and quite frankly, a whole lot less painful. Dreams were not only the playground of the subconscious; they were also the proving ground of emotions, and no one could manipulate emotions in dreams like his father.

Andrew had to admit, he hadn't been the easiest son to raise, especially for a single father. Perhaps that was why the Admiral waited until Andrew graduated from college and started working at Dream Simply Enterprises to share his best kept secrets. After all, Andrew couldn't build a defense against the Admiral's techniques if he wasn't familiar with them. Still, the openness of the dream world had brought closeness to their relationship that few could rival.

The Admiral's infectious smile had always welcomed Andrew into his presence, even on his hardest days. Although he rarely allowed conversation to drift towards himself and especially not about his work for the government, the Admiral always wanted to hear about Andrew's accomplishments, triumphs, and newest ideas. He seemed genuinely honored to listen to Andrew's problems, disappointments, and failures. How many times had Andrew sat in the wingback leather chair in his father's office at Dream Simply Enterprises, talking about nothing in particular, never fathoming that one day that luxury would be gone?

In his room, Andrew called Payne and asked him to find out everything he could about Omega, stowed his gear, and took a quick shower. Then he studied Hector's personnel file and visited his office, noting every detail. Hector Kilgore had worked in the underground bunker for the last nineteen years on various projects without incident.

Andrew could tell by his psychological profile that he would be fairly easy to access. Deciphering the dreams of a scientific genius, on the other hand, might be another matter, though he'd had some experience doing just that with Jon, his unlikely college roommate. Andrew wondered, besides Omega's possible involvement, if his friendship with Jon had some bearing on Faeder's choice to let Andrew work with Hector. Either way, Andrew imagined Faeder had an extensive file delineating everything that might motivate him to be more compliant in his duties and less aggravating to his ulcer.

Before lying on his back on his twin bunk, Andrew opened the envelope Faeder brought him and removed a small lock of Hector's curly brown hair. He didn't need Hector's hair to access his dreams, but it made it easier to focus on him, and therefore easier to find his dream. The hair, like a needle on a compass, pointed him in the right direction. He rubbed the hair thoughtfully between his fingers and closed his eyes.

4

A WALK WITH HECTOR

Andrew entered the dark gulf between his dreams and the dreams of others. The paths stretched before him, familiar as the streets of his hometown. Only the destination was new. His passage made wakes and eddies in the darkness that he could feel, like ripples in a pool of water. As he imagined, he reached Hector's dream with ease. He walked the perimeter, watching, taking his time deciding on the least intrusive entry point. He didn't want to startle Hector. Even if he was drugged, dreams were delicate. It took poise and finesse to enter them unnoticed.

Hector's office almost mirrored Andrew's memory of it. Graphs, genomic charts, a large calendar, and a smudged whiteboard filled with annotations—things one might imagine would be found in a scientist's office—covered the drab, battleship-gray walls. Amid the officious trappings, Hector stood out. He sat at his desk in a worn, wheeled chair that leaned dangerously backwards and to the left from years of Hector sitting askew while he labored over the building blocks of mankind. He wore a white lab coat over plaid pajamas and on top of his head, a multicolored balloon hat, the kind that a clown might make at a child's birthday party, bounced and bobbed as he worked.

Hector's eyes, exaggeratedly large behind the thick, convex lenses of his glasses, focused on the object perched on the palm of his hand. He twirled a Rubik's cube, looking at it slowly from every angle, occasionally twisting it a couple of times and then frowning in frustration. The colors mirrored his balloon hat and jumbled in kaleidoscopic patterns on each face.

One other thing stood out just as conspicuously as Hector. On one wall hung a poster of a perfectly proportioned woman dressed in a shimmering black sleeveless dress. Her face was completely obscured by a mask of white feathers except for her perfect pale chin and luscious red lips. She was a dream worth pursuing, not only because of her beauty, but because that picture wasn't part of Hector's normal décor.

While most dream walkers avoided getting close to their subject's environment so as not to pollute their findings, Andrew's father had made it a point to visit them. *The answers lay in the small things,* he had said, *the minute differences, things others would overlook as dream refuse.* While other dream walkers questioned the subject, the Admiral taught Andrew to question the dream. The Admiral had disagreed with Sojourner's—Faeder's—policy which kept dream walkers separated from their subjects and each other. That was one of the things that made him so successful. He took risks.

Andrew added a lab coat to his appearance and entered Hector's dream. He also added a chair on the other side of the desk and sat down.

"How've you been, Hector?" Andrew asked.

Hector didn't look away from the cube. "I've been better," he said. "I think someone's messing with me. They've scrambled the colors on my Rubik's cube."

"I'm sure you can work it again," Andrew reassured.

"No. I could work it if they'd just scrambled the cube. They've moved the colors." He set the cube on the desk in front of Andrew and sighed. "It can't be solved like this."

"Maybe I could help you figure it out," Andrew said helpfully, wondering how the cube fit into his recent break in sanity.

Hector looked at him for the first time. "Do I know you?" he asked, the edge of his dream thinning.

"I'm the new guy. I was just hired," Andrew said calmly. His voice, reassuring and smooth, put Hector at ease.

Hector regarded Andrew for a moment, considering his presence. "Vince's new assistant?" he asked.

"That's right," Andrew answered, allowing Hector to incorporate him into his dream instead of forcing himself into it.

"I hadn't realized they'd filled the position so quickly," Hector said. The edges of his dream firmed as he accepted Andrew's identity and continued with the observations of the cube. He leaned across the desk toward Andrew, "But what Vince wants, Vince gets. Am I right?"

Andrew nodded, hiding his amusement at the office politics.

Hector took his balloon hat off and laid it on the desk. As he did, the balloons twisted themselves into the familiar shape of a DNA double helix. The DNA slowly spun in midair, defying gravity. Hector scowled disgustedly at the double helix and then looked at Andrew. "Do you know who did this?" Hector asked, pointing at the cube.

Andrew shook his head. "No, I can't imagine anyone wanting to."

"Me either," he agreed, picking the cube up again and spinning the colors a few times. He shook his head. "Not possible."

Andrew, realizing that Hector was slipping back into his contemplations and that he was losing ground, changed his approach. "That was a pretty cruel joke to play. I bet there aren't very many people you know who would do that."

"No," Hector agreed. "No one I know would do that. It's unethical."

"Then someone you don't know, or maybe that you just met, must have done it," Andrew said.

Hector's eyes narrowed and he looked at Andrew suspiciously. "Do I know you?"

"Yes. We've met, remember?" Hector seemed skeptical, so he continued. "Vince's assistant. Truthfully, I'd rather be yours."

The stroke to his ego worked. He settled back into his musings. "I could certainly use you. I get very little help, and even less funding. No one really believes in my research."

"I do," Andrew said, hoping his encouragement would lead somewhere. "You were going to tell me who you thought messed with your Rubik's cube."

Hector nodded slowly. "I don't know very many new people. I don't get out much."

"Maybe not, but you do get out some," Andrew said, pointing toward the poster of the woman on the wall. "You had to get that somewhere."

Hector nodded.

"I hear there's a zoo topside. Have you been there?" Andrew asked.

Hector shook his head. He set the cube down on his desk again and looked closely at the poster. "Do you like Karaoke?"

"I guess," Andrew said. "Is that something you enjoy?"

Hector nodded and vaguely familiar music played from somewhere in the distance, though it was too quiet to make out.

"Is there a good place to go for that around here?" Andrew asked. "Maybe somewhere you've been recently?"

The edges of his dream changed, and a dimly lit bar materialized around them as the office faded. Glasses clinked and low conversations murmured, punctuated by the whoosh of seltzer being sprayed into glasses. Hector's pajamas faded as well, leaving a wrinkled pair of gabardine pants and a white oxford shirt in their place.

"Seems like a good place to have a little fun," Andrew said, taking in all the details. So far his luck was holding out. Suggestions in a dream might or might not take you where you wanted to go. He was hopeful. The better his results, the more access Faeder gave him to the information and privileges he wanted, things that could help him find out what really happened to his father. "What's this place called again?"

"You picked this place to meet, Quin. How much have you had to drink?"

"Too much, I guess," Andrew said, making a mental note of the new name. "I'm just a little confused."

"We're at Mei Mei's. You said you wanted me to meet someone. Someone special. Is she here?" Hector picked up one of the beers on the table and took a drink.

"Yes. She's here. She's excited to meet you. She'll be right over." Andrew said, taking a drink of the beer in front of him.

The sound of snapping fingers and piano chords broke loudly into the middle of their conversation. The floor lights on the stage lit up suddenly. Hector nodded toward the stage. "Of course. You said she likes to make an entrance," he said over the music.

A girl stood on the stage, her bare back to the bar. She wore a blue-black wig and a black sleeveless dress that touched the floor with slits up each side to mid-thigh revealing smooth muscular legs and dainty feet in stiletto heels. Her voice hugged Andrew like the satin arms of a lover as she began the words to Killer Queen. When she turned, her eyes peered mysteriously through a large white feathered mask; only her inviting rose red lips and pert little chin were visible beneath the feathers. As she sang, she looked directly at Hector, and he seemed unable to look anywhere else. Who could blame him? She was enchanting, even with the very minimal view she allowed of her face, perhaps more so because of it.

When she finished singing, she walked to where Hector sat and teased her fingers through his hair, causing him to swallow nervously. The pupils of his eyes dilated slightly as she traced a delicate finger over his lips. She leaned as if to kiss him, and instead pulled away and laughed. "I'm not that easy," she said. "You must earn my love. I'm worth it, aren't I?"

"I'd follow you anywhere," Hector whispered, completely enthralled, mesmerized even.

She was just a projection, a part of Hector's memory, but what a memory. If someone could ravage Hector mentally, she could do it, and if she was what he was dreaming, Andrew could understand wanting to stay unconscious.

"What's your name?" Andrew asked her.

She looked at Andrew angrily through the mask of feathers, made a production of turning her beautifully sculpted back to him, and walked away.

When she disappeared, Hector looked at Andrew, his face filled with confusion. "What did you say your name was again?"

"Quin." Andrew said, "I asked you here, remember?"

Hector nodded. "You wanted to know about my research," he said. His dream morphed into his office again. "No one ever wants to know about my research." He ran his fingers over the double helix strand of DNA swirling above his desk and it twisted back into a multicolored balloon hat. He placed the hat back on his head without looking at it. His eyes focused on the Rubik's cube. He picked it up, looked at the colors, and shook his head. "Somebody's messing with me. Everything's scrambled," he said sadly.

Andrew nodded. "I'm sure you can figure it out. Just keep trying."

Hector shook his head and turned away.

Andrew left his dream, returning the way he came and settled back in his own consciousness. He opened his eyes and looked at his watch as he sat up. The night was almost gone. Time warped in the dream realm. The search for Hector's dream, which had seemed to go by quickly, would have taken the most time. The dream itself might have taken place in seconds. Still, the process left him tired. He went to his desk and picked up the phone, dialing Faeder's extension.

Faeder answered the phone on the first ring. He'd been waiting for Andrew's call. "What did you find out?" Faeder asked eagerly.

It wasn't a quick and dirty answer, but it was something. Hopefully it was enough. "You'll want to start your search at Mei Mei's bar in Colorado Springs," Andrew said.

"I know the place," Faeder said. "Anything else?"

"Two people of interest. A man named Quin and a very beautiful woman. The woman may sing at the bar."

"There aren't any Quin's on our roster here at the base."

"I don't know," Andrew said. For some reason the name seemed familiar. Had his father ever mentioned a Quin? He didn't think so. "Could be an alias, but I have a feeling he doesn't work here. Double check it anyway. Hector said he was interested in his research. Oh, and Hector had a preoccupation with a scrambled Rubik's cube. Not sure what that represents, but I think it has to do with his research.

I might be able to learn more, but not tonight."

"Sure. Get some rest, and thanks Andrew," Faeder said. "We'll let you know what we find."

"I'm sure you will," Andrew said and hung up the phone. Then he made a second call to Payne, telling him the same things, adding, "If you could get a copy of his research for me, maybe I could get Jon to look at it."

"I'll see what I can do," Payne said and hung up.

The government never slept, and the workload seemed endless, though this was Andrew's first assignment that might involve Omega. The possibility that he would finally find out what happened to his father drove him onward. The man he knew as his father was kind, generous, and dedicated to helping people. Who would want to kill him? Certainly not someone in the private sector. It was here, with the government, that the answers would be found.

The mysterious woman in the black dress might just be the best lead he had yet. After all, if the Government knew for sure what had happened to his father, they wouldn't have *presumed* him dead. Someone somewhere knew something. And this killer queen was certainly the most unusual individual he'd encountered in his search. He had a new place to start, but not tonight.

Andrew went back to his bunk, this time only looking for relief from his mental exhaustion.

5

LEAD THE WAY

When Andrew awoke, he found a folder on his desk from Payne. Despite Faeder's lack of confidence in the mongrel's, Andrew was glad they were on his side, especially considering how easily Payne had slipped into and out of his room while he was sleeping.

What little research Payne had been able to do on Omega Industries led him on a circuitous route to nowhere. Omega Industries was just a conglomerate of odd companies on paper—on paper being the key. The industries mostly involved the legitimate businesses in the medical field—health insurance, pharmaceutical and hospital equipment manufacturers, infertility clinics, cosmetic testing laboratories, etc. Besides a tremendous amount of cash flow and a few red flags by the FDA, there was nothing particularly glaring about Omega's operations. Nothing that he could find tied his father to any of the companies or their subsidiaries.

Locating anyone involved in Hector's mental ravaging had been a problem also, for Faeder as well as Payne. The name Quin had been a dead end. No one at Mei Mei's karaoke bar could remember either a Quin or any other man with the woman in the black dress, and only had a vague recollection of Hector. Everyone, however, remembered the beautiful, mysterious woman, though all their accounts of her seemed to differ. She was everything the women wished they were—

intelligent, confident, and beautiful—and everything the men wished they could possess.

Further walks with Hector divulged no further useful information. In fact, Andrew could not recreate the scene in the bar or the mysterious Quin, no matter what he did. Besides the calendar that remained on Hector's office wall, the visions of the woman had disappeared, too. It was as if the memory had been forgotten, erased, or never happened. Beyond Hector's preoccupation with genetic anomalies that Andrew felt had something to do with the woman, there was nothing tangible about the girl that could be acquired.

After a quick search through the usual places, Andrew found Faeder in the mess hall eating lunch and sat down across from him to argue his point for the third time since his first dream walk with Hector. "Faeder, I'm telling you, Hector's dream, his problem, this girl—they all have something to do with genetic anomalies."

"His job is genetic anomalies, Andrew," Faeder said, shaking his head dismissively. "Of course his dreams include genetics! And you knew that before you entered his dream. You went to his office. Foreknowledge taints a dream."

"This is more than that," Andrew insisted. Trying to convince Faeder that Hector's interest in genetics was more than just an interest in his work further fueled Andrew's belief that Faeder was an imbecile.

"Unfortunately, Andrew, you seem to be the only dream walker on my team that can form an opinion," Faeder said. "I can't verify your data."

So, others had tried to access Hector's dreams and failed. "But what I told you about Mei Mei's. The girl…"

"But there was no other man and the girl seems to have disappeared from the face of the earth," Faeder said. He pushed his plate away and pulled out his antacids. "Look, Andrew. Dream walkers are just that. You give us your best guesses, and we take it from there."

"But…"

"Eating in the mess hall is hard enough without you trying to tell me how to do my job," Faeder said.

"And yet you want to tell me how to do mine. You brought me

here for more than just parlor tricks. You know Dream Simply Enterprises does more than broker information. We secure assets for our clients. Your assets are your people."

"It doesn't matter. We're transporting Hector out to a secure medical facility tonight."

"More secure than this?" Andrew asked incredulously.

"We need the space in the infirmary," Faeder said simply, waving his hand in dismissal.

"Need it for what? Hangnails and paper cuts?" Andrew said tersely. The words escaped his mouth before he could call them back.

Faeder's eyes narrowed dangerously, his gaze burning into Andrew's. "God knows trying to instill some military discipline in you hasn't been easy," Faeder said, the red splotches in his face darkening. "Most days I've felt somewhere between a babysitter and a mustang wrangler, and I told the commander as much this week in my briefing. On top of that, you know I have no love for those mongrels you keep around. So don't push me."

"Look," Andrew said, softening his tone, "just give me a week. I can help him, I know it."

"He's slipped into a coma, Andrew. How are you going to help him?"

"You'd have given Dad more time," Andrew said.

"Your dad wasn't a spoiled..." Faeder stopped and took a deep breath, letting it out slowly before beginning again. "Your dad knew his duty."

"And so do I," Andrew countered. "My duty is to the people of this base. You need every resource you can get, and that includes Hector. Awake."

Faeder's eyes bored into Andrew's as if he was used to changing people's minds with a single look. Andrew didn't flinch but held his gaze with what he hoped would come across as sincerity. He'd never imagined how badly bureaucracy would override good sense when he'd first been called upon to join Sojourner. Inheriting Dream Simply Enterprises after his father's death was vastly different than being a cog in the government's machine, a spoke in Faeder's wheel. No one could fully understand the danger in this kind of work, except a dream walker. Still, when Andrew was willing to take the risk, Faeder seemed unwilling to let him.

Faeder shook his head slowly back and forth as he looked at Andrew. He took a sip of his drink and swished it in his mouth and swallowed. "What if Hector does wake up? What then? Do we just let him go back to work like nothing happened? Either way, he's been compromised, and can't be allowed to continue here."

Andrew sat agape for a moment, shocked by Faeder's statement. He wondered if he shouldn't have added ear washes to the paper cuts and hangnails the infirmary saw. Could he have possibly heard correctly? Even as the question occurred to him, he knew he had heard Faeder perfectly.

"So, you'd prefer to leave him trapped inside his head?"

"It didn't sound that bad. According to you, he's working. It could be worse."

Andrew closed his jaw slowly and nodded. "Maybe you should let all your scientists have a few days off. See what happens then. The way I see it, no one is safe while these two people, Quin and this girl, are out there."

Faeder rubbed his hand over his mouth as if considering the implications of Andrew's words. "Leave can be canceled."

"People need to blow off steam. I can help you with that. And I can help you with Hector, too. Wouldn't you rather Hector be here when he wakes up than some backwoods facility where you couldn't question him right away? Give me one week, Faeder, to bring him back. After that, awake or not, he's yours."

Faeder's hand unconsciously went to the back of his head and started rubbing, signaling Andrew that he had won. "One week," Faeder conceded, frustration thick in his voice.

Andrew wondered if Faeder's irritation was because he had lost the argument, or because he knew Andrew was right. Had it even occurred to Faeder to wonder who would be next?

Although Andrew had never worked with coma patients before, he felt he could reach Hector. There was something odd about his confusion, his preoccupations, his circular logic. Andrew credited his fondness for the painfully awkward scientist to his similarities to Jon, and he was determined not to give up.

Nightly Andrew slipped into the liquid blackness in search of Hector's dreams. He spoke calming, reassuring words and joked about Sojourner, Vince, and Faeder. Andrew even taught Hector to play racquetball, though the physics in the dream were far different than in the physical plain. Hector became more and more comfortable following Andrew from one adventure to another, never understanding that Andrew was leading him closer and closer to the edge of reality.

While Faeder and the doctors gave up on Hector's recovery, Andrew refused to be defeated. Andrew worked until Hector let go of his preoccupation and confusion, and relaxed. Andrew continued until Hector found the way back to the place between dream and consciousness that led to the real world.

When Hector finally awoke and understood what had happened to him, he asked to see Andrew. He thanked him for his friendship and for not giving up. Unfortunately, awake, Hector had no memory of the R and R days spent off base, or of the woman who seemed to be the cause of his malady, or anyone named Quin for that matter. Much like the inherent forgetfulness that accompanies waking from a dream, it was as if the encounter had never happened.

Andrew, though, could not forget. The memory of the girl haunted him. Perhaps she was the key to finding his father's murderer. Perhaps she was his killer. Either way, he had to find her, and he would not relent until she told him everything she knew.

JUST KRIS

6

MISSING PIECES

The blood red wisp of material Lex wore could hardly be called a dress. There was scarcely enough to cover what had to be covered, never mind what should have been. The front fastened around her neck and dropped dangerously low before coming together just below her navel. The back began at the skirt, which wrapped itself around her like a designer glove, and ended well before mid-thigh.

With one last approving look at herself in the full-length mirror in her room, Lex heard the door open. She didn't turn around. The quiet footsteps were unmistakably those of nurse Ophelia. Hers was the first face Lex remembered seeing when she woke frightened and confused in the Omega compound three years ago. Ophelia held her hand through the pain, hummed soothingly through the nights sitting up with her.

Ophelia was the closest thing Lex had to a friend. She often imagined what her life might be like if Ophelia was her mother and she had never heard of Omega, not that she was allowed to voice her wishes. Tonight was no different as Ophelia took the hair brush from Lex and drew it slowly through her long hair, the same golden brown as Ophelia's. As she brushed Lex's hair, she hummed in her soothing alto tones.

Ophelia stopped humming abruptly. "It's been said that your

target tonight is a dreamer."

"That's not a luxury I've been afforded," Lex said dourly, her eyes flitting to Ophelia's gaze in the mirror.

"That's not exactly what I meant," Ophelia said, easily sidestepping Lex's sarcasm. "It's said that he can visit your dreams. Talk to you, like I'm talking to you now, while you're asleep."

Her target already seemed like a dream, a larger-than-life fantasy. This new information only added to the superstition surrounding the fabled Andrew Mosby. Was Ophelia trying to frighten her? Tease her? Lex met Ophelia's gaze steadily in the mirror before her. She had never looked so serious.

Lex shifted her gaze to her own eyes. The idea that someone could invade her dreams sounded like a bad joke—or a nightmare, and she had enough of those already. Awake, she was confident she could hold her own. She could even wear this wisp of a red dress and wear it well, even if it did irritate her to be esteemed based on her looks. She was smart and Omega knew it. Still, it hadn't been her brain that they'd chosen to use; it had been her looks and the effect she had on men when she was in their presence.

"If what you are saying is true, how will I know if I am awake or dreaming?" Lex asked. She turned to face Ophelia, not trusting the mirror to speak the truth.

Ophelia handed Lex the brush and took a deep breath, letting it out slowly before she spoke in her rich alto voice. As she spoke, she seemed far away, as distant as an old movie coming across the years from a faraway time and place.

"I understand," Ophelia said, "that it is not an easy concept to teach—knowing the difference between what's real and what's dream. Our subconscious enjoys the peace and quiet of our consciousness not constantly fighting to be in control. The subconscious part of our minds does everything it can to keep our conscious mind in the dark."

"You really believe he can do it—enter my dreams—don't you?" Lex asked.

"If you can't control him, Lex, you'll put us all in jeopardy."

"And if I can?" Lex dared to ask. "Will you finally tell me about my life before I came here?" Silence stalked the room. Lex counted her heartbeats, waiting, hoping.

"You had no life before you came here." Ophelia finally answered, the chill in her voice as cold as the iceberg that sank the Titanic. "It's best you accept that."

Swallowing her disappointment, Lex gave the only acceptable answer. "Yes, ma'am."

Turning Lex around for one final look, Ophelia asked, her voice deep and rich with Southern charm again, "Are you ready?"

"As I'll ever be, though I'd like to have a chat with the person who picked out this dress."

Ophelia smiled and nodded. "It's quite the piece, isn't it?" She produced a small red handbag, pulled out a tube of lipstick, and handed it to Lex.

"*Piece* is *all* it is," Lex said, frowning at her reflection in the mirror. "I'm still looking for the rest of it. Just once I'd like for someone to look at me and see more than this." She swept her hands along the length of her body.

"You pull it off splendidly," Ophelia said with satisfaction. She took a perfume bottle from her pocket and spritzed Lex. "Now buck up. You need to nail this one."

Lex nodded at Ophelia, her only friend and mentor. She took the lipstick, the same deep red as the dress, and applied it to her lips. She pinched her lips together, sliding them back and forth to make the lip color even. Despite Ophelia's odd forewarning, she was ready. Regardless of Lex's fashion preference, she had more than enough training and raw nerve to pull off this persona.

Lex stood, back straight and eyes determined, ready to do what it would take to make Ophelia proud. She wanted more than just Ophelia's approval. She wanted more freedom within the strict regime of Omega. That, and answers about her past, if she had a mother, a father, a home. Perhaps with this assignment she could finally earn those things.

Ophelia took the key from her pocket and unlocked Lex's door from the inside, letting them out into the hallway where Ray, her handler, waited to escort her to her assignment. "Don't let us down. Show that Andrew Mosby what you're made of."

Lex smiled, her lips the color of blood. "With pleasure."

7

MEET THE OBJECTIVE

As objectified as she felt, Lex had to admit, the crimson dress made her feel dangerous. On her way out of the Omega compound, she decked two guards with wandering eyes, just on general principle.

An hour later, a grey stretch limo materialized through the mists of evening at the corner of Seventeenth and Union Streets. Five svelte shadows, hired through an escort service waited. According to her handler Ray, the same scenario had played out every Friday for the past month, often with different women and always with different locations. The shadows hardly noticed when Lex joined them. She pulled the collar of her trench coat higher to keep out the haze.

A stone-faced chauffeur got out, circled the car, and opened the door. The women slid inside without a word. They rode silently toward their destination as the fog outside swirled around the tinted windows. For the women hired by the escort service, the night meant easy money. For Lex, it was simply a step toward her objective to control Andrew Mosby.

As the limo slid liquidly through the darkening city, Lex considered what she knew. A recent string of incidents involving government employees and, particularly, a certain geneticist, created the need for in-house entertainment. Her target, Mr. Andrew Mosby, recommended this precaution when he undertook the work of finding the mysterious woman responsible for the near mental massacre of their brightest, albeit awkward, scientist. A restriction in leave had been implemented immediately, with any and all entertainment now contained and provided in secure locations.

Lex smiled at the thought of her part in creating the need for heightened security. She enjoyed her work and the rewards and freedoms that success provided in her encapsulated world. However, pretending to be someone with a past thrilled her most. On assignment she could pretend, if only for a little while, that she knew who she was before belonging to Omega.

In the silence, Lex thought about the purpose of her foray into the evening mists. She had heard her mark's name mentioned in hushed conversations before Chief Jones called her into his office and gave her the details of her next assignment, a job usually relegated to her handler. Her target, Mr. Andrew Mosby, was somewhat of an enigma, even among the people who knew him. Recently, his accessibility became nonexistent and he very secretive. Few in Omega knew much more about him than his name. Ophelia's recent assertion that he could enter someone's dreams made him even more chimerical.

Even Chief Jones, the official figurehead in the Omega compound she knew as home, thought the assignment important enough to speak to her. Without looking up from his computer, Chief Jones had motioned for her to sit. He spoke into the telephone, evenly delivering a series of "Yes sir's" to someone that his perfect posture indicated made him nervous. As he hung up, he relaxed into his executive chair, but he still didn't look at her.

"I congratulate you on your initial contact and inevitable conquest of the government scientist last month, Gamma," the Chief said. "We are very pleased with your latest success as well. I trust you are rested and ready for a more difficult assignment?"

Lex frowned at the chief's use of her codename, but answered politely, "Yes, sir." She couldn't remember having any other name. She'd chosen the name Lex because it felt right, though she couldn't say why, and no one dared call her Gamma to her face except the Chief. Gamma sounded like grandma and made her feel old, though she was only nineteen, or sixteen, or twenty-one depending on the letter sized manila envelope her handler Ray gave her at the beginning of a mission.

Once when sparring with Ray, she asked when her birthday was. He had only said, "It's what we tell you it is, Darlin'." She'd kicked at him in frustration, and he'd used her lack of self-control to send her sprawling on the floor. She'd lost privileges for that slight break in protocol.

"Ready and able, sir," Lex said when it seemed that the Chief, engrossed by the data on his computer screen, had forgotten her. Her skin thrummed with the excitement of escaping the compound again, if only for an evening.

"Excellent," Chief Jones said, still looking at his computer screen. "Ray has the details. Close the door on your way out."

When Lex turned to leave, the Chief looked up from his computer screen, "And Gamma," he said gravely, his eyes locking with hers. "Don't fail us. We are placing a great deal of faith in your abilities. Our benefactor is counting on your success."

"Yes, sir," she said, wondering who that benefactor was and why talking about him made the Chief stiffen in his seat. He nodded and returned to his work without another word. She felt the tension, like static electricity, sparking around her. Later, Ophelia's insistence on Lex's success had only added to her resolve to prove herself to the only family she remembered—or was allowed to remember—dysfunctional as it was.

Lex rode in silence in the back of a limo, her mind buzzing with a multitude of questions. *Why had Omega chosen her? Why Mr. Andrew Mosby? And what was so different about tonight?* Ray had been less than forthcoming when she questioned him. He'd given her the barest of details about her mark and her assignment, and then left her contemplating the barest of wardrobes for the evening.

The limo pulled into the parking garage at the Hotel de Shay, a luxury hotel on the affluent side of the city. Two other limos with more women pulled up as they did. As the women exited the limos, a muscular guard with neat, sandy hair looked at each one emotionlessly, dividing them into two groups and showing them to the elevators. Lex's elevator traveled down to the bottom of the parking garage where two windowless vans awaited them. As she exited the elevator car, Lex looked back at the numbers lit up over the elevator doors. She noted that the other elevator had stopped on the eleventh floor. If her elevator ride failed to produce the elusive Andrew Mosby, she would return here.

Another guard quickly appraised the women before scanning them with a handheld metal detector and motioning them toward the vans. The women rode in silence, one toying with the charms on her bracelet, one staring at her hands, several others simply closing their eyes for the entire ride. After about an hour, the van pulled to a stop and deposited them beside a worn brick building with a faded wooden sign which read *Canteen*. The same sandy haired man with the unreadable face helped them out of the van.

As Lex exited the van, she noted the high, chain-link fence topped with barbed wire that surrounded the complex of buildings. She scanned the guarded facility for escape routes. The only visible entrance was defended by machine gunners in a guard shack just inside the fence. They sat behind a wall of sandbags, hands on their weapons, their sights trained on the gate. Here and there armed guards patrolled the grounds, a few glancing toward the women with scornful looks, or perhaps masked jealousy.

A light rain began to fall as they passed through two sets of doors and entered a dark, smoky room equipped as a nightclub. The other women took off their coats and began to mingle with the men awaiting their arrival; obviously this wasn't the first time for the women, or the men. Lex removed her coat and hung it up by the door, revealing more faultless fair skin than crimson dress. She shook the rain from her hair, aware that every eye in the room drifted unconsciously to her as she did so. Owning her new persona, she walked casually to the bar and sat on a black leather stool.

"Apple martini," she breathed to the powerfully built man behind the bar.

The bartender poured several liquids into a carafe and began shaking it, then poured her a glass of the concoction, placing it on a drink napkin in front of her. He dropped a thin slice of green apple into the glass. "You like living dangerously, don't you?" he said, picking up another glass as someone else approached the bar.

"Is there any other way?" she asked, her eyes scanning the room from the mirror behind the bar. Sallow light from a few small wall sconces dimly lit the room, though there were other lights hanging above the tables that weren't currently being used.

The bartender mixed a bloody Mary and a fuzzy navel and handed them to a stubby bald gentleman. "Evening Faeder," he said as he handed him the drinks. As Faeder walked away, the bartender continued, "You don't look like you belong here. You're not Mosby's type."

"Oh?"

"The girls he hires for these things aren't usually..."

"Did I hear my name?" A man dropped his hand onto the bar beside Lex, his eyes fixed on her, like an artist studying a sculpture.

The bartender plucked up another glass and began fixing a soda water with a twist of lime. "I was just telling the lady that she was too beautiful to get hooked up with the likes of you." He placed the drink on the bar in front of Mosby, who hadn't flinched in his gaze since arriving.

Mr. Mosby chuckled at the bartender's sarcasm, though his eyes never left his scrutiny of Lex. Grabbing another glass, the bartender winked at Lex and moved away to assist someone else with a mind-numbing mixture.

"You must forgive Tom," Mr. Mosby said, picking up his drink. "I'm afraid he doesn't like me very much. I always give him a beating on the racquetball court. You can call me Andrew."

Lex looked at him in the mirror behind the bar. She studied his features carefully, memorizing every detail. His hair reminded her of raven feathers. Ebony and rippling, it flowed across the top of his head and down over his forehead in soft waves. His eyes were an enchanting hazel grey, mutable and fathomless. An expensive black tux and crisp white shirt were tailored to fit perfectly. She imagined that underneath the clothes his body rippled as much as his hair and could almost see the muscles bulging and straining on the racquetball court as he lunged for the ball.

Where his tux left everything to the imagination, she was suddenly aware that her dress left almost nothing that could not be seen. She took another sip of her drink, considering the potable a less potent adversary than the man whose sudden appearance chinked her confidence.

"Shall I assume by your silence that you, too, find me unsuitable as company?" he asked, amusement in his voice.

Lex set her glass on the bar and turned her head to look directly into his deep hazel grey eyes for the first time. Her hand trembled as she set her glass on the bar to steady it. "I guess that depends."

His right eyebrow raised almost imperceptibly as his eyes probed hers for any hint they might give. "Depends on what, might I ask?"

She turned her body toward him, "On what you want and what you have to offer."

He laughed softly, his eyes following the curves of her body as gently as a lover's caress. "What's your name?"

"What would you like it to be?"

He paused for a moment, his eyes darkening to a browning grey. "I make it my business to get to know all the new girls," he said, taking a sip of his drink. "Your name," he commanded.

Something in the way he said "*all the new girls*" made Lex flinch. She looked at him, her eyes narrowed as she tried to reach the depths of his, to find the mirth that had so quickly faded. "Nicolette…but my friends call me Nikki."

"Nicolette…that's pretty." He took a stray strand of her hair in his manicured fingers and moved it behind her ear. "Is it really your name?" he asked.

Lex forced herself to remain calm despite his touch and focus on the mission. She smiled a very devilish smile, and her eyes sparkled. "It is tonight, unless you would prefer something else."

"No," he said, coolly. He looked around the dimly lit bar taking note of each man and woman, "that will do."

She followed his gaze which so quickly abandoned her. She committed to memory every detail of the men present, randomly dressed as if plucked from every era's fashion casualties. They were mostly awkward and self-conscious. The women were beautiful and graceful, but their faces held a gentleness that seemed to make the men more at ease. Most were talking. One couple danced; the man's hands nervously rested on her waist as if he was stuck in a nightmarish middle school dance. His dance partner looked at him with gentle eyes, encouraging him. If she didn't know better, Lex would have thought the girls were grade-school teachers, giving lessons in social graces.

Observance of the other women in the room while sitting so close to Andrew made Lex unexpectedly and painfully aware that the others dressed more sensibly. *"Damn the Chief,"* she thought angrily. *"And damn Ray, too! They're probably having a great laugh at this moment."* She made a mental note to find out who was in charge of choosing her clothing for the night when she got back to the compound…and beat them senseless. She took a deep breath and smoothed out the edges of her face, like ironing the wrinkles out of a shirt. If this was one of their tests, she was determined to pass.

Lowering his voice, Andrew leaned his head close to hers. "Do you know why you are here, Nicolette?" he asked.

Lex's heart raced, as if his lips had traveled slowly up her cheek bone before filling her ear with his warm breath. She felt the blood rising to her face as her body reacted to his nearness. She was not used to feeling this way. She was used to making men feel this way. She was used to being in control.

To give herself a moment to calm down, she took a slow breath in and let it out, fighting the urge to turn her face to his, concentrating on slowing her heart. "Because I'm beautiful and you're rich," she said at last, taking the slice of apple in her fingers and wrapping her lips around it leisurely before biting off the tip.

"Beautiful, *yes*," he said, his eyes flickering over the length of her body. "However, you were hired as entertainment." Then he leaned away from her, his eyes surveying the others in the room again, specifically that man the bartender had called Faeder. The bulbous bald man had delivered the drinks he acquired to a couple of girls and introduced them to some of the awkward men in the room. Now he stood talking to a uniformed man who had just entered from a side door near where she had hung her coat.

With Andrew Mosby's eyes safely focused elsewhere, Lex dared to gaze at him closely. His face was freshly shaved, and his gently curving lips looked as if they would be soft and pliant. His strong hand still rested easily on the bar beside her, his veins thrumming silently with his heartbeat. The music played softly in the background, and she wondered how it would feel to be in his arms.

"Perhaps you'd care to dance?" Lex asked. When he didn't answer, she grinned mischievously. "I'm afraid you wouldn't like my singing. Perhaps a rousing game of Zoom, Schwartz, Profigliano?"

He turned his head sharply and she fell into his hazel grey eyes. The barest hint of amusement and curiosity danced in those deep wells. She suddenly felt naked, as if his gaze stripped everything away, and he could see what she was thinking, could hear her heart betraying her, could see even to the very reason she was there. The reason she was there. His nearness made it difficult to focus. Why was she there again? She wondered if he could see the lump that had formed in her throat.

"Theirs," he said resolutely, tilting his head toward the room of awkward men. "Not mine."

"What? Prefer to watch?" she asked, her words tipped in sarcasm to hide her disappointment.

Andrew let out a hearty laugh, surprising the rest of the guests who turned to look at him briefly before returning to their conversations. "No, my dear Nicolette." He looked into her eyes, brushed the hair off her shoulder, allowing his fingers to trace the edge of her hair down the silky skin of her back. Lex drew in a shallow breath at his touch. Amusement flickered in his eyes at her reaction, and for a moment she thought he might waver, might give in to her. Her lips parted and her chin tipped almost imperceptibly towards his. His hand dropped to his side and his eyes left her as he looked back toward Faeder.

Her heart pounded in her ears like ancient tribal drums. Beyond needing to be successful, to please the Chief and Ophelia, Andrew Mosby's nearness evoked a desire within her for his attention. Equally she wanted to force him to do her bidding and to surrender to his touch. Her body ached for his fingers on her back again, and for his lips to caress hers. "Don't you want me?" she whispered, fighting to keep the sounds of desperation out of her voice. Wasn't that why she was here? To make him want her? Wasn't that what she excelled at?

Andrew glanced at her distractedly. "No," he said. "While I assure you, I am affected by your beauty, I never mix with…well…business with pleasure." He nodded his head toward the rest of the room. "You were hired to mix with the guests at the party— *I* am not a guest. And Tom was right: You're not my type."

Lex looked back into the mirror, this time at herself. A cheap commodity stared back at her. Was that who she really was? Is that what Ophelia and the others refused to tell her? His words, like poison tipped daggers, ripped away what little dignity her dress allowed her to maintain. She was trembling, and just to have something to do, she lifted her glass to her lips, drained it, and set it back on the bar. Her voice, cold and distant, spilled from her mouth. "You must excuse me. This is my first time here. I didn't realize…"

Angry tears threatened to break free and declare her weakness. *Who does he think he is? Better yet, who do I think I am? I have to get a grip*, she thought. She stood to move away from the mysterious man who could so lightly dismiss her.

"Nicolette?" His voice was gentle, quiet, like a summer evening breeze, and so close to her ear that she dared not turn toward him. His hand nestled into the bare small of her back, blocking her escape. She shivered in ecstasy at his warm touch. When he was near her, a chasm rived her chest—a chasm she longed to fill with him. When he touched her, she became the chasm, empty and void of all except her desire for him to touch her again. She stood still, fighting the conflicting desires to cry, to kill him for making her feel so weak, and to wrap her arms around his neck and kiss him.

"Nikki," he said softly, his voice drawing her face towards his, despite her attempts to avoid doing just that.

Lex looked into his eyes, her heart pounding out the primitive beats of her emotions. His eyes narrowed and he looked deeply into hers, as if reading her intent, seeing her purpose for standing there in his presence. She forced her head away from his gaze, frightened and ashamed and enthralled, fighting the emotions that warred within her. She closed her eyes and fought to control her breathing, her heartbeat, her impulse to run from the building, her desire to taste his perfect lips. She wanted to run far away from the man who made her feel this way, but his hand was still on her back, his touch paralyzing her like the tentacles of a sea anemone anesthetizing its prey.

Faeder approached Andrew. "When you're ready to take a walk," Faeder said, "everything's ready for you."

Andrew exchanged harsh whispers with the man called Faeder, and then Andrew's intoxicating voice fell again on Lex's ear, the warmth of his breath exciting every nerve in her body. "I'm needed," he said, his arm guiding her back to her seat at the bar as if she were a puppet and he held the strings. "Wait for me here." Turning to Tom he motioned for her drink to be filled.

Lex sat down and stared at her glass, unwilling to meet his eyes, even in the mirror. "I…was purchased for your guests," she said, forcing her voice to stay steady. "I have work to do." Then she was silent, angry at herself for her weakness and the effect that she allowed his voice to have on her. Turning her head away from Andrew, she looked toward the opposite end of the bar where an awkward man was standing alone, waiting for Tom to serve him. She felt sorry for the shy man in a way she'd never imagined before that moment. Tom placed a fresh drink in front of her, and she was glad to have the distraction.

Faeder began whispering more urgently and Andrew nodded. Then Andrew's mouth was beside her ear and he breathed a tender command, "Wait. I won't be long," and then followed Faeder out of the room, pausing just a moment at the door to look back at her curiously.

When they were gone, Tom said, "I told you you weren't his type."

"I guess you were right," Lex said, her strength and boldness returning with Andrew's departure. She glanced in the direction he had disappeared. Where had he gone and what did he know? There was something unnatural in the way this man affected her, made her desire him with a word, or a touch. She needed time to think, and the safety of distance from the man who made her want him.

"I, on the other hand," Tom said smiling, "Would be happy to make sure you made it home safely tonight."

"Thank you for the drinks," Lex said coolly. "But I think I'll pass."

Tom shrugged. "Your loss."

"Tell Mr. Mosby... Tell him, 'Time and Nikki wait for no one.'"

"You can't get out of the compound," Tom said as he picked up a glass and filled it with liquids from several bottles. "And even if you managed to, he would find you."

Lex smiled, her confidence returning with each passing moment that Andrew was away. She drained her glass and stood. "Perhaps. Then again, perhaps I just need to get some fresh air." She stood and walked to the door, took her coat from the hook, and with one last look around the room, disappeared into the mists.

The party continued. Only Tom watched Lex go.

8

TIME AND NIKKI

Thirty minutes later, Andrew returned to the room, his eyes scanning every crevice in an instant and then locking with those of the bartender, Tom. "Where is she?"

"Gone," he said as he wiped the bar with a crumpled gray bar towel.

"Gone? Where did she go?"

Tom shrugged. "She said to tell you, *Time and Nikki wait for no one.* She said she was going to get some fresh air. That was twenty minutes ago."

"And you didn't think to come get me?"

"Where could she go? She's probably outside getting a smoke."

Andrew crossed the room in a few long strides and pushed through the doors, quickly exiting the building and rushing into the street. There was no one—only the gloom of night and the swirling fog from the recent rain. He crossed to the guard shack and inquired, but none of them had seen anything, certainly not a beautiful woman. They were looking for a threat outside the compound, not inside, and no one had left by the gate. She had simply disappeared.

9

THE KEY

The iridescent lights thrummed steadily over Andrew's desk in his pigeon-hole office under the mountain where he did his preparation for the real work of Sojourner. Back in Las Vegas, his office had two complete walls of windows looking out over the less glitzy part of the city. Daily since he'd arrived, he gave thanks that he wasn't claustrophobic.

On his desk was a stack of mail dutifully sent by Helen—not work mail, because she took care of all of that, but personal things like his sports catalogues, business magazines, a tin of Helen's famous chocolate chip cookies, and a dozen or so condolence cards addressed specifically to him along with a note from Helen that read, simply, "Call your sister."

Andrew picked up a cookie and tapped it over the tin, letting the crumbs fall, then took a bite and tried to imagine himself at his office window watching the street vendor on the corner. His office in Las Vegas smelled vaguely of lavender instead of stale air and his lights never buzzed. He needed to escape before the monotony drove him crazy.

From the stack of cards, Andrew plucked the last unopened envelope which was thick and smooth like an expensive wedding invitation. It had no return address. He turned it over and slid his finger under the flap and removed the card, an elegant white stationery with no markings on the front. He opened the card and traced his finger over the neat cursive penmanship.

It read, "Your father's death was a great disappointment. If I can be of any assistance, feel free to call. My sincerest condolences, Dr. Polk." He flipped the card over, but the back was as clean as the front. Nothing more, just those words. He looked at the envelope again. There was no return address, but as he flipped the envelope over, a business card fell out. It listed Dr. Polk as a Fertility Specialist and included a phone number and address in Florida. Andrew remembered the odd man at the memorial service, the one who wanted to know about the closed casket. Andrew wondered what possible need Dr. Polk could think he had of a fertility specialist.

From the hallway, Faeder knocked on the door. When he had Andrew's attention, he entered without waiting to be invited. "Andrew, I need to talk to you. You got a minute?"

Andrew scowled at the intrusion. "Just going through my mail." He held up the card so Faeder could see it. "This guy was at Dad's memorial service. Said he knew Dad back in the day. What do you think he meant?"

"Probably went to high school together. Or an old client. Who knows."

"Maybe."

"Look. Most of the people your Dad knew outside of Sojourner had a screw loose. You need to forget about his civilian life for right now and focus on his work here at Sojourner. The more time we waste, the further away his killer gets."

Andrew nodded. He picked up the stack of sympathy cards, fishing out the one from Jon that asked him to visit soon, and dropped the rest into the trash can, including the one from Dr. Polk. The guy was odd, but Faeder was right. Most of his father's clients were eccentric in some way.

"What do you need?" Andrew asked.

Faeder dropped a folded newspaper on Andrew's desk, folded specifically at an article concerning the death of a certain young female escort. Andrew stared at the grainy photograph beside the article. She looked young, innocent even, as if the photo had been plucked from the pages of a high school yearbook.

It was, of course, the same woman—the same sultry, mysterious woman who had been at the party just a week ago. Saucy and audacious, she was nothing like the conventional girls he requested from the escort services. She'd asked if he wanted her. He'd lied and said he didn't.

"I'm sorry I don't have better news for you," Faeder said, rubbing the back of his bald head with one hand as he peered over Andrew's shoulder at the newspaper.

"Have you learned anything else about her?" Andrew glanced at Faeder hopefully. The article only supported what he already feared. Since she'd disappeared, he'd searched for her in the dream dimension with no luck. She had vanished without a clue to her identity, much less the reason she crashed his party. And now, it seemed, he would never know.

"There's not a lot to tell," Faeder said, pulling a chair up beside Andrew, which meant that there was really a lot to tell, but nothing good. "None of the other escorts knew her. No one at the party had ever seen her before. No one invited her. She wasn't on the roster of any of the escort services we've been using." He cleared his throat and skimmed the details of the article again. "I checked at the morgue. Her death was determined to be an accidental overdose. The body was identified and cremated at the request of the family. They paid cash."

"She didn't look like your typical user," Andrew mused.

"It seemed odd to me, too."

"What about the newspaper? What could they tell you?"

"No luck there either." Faeder's face reddened in splotches, perhaps from the warmth of the air, or perhaps from embarrassment that he had been the one to pull Andrew away from the girl that night, and over a dead end no less. He looked at the floor, rubbing his left temple with the stubby fingers of his left hand, not meeting Andrew's eyes. "The article was credited to a reporter who swears he didn't write it. And no one else is taking credit for it either."

"And no one here saw her leave the compound?"

"Not a soul. Not even the security cameras caught anything. It's too clean to imagine anything but foul play. The way I see it, there are two possibilities."

"And they are?"

"One, someone on the compound is responsible for her disappearance and death."

"And two?"

"She was no ordinary escort."

"So, you're thinking Omega?"

"Aren't you?"

They both looked back at the picture in the paper. "Anyway, it's a moot point now," Faeder said. "Whoever she was seems to have caught up with her. Put her out of your mind."

"Maybe," Andrew said, his eyes never leaving the photo. He glanced at his duffle bag beside his office door, wondering if it was worth one more dream-walk to be sure. Was this girl really connected to Omega Industries? There was something different about her, something unforgettable and raw.

Faeder looked at Andrew meaningfully. "Omega doesn't leave loose ends."

"What is Omega?" Andrew asked, his words dripping with irritation. "I can't help if I don't know what I'm up against."

Faeder sat back in the metal office chair, perhaps considering how much to tell Andrew, perhaps wondering if he should tell him anything at all. "Your father used his talents to monitor our country's infrastructure and certain corporations and their cash flow on our home soil. One of those corporations was Omega Industries. Omega has slowly been amassing a large amount of capital and your father was keeping an eye on their movements."

Andrew nodded. "Sounds very familiar. Same type of stuff I've been doing for you."

"Almost as well as your father, too," Faeder said wryly. "And you haven't been doing it as long."

Andrew shook his head dismissively. "Then why Omega? Why

not one of the other companies he was researching? Or a personal project?"

"He didn't share a lot with me about his personal projects. Quite frankly, as long as your father gave me the results I needed, I didn't care what he did with his free time. It's how the program works. Dream walkers sometimes even work from home, but you know that."

"Again, why do you suspect Omega?"

Faeder sighed. "When you father registered his last cruise, the one where he disappeared, he registered it as a day trip *to Omega.*"

"That's not exactly a location on maritime charts," Andrew said.

"I checked. There is an Omega Island, but it's part of the Palmer Archipelago in the Antarctic," Faeder shook his head and shrugged. "Since it's a sure bet your father wasn't headed there from California, the obvious conclusion was that he was meeting someone from Omega Industries."

"Still, he would have told someone what he was doing, wouldn't he?"

"I've questioned your father's mongrels, and they know nothing, or are admitting to nothing. I suggest you ask them."

Andrew winced. Even if they had adopted the name, there was something disturbing about the way Faeder said it. Regardless of the feud between Faeder and the Admiral's men, Andrew doubted they would hold back on purpose, at least not when it mattered. Certainly, if his father was researching Omega, he would have used his men to verify his research. Maybe the mongrels did know something, they just didn't realize it.

"Speaking of your mongrels," Faeder said, "I haven't seen the pack leader in quite a while."

"It's what you wanted, isn't it?" Andrew asked. "My mongrels out from under foot?"

"Anything I should know about?" Faeder probed.

"A personal project," Andrew answered. Finding out what happened to his father was very personal.

"So, the government is just supposed to pay their salaries to pick up your dry cleaning and play racquetball?"

"If the government wants me? Yes. Their salaries are pocket change compared to what the government wastes daily on the defense contractors you had me research. The mongrels are good men whether you believe it or not."

Faeder scowled. "They're reckless. You can't control them."

"I don't have to. They want what I want—what you want, I thought. To find my father's killer."

"And you're ok with their methods?"

"You brought me here to get a job done, and I intend to do it." Even as he said it, Andrew wondered how far he would go to find his father's killer.

Faeder shook his head. He stood and started pacing the five steps back and forth that Andrew's sparse office allowed. "I'm just saying I'd be careful where I put my loyalties if I were you."

"Do you have anything useful to tell me about Omega or the girl? If not, I have work to do."

Faeder stopped pacing. His face—the same dark crimson of Nicolette's dress the night Andrew met her—contorted in a war between anger and disbelief. Andrew thought he had pushed too far, but Faeder's face cooled to a mottled pink, and he spoke again. "Omega recently made a rather large acquisition in the farming industry in Texas. The company they purchased is known for its use of cloning technologies to improve food sources."

"Cloning?" Andrew laid the newspaper with the picture of Nicolette on his desk and feigned interest. "That's odd." It had sounded odd the first time he'd heard about it, too, right before the Mongrel's pack leader, as Faeder called him, left the base to run some errands.

10

THE TASTE OF FAILURE

Hidden among the dangling clothes and haphazard pairs of stiletto heels, leather boots, running shoes, and a rainbow of fuzzy slippers, Lex sat in the closet of her quarters and contemplated her failure. She often hid there when she needed to think, and now she had a lot on her mind. She hadn't slept well since she returned to the Omega compound. When she closed her eyes, the hazel grey eyes of Andrew Mosby searched for her in the mists, and she awoke wet with sweat. Even awake, the memory of his disapproving eyes haunted her. Could he really enter her dreams as Ophelia had suggested, or was Lex imagining him there?

A week had passed since her first encounter with Andrew Mosby, and yet Lex still couldn't get the events of that night out of her mind. Her stomach ached as she thought of his hand on her waist, encouraging her to sit at the bar and wait for him. His presence intoxicated her. She hugged a lavender fuzzy slipper to her chest and wondered if this was how she made her other targets feel. The thought of being so flippantly quashed angered her and scared her a little.

Part of her, the exhausted part, refused to let Ophelia's words frighten her away from the deliciousness of sleep. She closed her eyes. As her heavy lids slid shut, she saw his eyes looking deeply into hers, searching, laying her soul naked before him. Her eyes popped open, though it took sheer will to keep them that way. She trembled like she was caught in a perpetual earthquake. He'd dismissed her so easily, without a second thought.

He was supposed to kiss her, to fall for her and fall hard. Yet, he hadn't. Wasn't subliminal manipulation her area of expertise? She could suck information from a man like one long draw on a cigarette and leave him spent. She'd done it dozens of times for Omega. Mr. Andrew Mosby had been the exception.

Her mission to penetrate the Sojourner program at a level that normal agents could never go, to destroy them from the inside, had failed, something the Chief would not accept and something the benefactors would see as unpardonable. While she could now put a face on the enigma, a face that haunted her dreams, what else had she accomplished? Andrew Mosby viewed her as a cheap escort, unworthy of associating with him. She might have been flattered that she was pulling off her cover so well if the memory of his rejection hadn't wounded her so deeply. Worse than that, despite his dismissal, she longed to feel his touch and to hear him say, "Nicolette," again, even if it wasn't her name.

A brief knock rattled the door to her room, then silence. Lex braced herself as her closet door swung open and a familiar sun-weathered face with insufficient eyes peered at her through the tangle of clothes. Her handler Ray knew where to find her. Even her safe place wasn't protected from his presence in her life. Lex closed her eyes and slunk further down in the dangling clothes.

"Come on out of there darlin'," Ray said, running a hand through his sandy hair. "You look like E.T. in there, which is why I'm here. You haven't phoned home in a while. The big man sent me to check on you and get you back in the game."

"Go away, Ray," Lex said. Two years ago, Ray had been assigned as her liaison with Omega when she was on assignment. He had been with Omega longer than she had, though when she pressed him for information about her past, he simply said, *some tales are best left untold.* She'd learned the hard way not to ask too much. Despite his small frame, his strength and training made him dangerous. Still, she wondered.

"Come on out of there and check out your picture in the paper," Ray said. "I think they got your good side." When Lex didn't move, Ray threw a newspaper at her where she sat brooding among the shoes. It was folded to an article about a hooker found dead in an alley somewhere downtown. She looked at the photo a moment—an almost normal teenage headshot—and threw it back out of the closet. The faked photo was almost as cruel as the feeling of failure that haunted her. She would give anything to remember having a normal teenage life, with normal teenage problems.

"I said go away," Lex said, her whining turning to irritation. "I'm not in the mood."

"So, what's different?" Ray said, his laughter filled with sarcasm. "Though I think I remember you saying once, 'over my dead body.' Your death was a success, and I'm ready any time you are. Never thought of myself as a necrophiliac, but for you I'd make an exception. What do you say? Be my zombie queen?"

"Leave me alone," Lex growled, and picked up a six-inch crimson stiletto pump and hurled it at Ray.

He easily side stepped the projectile and turned to wag his finger at her before continuing. "Now darlin', you know we can do this the easy way or the hard way." An evil glint reflected in his eyes as he said *the hard way*. "But one way or another you are coming out of that closet. We've got work to do. Besides, I brought your favorite, fresh bagels and strawberries."

"With cream cheese?" Lex asked, her mood softening a little. She'd eaten very little since the night she met Andrew Mosby.

"Of course. Nothing but the best for my girl," he said, opening a bag from the bakery and waving it gently around the closet doorway. The smell of ripe red strawberries and fresh baked multigrain bagels wafted toward her.

Lex pushed the clothes aside and stepped to the door of the closet. She looked at her handler and then at the bag. "I'm not your girl," she said, her bottom lip protruding in a pout.

"Yeah, whatever. You know you love me," he said holding out

a fresh strawberry in his palm, as if trying to entice a wild horse closer with a slice of apple. "I've got your new identity here, too."

Lex walked out of the closet, her lower lip still projecting her displeasure. Ray smiled and set the bag of bagels on the table. "Pull up a seat, darlin'. We've got a lot to talk about." He bit into the strawberry he held and nodded appreciatively.

The room, not much bigger than her closet, throbbed beneath the failing fluorescent bulbs in the ceiling. Lex sat down at the small Formica table against the wall, pulling the contents of the bakery bag out and setting them neatly in front of her. She took a plastic knife from the silverware tray that she kept in the middle of the table and spread an ample amount of cream cheese onto half of a still warm bagel. Ray laid a thick manila envelope on the table beside the bagels. He started to speak, but she held her hand up to him, her eyes warning him not to interrupt. She sliced several juicy strawberries and placed the slices on top of the cream cheese. When she was satisfied with how it looked, she took a large bite and chewed with her eyes closed for a moment. Then she opened her eyes and nodded to Ray.

A combination of irritation and amusement danced in his eyes as he began. "Your next assignment is taking us to Texas."

"Texas?" Lex asked. "What's in Texas besides tumbleweeds?" She wondered how she knew about tumbleweeds, and the thought of going to Texas suddenly seemed interesting, though she wouldn't readily admit that to Ray. His misogynistic bigotry repulsed her, but he helped her get out on assignments, and he brought her fresh strawberries, cream cheese, and bagels, things she couldn't get for herself.

"A lot actually." Ray watched his forearm admiringly as he flexed his muscles, making the veins seem to thicken and relax. "Especially in San Antonio. But we're only interested in Theodore Bailey. He's being held for questioning by some friends of ours. We need to know what he knows. Besides, a change of scenery will do you good."

Lex frowned at his obvious allusion to her recent failure. "What if I'm not ready.

"What do you mean not ready?"

"Maybe I've lost my touch."

"Not the way I hear it, darling'. Talk in Omega is that Mosby had men combing the streets for you until the article came out in the paper. You've still got your touch, my little *killer queen*!"

"Maybe," she said skeptically. She picked up the last strawberry and bit the tip off, enjoying the sweetness of its juice and the pop of the seeds between her teeth. "I guess I could use some fresher air." She frowned as her words reminded her of the night when she'd left the bar, telling Tom she needed fresh air to avoid further contact with Andrew Mosby. Was she running away now, too?

Texas would be the furthest she'd ever been from home, or at least the sparse buildings of the Omega compound she called home. She wondered how far Omega's power reached, if she could disappear into the crowds there, or if Ray would still find her.

"Since you're dead anyway, it makes sense for you to disappear. At least for a while."

Picking up the envelope that contained her new identity, Lex asked, "So who am I this time?"

"Victoria Farrington," Ray said casually.

"Victoria?" Lex winced at the irony of the name and wondered if Ray had chosen it. What victory had she accomplished? The name couldn't have stung more if it had been Failure Farrington. Still, when she wore that name, she would carry its dignity and make it her own.

"Yes," Ray said, his voice not changing. "On vacation with your brother, Ray Farrington."

"My brother? Have you looked in the mirror lately? You're a little old to be my brother, and we look nothing alike."

"Half-brother. Or I could be your secret sugar daddy." Ray leaned back in his seat, his lower vantage point giving him a better view of Lex's legs. "Either way, we'll be traveling together under those aliases."

"Together?" Lex snorted. "Great! Making sure I don't make a mess of things again?"

"Darlin' you know I love being your handler. In fact, I'd love to handle you in more ways than one, believe me. And maybe we can work that out if you are interested…make the sugar daddy cover more believable."

"Don't make me hurt you." Lex said, unconsciously shifting her legs further under the table and at the same time centering her balance. She didn't like this lecherous side of Ray, and unfortunately it was a side she'd been seeing more and more recently.

"But," Ray continued, sitting back up and addressing Lex in a serious tone, "I've got my own fish to fry this time. You're just eye candy for the ride unless I need backup."

Lex stood and went to the small cube refrigerator in her room and retrieved a bottle of water. Besides being thirsty, it gave her an excuse to move away from Ray. She drained half the bottle and then looked back at him. "When do we leave?"

A slow, crooked smile took shape on Ray's face. "How fast can you pack?"

11

THE LIVING DEAD

The cinderblock cell holding Theodore Bailey extended six feet by four feet, being generous. A seatless toilet covered in a sickly grey film stood in one corner and stains which he didn't care to identify splotched the putrid yellow walls. Theo sat on the floor with his knees to his chest and his head bent, the one-hundred-ten-degree temperatures making sweat drip from his nose and eyelashes. He glanced through sweat-bleary eyes at the boarded window, trying to figure out where the sun languished in the sky.

Whatever time it is, he's late, Theo thought, his muscles tightening in anger. Texas felt like hell to the living dead.

Shouts echoed in the corridor outside his cell, followed by gunshots, and the familiar thunks of bodies falling to the floor—all the sounds of a successful raid. Cell doors rattled; feet pounded on wood. The thunderclaps of automatic gunfire blowing away locks reverberated through the prison.

Theo stood, scratched the wet scruff on his face and a couple of other places, and, despite his discomfort and disheveled appearance, he forced himself to look commanding. The sound of footsteps reached his door, and the report of gunfire and the ricochet of the lock being shot off rang through the air. The door swung open revealing a tall, slender man in camouflage fatigues with a crew cut.

"Hello Payne," Theo said brushing past him. "It's about time."

Payne snapped around and followed behind, waving his nine-millimeter to punctuate everything he said. "Had a hell of a time finding you, Theo. We were looking through Omega's max-security places, scoping out the known warehouse compound, that sort of thing. Who woulda thought they'd stick you in some backwater cement block in the middle of a salt flat? Farming industry my ass. Nothing growing out here but sand dunes."

Theo sniffed and brushed away the love-struck flies that followed him out of the cell. He started to reply and realized his throat was full of dust and his tongue so dry it stuck to the roof of his mouth. "Got any Kentucky bourbon?" he asked, forcing the words out. "I want something smooth."

Payne took his canteen from his hip. "That'll have to wait. Water's all I've got."

"Never mind. There's something in the *warden*'s office." He said the word warden with contempt, for the rotund Omega man was no law enforcement officer. He pushed open the door of the warden's office and went to the refrigerator. He took out a bottle of cheap white tequila. "Damn shame," he said reading the label. "I guess this will have to do. Got a cigarette?"

"You keep mixing fire and alcohol, and you're going to have an explosion," Payne said. He grinned and handed Theo a half-empty pack.

Theo relieved the warden's chair of his lifeless body and sat down. "So, how'd you finally find me?" He asked. He tamped the pack of cigarettes casually as he thumbed through the files that littered the top of the warden's desk.

"A little birdy told us."

Theo nodded, "I thought maybe. The kid's almost as good as his father."

"I was kind of disappointed," Payne said. He frowned thoughtfully. "I was all set to *persuade* the information out of a federal agent we encountered on Omega's payroll."

Theo pushed papers around the warden's desk until he found

the envelope he wanted, the one with his mug shot, forged stats, and traveling papers to a hospital in San Antonio where he was supposed to go when the agents got there, tomorrow according to the papers. With the heat outside, the first thing they were likely to meet was the smell of the guards. He pulled the information about the hospital from the file and handed it to Payne.

Theo set fire to the rest of the file and tossed it in the metal trashcan. Having disposed of the file, he fought the impulse to dispose of Omega's jail in the same manner and followed Payne outside. Two more mongrels stood guard at the entrance to the building—Martin and Tucker. With a nod from Payne, Tucker spoke into a radio and a helicopter appeared above the horizon.

Theo climbed into the cockpit beside the pilot while the others slid into the bay, their guns still pointing toward the building where Theo had been held. The pilot dropped Payne and Theo at a private airport near San Antonio where Theo changed into a fresh set of clothes, though it did little for his disposition. He wanted a shower, but that could wait until he got to the hotel. Theo and Payne plunged back into the sun-bleached desert and entered a white limo, happy to be away from the noise of the helicopter and in the cool air conditioning.

Theo let the authority ebb out of his shoulders as he sank into the leather seats. "You got it?" Theo asked at last.

Payne grinned. "I got it."

For the first time in days Theo breathed a sigh of satisfaction and let the air conditioning soothe his tension away, if only for a moment. Then he pushed forward, unwilling to let the minor victory distract him from his purpose—avenging Admiral Mosby.

"So, where is it?"

"Right here." Payne handed Theo a cowhide leather briefcase. Then he opened the limo's wet bar, produced ice and Kentucky bourbon, and poured them both a drink.

"Did you have any trouble getting it?" Theo asked as he pulled a manila folder from the briefcase and flipped through the file.

"No. It was right where you said it would be."

Theo tucked the folder back in the briefcase and laid it across his lap. He took the tumbler Payne offered and sipped, smiling his approval. "Now that's smooth." He closed his eyes for a moment, letting the events of the past few days slowly come together in his head. He had spent two days in that hell of a cell, but he hoped the file would prove worth it.

Theo looked at his watch. "When will our guest be joining us?"

"Tonight. Flying into San Antonio at sixteen thirty."

"I trust all the arrangements have been made."

"Just like you wanted, but…" Payne paused dramatically.

"But what?" Theo hated it when Payne tried to set him on edge.

"I'm not sure. It may be nothing."

"Spit it out." Theo said, annoyed.

"I may not have found you talking to the federal agent, the one on Omega's payroll. But I did learn something. We might have a bit of a problem at the airport."

"What kind of problem?" Theo asked, his irritation growing.

"We might be having other company. It appears operatives from Omega are on their way here too, on the flight at sixteen hundred." Payne grinned. "They want to ask you a few questions."

"I guess they'll be disappointed." Theo took a sip of his drink, and a gleam of sheer delight entered his depraved eyes. "It seems we need another suite at the hotel. Arrange it. And have a limo waiting for them at the airport."

Payne looked at him dubiously. "You want me to bring them to the hotel? I think you fried a little too long in that cell."

"Maybe." Theo said, smiling, "But a very wise man once said, 'Keep your friends close, and your enemies…'"

"Yeah, I know, 'closer.' But don't you think this is a little too close?"

12

OH, MEGA!

Body washed, face shaved, and throat refreshed, Theo strolled into the airport alone and checked the vidterm: Flight 701, arriving late 4:15 pm. He looked at his watch. *Sixteen ten. Cutting it close,* Theo thought. *But what a ride!*

Omega operatives, although he didn't know who they were or what they looked like or how many, would debark any moment now. He trusted his instincts and waited casually in the seats near the gate for the passengers that came through the terminal.

He took in everybody that walked through: their faces, their mannerisms, their eyes…their lips, their thighs, their hips, their…hell, now *that* was a body. He followed the long, perfect legs to the almost revealing edge of a black leather miniskirt drifting over her hips to her gossamer white blouse, the natural curves that flowed through her neck to her cheeks and eyes and then plunged down again recklessly in her golden brown hair.

"Ohh Mega!" he breathed, his eyes captured and held for ransom by her beauty. She had almost gone out of sight before he realized that she wasn't alone. A muscular man in black slacks and white polo shirt followed a step behind and to one side with two carry-ons, as if he knew she was way out of his league and needed to protect his interests with a show of force.

The sliding doors opened out to the area where taxis and limos parked awaiting their passengers. A row of chauffeurs wearing dark suits and black caps with shiny visors stood holding placards with names scrawled in black marker. One fellow who might have been a college student working for the summer held out his sign marked in blockish letters that couldn't be missed: OMEGA. In seconds Theo would know if his instincts were correct.

The skirt and her shadow stopped uncertainly, glanced at each other, and then back at the driver. He tucked the sign under his arm, and they followed him to a limo parked not far away. The rear view of the skirt was just as lush and pleasing as the front, and Theo couldn't help lingering to watch her legs fold into the car; the black leather micro-mini tantalizingly rose just a bit as she eased down onto the seat.

The driver closed the door, and the spell seemed to be broken for the moment as Theo remembered the second plane would be arriving momentarily. He left the limo driver to deliver his luscious package to the hotel while he returned to meet his real objective.

Theo had hardly returned to the terminal when flight 804 began unloading its passengers. The first one through the gate was Mr. Andrew Mosby. They greeted each other with a firm handshake and a smile.

"How's my favorite mongrel?" Andrew asked.

Theo grinned at his joke. "Never better."

"I wasn't sure you would be here," Andrew nodded toward the exit doors. They began walking. "I trust your brief incarceration ended well?"

"Nothing I couldn't handle, though I understand things went smoother thanks to you."

"Just glad I could help."

"Still, I'd appreciate it if you didn't make a habit of poking around in my head too often," Theo said. "It gives me the willies."

Andrew laughed, "That's not what you said at Dad's funeral. If I remember correctly, you gave me an invitation when you didn't give me your name."

"Desperate times and all that."

Andrew sobered. "Yes. And all that."

13

THE GAME

As Victoria, Lex felt different the moment she disembarked from the plane and entered the terminal in Texas. No trace remained of the weakness that consumed her as Nicolette or the pouting broodiness of Lex. She passed into the new persona Victoria as if walking through a door, closing it on all of what she had been, and embracing her new identity. Her demeanor radiated pride and self-assurance. She allowed nothing to faze her as she walked through the terminal with Ray; not the lustful glares of the men, or the haughty glances of the women who whispered disapproval to hide their jealousy—not even the heat affected her poise.

When she saw the limo boy holding the sign that read in bold black letters, "Omega," she paused only a moment to glance at Ray with a raised eyebrow, silently asking, *Are you coming with me or not?*

Ray swallowed hard and nodded, putting the bags in the trunk as she liquidly slipped into the back of the limo.

When he joined her on the black leather bench seat, she tilted her head toward the driver and asked, "Yours, Ray?"

"No, Victoria," Ray said, shaking his head.

"I thought you said this was a vacation." She opened her purse and pulled out a small compact mirror, checking to see that the heat hadn't affected her makeup.

"Sorry, Sis. Vacation for you, but I still have to work."

"Should I be worried?" she asked, glancing at him in her mirror before returning the compact to her purse.

"Let's just see where this goes," Ray said. His temples throbbed as he clenched and unclenched his teeth. Whether she needed to be worried or not, his concern pulsed just below the surface.

Lex leaned forward, "Driver. Where are we going?"

"The San Christopher Hotel," he told them. "It's one of the swankest places in town. I've never stayed there…can't afford it…but I hear it's unbelievable."

"And who sent you?"

He shot a confused glance at them in his rear-view mirror. "Didn't you?"

She leaned back against the supple upholstery and crossed her legs away from Ray's drifting eyes. He swallowed thickly and forced his gaze away from his *sister*'s thighs and toward the heat coming off the road ahead of them.

Lex wondered if he ever intended to maintain their cover as brother and sister, or if he was counting on no one believing it. She noted the gleaming gold band he had added to his ring finger. Perhaps the cover of fake sister/mistress was his way to get what he wanted. Since her failed mission, his eyes increasingly wandered to places a brother's never would. If only she could see into his mind and know what he refused to tell her.

"Any idea who our benefactor might be?"

He flashed a forced smile. "Let's just play the game, see where it takes us, Victoria," he whispered.

"Sounds delicious," Lex said. "Although I *was* hoping for at least one evening to relax."

Ray nodded. "As had I, Victoria. As had I."

14

VICTORIA

The San Christopher, a masterpiece of Spanish architecture, gleamed in the Texas sun. Alabaster walls stood out against the building's duller neighbors, and its gilded columns produced a golden glow and swept skywards to double domes that shone with burnished bronze. A canvas awning covered a crimson carpet that stretched from the limo to the oversized bronze doors that opened automatically as Ray and Lex approached.

Inside the hotel lobby, Lex and Ray paused to take in the magnificence, or rather take inventory of the space and anyone who might be expecting them. The lobby extended up for two stories. A balcony with glass tables and cushioned chairs circled the lobby. Several men in business attire sat separately at the tables reading newspapers or working on laptops. One couple sat holding hands and staring into each other's eyes as they whispered to one another.

"Nice," Lex said, wondering which of Omega's enemies had arranged their stay—perhaps watching them even now as they entered—and looking forward to a chance to redeem herself.

"Yeah. Too bad I have to waste a trip like this on my sister," Ray said, his eyes twinkling.

"You know you love me," she said, echoing his words from that morning. She smiled and playfully punched him in the arm as they walked to the front desk.

Ray set their bags on the floor and addressed the clerk behind the counter. "Our company made our arrangements. I'm not quite sure what name the reservations would be under. I'm Ray Farrington, and this is my sister, Victoria Farrington."

The clerk's eyes swiftly passed over her figure and then winked at Ray. "Nope. Nothing under either of those names. Perhaps there is something else you would like me to try?"

Lex, who had been looking at the people on the balcony, caught the clerk's eyes wandering dangerously over her body. She cleared her throat and the clerk's eyes met her molten glare. He forced his gaze back to the safety of his computer screen.

"Try Omega Industries. We are here on a business trip."

The clerk's fingers clicked across the keys. "Got it," he said. "Looks like you are in one of the penthouse suites, suite 601." He produced two sets of keys for the room and the elevator and rang the bell for the bellhop. "Have a wonderful stay, and if we can do anything to make your stay more pleasurable, just let us know."

"You can start by sending up some whole wheat bagels, cream cheese, and fresh strawberries, washed but not capped," Lex said, maintaining her fiery gaze, "oh, and a bottle of your best white wine, German if you have it."

"Yes, ma'am," said the clerk, scrambling to write her requests on a piece of paper.

Upstairs Ray tipped the bellhop well, promising him more where that came from if he kept him informed about the other guests in the suites. The bellhop fingered the bills and nodded.

When the bellhop left, Lex relaxed and looked at Ray for direction. "What now?"

"Just settle in. I'll do all the work. For now."

While Ray swept the suite for bugs, Lex explored. A large living area with crimson couch and chairs opened on either side to a private bedroom and bath. On the side opposite the entrance, large curtains covered the wall. She threw her suitcase on the bed in the room to the right, paused to examine the print on the plaster wall of a brave matador facing a charging bull, and then walked back to the main room.

Pulling back the curtains, she clapped her hands in excitement when she saw the pool that could only be accessed from any of the four suites on top of the San Christopher. Swimming had been a luxury at Omega, and even then, it was always centered around training and stamina building in a lap pool hardly bigger than a hot tub. She hurried back to her room and dug through her suitcase looking for her bathing suit, a black string bikini. She put it on in her bathroom, admiring how it looked in the mirror before piling her hair on top of her head and securing it with a series of scrunchies. She grabbed a towel and the complimentary bottle of sunblock from the bathroom counter and went back to the entrance to the pool.

"I'm going swimming, Ray," Lex called as she opened the glass door that led into the pool courtyard. She was glad he was busy. Of late, he'd been less work and more Ray, and she just hoped for a few minutes to herself.

"That's fine, Victoria." Ray called back, unloading electronic equipment from his suitcase and assembling it. "I have some things to take care of and then I'll join you."

She sighed, relieved to have the pool to herself. In the courtyard outside the suite, a marble swimming pool reminiscent of a roman bath stretched across the roof. Neatly arranged around the pool sat plush white lounge chairs available for the guests of the four suites, but the courtyard echoed with emptiness. She tossed the towel and sun block onto one of the chairs as she walked to the edge and dipped her toe into the pool. The water, warm and inviting, sparkled in the sunlight.

Heat poured into the courtyard and swirled around her body like dancing flames. The scant bikini afforded little protection against the indifferent caresses of the sun. She picked up the sun block and looked at the bottle. SPF 50. She opened the cap and sniffed. It smelled like cucumbers, lavender, and an overripe coconut. She wrinkled her nose, glanced toward the sun, and squirted some into her hand. She slathered sunblock on the places she could reach, and then slipped into the pool. The water felt like a warm embrace, and she gladly sank in over her head and shoved off the wall toward the other end. Breaking the surface at mid pool and alternating her arms through the water, she gracefully pulled herself forward in a perfect free style. She wondered when she had learned to swim. Not at Omega. Somehow, she'd known before her first trip to the lap pool. She must have learned sometime before her memories began at Omega, but when? She dug through the water, lap after lap, willing herself to remember. She concentrated, but no revelations came.

When her muscles ached from exertion, she climbed out of the pool and collapsed on her stomach across a lounge chair, exhausted. She glanced around the courtyard to ensure she was still alone, and unhooking her top to avoid a tan line, gave in to fatigue. She lay precariously on the edge of sleep, so ready to fall, but afraid that she would get burned if she lingered too long in the sun. She hadn't been able to reach her back with the sunscreen. She should get up, go inside, and shower before dinner. She should at the very least roll over, but her body wouldn't listen to her. The weight of exhaustion held her to the lounge chair like an electromagnet.

With her eyes closed, and her thoughts so distant in the fog of fatigue, she wondered: was she awake now, or dreaming? She contemplated the strange conversation with Ophelia, about a man who could enter dreams, whose eyes she had felt searching for her in the mists of sleep since her first encounter with him.

Footsteps approached her from across the courtyard, as silent as the hours before dawn. Was she imagining them, dreaming them, or were they real? She waited, listening, fighting her helplessness, but exhaustion won. Maybe it was Ray, or perhaps this was simply some innocuous guest from one of the other suites. What if it wasn't either? But what could someone do with Ray just steps away. He might be a prick, but he wouldn't let anything happen to her, would he?

If, however, she was dreaming, and this was some spirit form of Andrew Mosby, then perhaps she could fight to wake up as she had so many times in the floor of her closet and force her eyes open. But what if she didn't block this intrusion? Could she learn something useful to Omega? Gain the knowledge that was carried on raven wings? If this was a dream, how would she know?

She allowed herself to forget her failures and fall into her persona. Her name was Victoria Farrington. She was on vacation with her half-brother. Although she couldn't see the person who had entered the courtyard, she could sense him as powerfully as she felt the sun on her back. Could she draw him closer?

"Ray, be a dear and put some lotion on my back. I'd hate to burn," she said.

The footsteps drew closer, and then the snap of the suntan lotion bottle opening echoed off the surrounding walls. Strong hands slid across her back and over her shoulders, working the coconut-scented lotion into her skin and the knots out of her muscles. When she was satisfied that hands weren't wandering to restricted areas, she yawned and relaxed into the ecstasy of the intoxicating touch.

"That feels so good," she sighed, sinking further and further into blissful relaxation despite willing herself to remain alert. Something wasn't right. Something didn't match. *Coconut scented*, she mused. But didn't it also smell of cucumbers and lavender?

She struggled to open her eyes, but the skilled hands and her many nights of sleeplessness worked against her. "Did you change sunscreens?" she murmured, trying to focus on why that would matter. No response came except the tenderness that felt so different than anything she had ever felt at Omega. Her tired mind reasoned that Ray had said he would handle the work, and she gave in to her exhaustion as the hands adeptly worked the tension out of her body.

If this was a dream, she didn't want to wake up. The hands seemed to know every muscle in her back, and slowly worked their way down her body, massaging lotion into her thighs and calves and finally her feet. The bliss each caress evoked, like a strong barbiturate, carried her over the edge of feathery blackness and into divine, dreamless slumber.

15

COCONUT

A familiar voice drew Lex out of restful sleep and back to the side of the pool at the San Christopher, "Hey darlin', you want me to put some lotion on your back?"

Lex opened her eyes and raised her head to see Ray standing there beside her in a bright orange bathing suit, bouncing his eyebrows at her.

She stared at him for a moment blinking. "Uh, no. I managed." Had someone else even been there, or had she been dreaming? She scanned the pool area for any clue that it had been more than a dream. She couldn't see anything out of place, but the sun had moved a considerable distance across the sky, and she felt rested and relaxed in a way she hadn't in over a week—or perhaps ever.

"Too bad," Ray said. "My massages have happy endings." He bounced his eyebrows again.

"Give it a rest, Ray."

"Suit yourself."

"I think I've been out in the sun too long already. Be a dear, brother, and fasten my top so I can go in."

"I just got here. You can't go in yet. Besides, there's no one here. You could turn over and tan on the other side." Here was the Ray she knew and loathed.

"Forget it," she snapped, and contorted her arms to hook her bathing suit behind her back. Too much time in the sun would have left a burn. As she arched her shoulders, she expected the sore pinch of sunburn and felt none. She hadn't been dreaming. Someone had put lotion on her back; and if someone had put lotion on her back, then who? She sat up and examined the pool area carefully, noting the direction that the footsteps and the skilled hands must have come. Did they come from the suite beside theirs or the access door? With both so close together, it could be either. "How long have I been out here?"

"A couple hours, I guess. I had some phone calls to make. I also checked in with the Chief. It seems our Mr. Theodore Bailey didn't like the accommodations our friends provided. Our visit may take a little longer than expected."

"I'm not complaining," she said. She looked toward the door opposite her suite. The curtains were drawn completely. "I think I could live here."

Ray rubbed a hand over the scruff on his face the way he did sometimes when he was trying to decide how much to tell her about an assignment, which was usually nothing. He shook his head. "I also went down to the lobby for a while to see if I could find out anything about who set up the rooms."

"Did you?" she asked. She picked up the sunblock, snapped the cap open and sniffed. It smelled like coconut. Just coconut. She set it down beside her, not knowing what she had expected to smell.

"No. The rooms were set up on the internet and paid with a cash transfer. Nothing useful," he said. "The guy at the desk said the other suites were empty, but I'm not so sure. I have a feeling our Mr. Bailey is as curious about us as we are about him. Tonight, after dinner, we'll see what we can find."

She looked at the three glass doors that led to the other suites and the solid door presumably for hotel maintenance. Why hadn't she looked when the strong hands that slid deliberately across her back didn't stray from their course?

Ray's eyes followed her gaze around the pool. "Hey, are you

ok?"

"What?" she asked, looking at him again. "Oh, yeah. I'm just not used to this heat. I need to go in and cool off. Maybe take a cool bath and clear my head."

"Yeah, sure," he said, keeping his eyes focused on hers. "You do that, darlin'. Dinner in a few hours, ok? Be thinkin' about what you'd like to eat."

"Sure," she said, smiling her *nothing's wrong* smile. She grabbed her towel and wrapped it around her as she headed for their suite. With one last glance backward, she slipped into the hotel room and closed the door, leaving Ray sitting on the edge of the pool, dangling his legs in the water and watching her go.

.

16

JUST BUSINESS

When Andrew reentered his hotel suite, he found Theo sitting at the table staring at the ice cubes in the crystal tumbler in his hand, slowly rocking it back and forth.

"That took a little longer than I expected," Theo quipped. "Did you enjoy yourself?"

Andrew scowled at Theo and turned to make sure the door was securely latched and the curtains drawn. Then he chunked a tube of sunblock on the suite desk beside Theo's military grade computer with various scenes around the hotel displayed across the screen.

"She could have drowned," Andrew said.

"She didn't."

"She could have."

"Is it her, or isn't it?" Theo asked, tossing him a bar towel.

"It's her," Andrew said, wiping the suntan lotion from his hands on one of the hotel towels.

"That's too bad," Theo said, taking a sip of his drink.

"Too bad?" Andrew tossed the towel on the edge of the desk with the sunblock. "Why is that too bad?"

Theo looked up from his drink, his eyes carefully studying Andrew. "I was hoping to have her for myself."

Andrew laughed without humor, "I don't think that's one you'd like to tangle with." This girl, Victoria or Nicolette, was beautiful, sexy, alluring, but she was more than that.

"She doesn't really seem to be your type either," Theo said, setting his drink on the table and focusing his full attention on Andrew. "This one's pure poison."

"I'm not convinced that she is," Andrew said as he poured himself a glass of Theo's bourbon. "There's something innocent about her. Almost naïve. Besides, this is business. I don't mix business with pleasure."

"So, there's hope for me yet. When you're done with her, toss her my way," Theo said, watching Andrew for a reaction.

"I know what you are doing. I am not compromised." Andrew took a sip of bourbon and frowned. "Ugh. How do you drink this stuff?" He set the drink down. "I just don't like drugging her. It doesn't feel right."

"We're going to do a lot more than drug her before this is over. You need to make peace with that."

"When I first met Faeder, he said Dad was doing some philanthropic work with missing girls. What if she is one of those girls?"

"What if she is the key to finding out what happened to your dad? We can't ignore that possibility just because she might be the victim of a crime."

"Just have someone follow her when she wakes up."

"Already arranged," Theo said. "There's no way we'll lose her, but you should have let us grab her while she was unconscious. It would have been easier."

"I didn't know the mongrels ever did anything the easy way."

"Hooyah."

Andrew sat down across from Theo, looking at him unwaveringly. "There are things we can learn from her, from her handler, before we take her. There's something more about her, something I hope your recent errands can enlighten."

"There's definitely something more. Several somethings more."

"So, you got it?"

"I've got what you want, for now. The girl's going to cost you extra."

Andrew smiled and nodded, "The usual case of bourbon?"

"You know me so well," Theo laughed.

"Let's see what you've got."

"Well, to start with, I believe Omega recruited her for her specific genetic profile."

17

POOR LITTLE DARLING

That night at the Iron Cactus restaurant on the River Walk, Lex couldn't escape the feeling that someone was watching her, though she couldn't pinpoint the source.

"Something wrong with your food, Victoria?" Ray asked.

Lex looked up from her plate and smiled. "No. The food is great. Especially the guacamole. I can't believe they make it right at your table."

"Then what's up darlin? You've hardly eaten a thing."

"I don't know. I just…" She shook her head and shrugged. She took a bite of her iron carnitas. The tender, shredded, marinated chicken was cooked to perfection, and the cilantro lime rice and bittersweet red chile sauce was a delightful sensation of opposing flavors. At least that's what the menu touted. Food like this was a real treat after years of eating what they served in the Omega compound.

"Just what?" Ray pursued the thought that danced at the edges of her mind.

"I just…at the pool today, I had the strangest dream. I asked you to put lotion on my back…"

"I like the sound of that," Ray said, leering at her.

Lex frowned at him. "Forget it." She took another bite of her carnitas and looked out the window toward the lush vegetation of the river walk.

"Hey, don't leave me hanging like that, Victoria." He downed the rest of his beer and let his eyes wander dangerously over her body. "It was just getting good."

Lex scooped another forkful of rice from her plate and ate it self-consciously. "I'm beginning to understand why brothers and sisters don't always get along," she said, her eyes focused on her plate. "You do remember that you're my brother, right?"

Ray laughed harder than usual, with an evil glint in his eyes. "You know you love me," he said, echoing her words from the morning, bringing them full circle. He leaned in closer and slid his hand up her thigh, "And one day…"

She bent forward to meet him, her hand descending on his like an eagle's talon. Her fingernails dug into his pressure points as she whispered, "Not in my *worst* nightmare."

His advances thwarted, he pulled his hand back sharply, the mirth having fled his face. He took a last bite of his food and a last sip of water and stood up. "I have to meet someone about Mr. Bailey," he said, taking his wallet out and throwing money on the table.

"Are you ever going to tell me why we're here?" she asked.

"You just enjoy yourself, darlin'," he said stiffly. "I'll see you back at the suite."

When she was sure that Ray was gone, Lex took another bite of her food, closing her eyes to savor the peculiar flavoring. Her mind wandered slowly along the river walk from the hotel to the Iron Cactus. The occasional wind that rustled the trees had been a welcome visitor, stirring up the sweet smell of the flower blossoms and providing a moment of relief from the heat. As she meandered along the river past the shops, the gondola tours, the couples walking hand in hand, something made the hair stand up on the back of her neck on more than one occasion. But what? Or who?

It wasn't the same feeling as the dream by the pool, a dream which left her muscles completely relaxed and smelling of coconut when she awoke, a fact she wouldn't share with Ray. She was being watched, and closely. When she'd mentioned it to Ray, he'd said, "Who wouldn't be watching that cute little tight ass of yours?" But still, it was more than the usual stares, something different. Hadn't she been trained to tell the difference? Not that Ray would give her credit for it if she did. To him, she was just a cute little tight ass.

"Excuse me, ma'am," the words of the waiter brought her back to the table.

She looked up at him and smiled. "Yes?"

He set a margarita on the table and said, "A gentleman ordered this Cactus Juice for you and asked if you would join him outside on the patio, last table on the left." He pointed at the glass doors that led to the tree-covered patio.

"Come back to apologize I suppose," she said, picking up the drink.

"I wouldn't know, ma'am," the waiter responded with a smile and left the table.

Lex took a sip of the margarita, savoring the sweetness of the Midori melon Liqueur and blue Curacao, and the bite of the tequila. A single strawberry perched on the edge of the sugared rim of the glass. She grabbed her purse and carried the drink outside.

It was dark now, and the lights from the restaurant windows gave a warm glow to the restaurant courtyard and reflected softly off the water. The air had cooled, and a refreshing breeze tugged at her hair. Tiered gardens and hanging baskets overflowing with flowering plants surrounded the tiled courtyard, like an oasis in the desert. It was so lovely, so different from the cool mountains she so recently called home. She was completely caught off guard when she sat down and the man at the table wasn't Ray.

"Hello, Ms. Victoria Farrington," a smooth voice said. "I'm so glad you could join me. I trust you are enjoying your stay at the San Christopher."

"Mr. Bailey, I presume," she said, setting her drink on the table. She studied his appearance, his closely cropped sandy brown hair, his clever eyes, the tiny scar on his left cheek, perhaps from a fight. "I trust you would know if I wasn't."

"I insist you call me Theo." He smiled and the tiny scar faded into a false dimple. "And you are very shrewd. I do make it my business to know things. For instance, I know that jerk-off that's with you doesn't understand just what a treasure you are. I'd watch my back if I were you. He thinks he has a chance."

Lex picked up her glass. "And you?" she asked, looking over the lip of her glass at him as she took another sip.

"Oh, I have more than a chance," he said winking at her, "but I'm not here after your body. I'm afraid I've already promised that to someone else."

Lex plucked the strawberry from the rim of her glass, twirling it in her fingers. "I'm hardly a commodity. I can't be bought or sold." Or could she? Ray had refused to give her the slightest hint about their mission.

"We shall see," Mr. Bailey said smoothly. "On both accounts." He reached into his pocket, took out a pack of cigarettes, and tamped them down on the table. "I do, however, have something you want…something you need." He picked up a glass of bourbon and took a swig, then set it carefully back on the table before continuing. "Your *brother* knows things he doesn't want you to know. Things you *should* know. Things I can tell you." He paused to light his cigarette and lingered long on his first draw. "Things like, how he always seems to find you, no matter where you hide."

The courtyard faded around Lex, and she leaned closer to the man who promised answers. If he knew how Ray tracked her, perhaps he knew more, like who she was. Mr. Bailey had her complete attention. "Who are you? And what business do you have with my *brother*?"

He bent his face just inches from hers, his cigarette breath assaulting her face. "Poor little darlin," he mocked, grinning wickedly. "Nobody tells her a thing." Without looking away, he put his cigarette out in the ash tray on the table, then stood up and threw down a couple of dollars. "I'll be in touch," he said, and walked away.

18

LOST AND FOUND

As beautiful as the River Walk was with its ornamental trees, cascading flowers, and brightly colored umbrellas and awnings inviting shoppers to stop and spend their money, its allure faded for Lex as she pondered what Mr. Bailey said. She walked slowly along the winding sidewalk beside the river, oblivious to the sweet scents of flowers mixed with humidity from the river. The boat tours had stopped long ago as the city and its inhabitants settled in for the evening. Most of the people had returned home or to their hotels, leaving her alone to think about her life, or what she remembered of it.

Her first memories were not of parents, or playing as a child, but of a sweat-soaked hospital bed in an Omega training compound. She awoke three years ago with an agonized scream and no memory before that moment. Her nurse, Ophelia, told her that she had been in an accident and had been in a coma for several months. Beyond that, Ophelia gave her no indication that she had a past beyond belonging to them and discouraged questions on the subject. She said she wasn't at liberty to discuss such matters, simply, she was sick, and then she wasn't, and now she owed Omega. No one else even bothered to give her that much. Certainly not Ray.

It took hard work, determination, and discipline to achieve her current level within Omega, though that level still left her feeling like a hostage even on good days. She exercised daily, practiced several forms of martial arts, studied languages and the arts, etiquette and poise, weapons and warfare, medicine and biomechanics, chemistry and mixology. Her favorite, though, was music. She worked hardest to earn time alone with the piano.

Still, here on the winding sidewalks that wove through the city by shops, restaurants, and hotels, she knew the people here enjoyed a freedom she could never achieve as an Omega operative. Every minute of her day for the first two years living in the compound had been carefully planned for her. Only in the last year had she been allowed to leave the compound under the supervision of her handler Ray. Even then freedom was limited, like being on an invisible leash. Here though, she imagined she could slide comfortably into any number of lives and be quite happy carrying on a very ordinary existence.

So, what made her so extraordinary to the people at Omega, that she would be so closely maintained for so long? Who was she, really? And what did Ray know that she wasn't supposed to? She wondered if the answer could be found in knowing the benefactor who made even the Chief nervous.

Deep in thought on a marble bench, Lex stared at the eddies dancing on the dark San Antonio River. She didn't flinch when she heard Ray's voice.

"I thought you were going to meet me back at the hotel so we could search the other suites."

She didn't look up, but continued staring at the water. She knew he would find her eventually. He always found her. Did Mr. Bailey really know how? Ray sat down beside her and flicked a flower blossom into the water. "What's up, darlin?" he asked.

She winced as Theo's words echoed in her mind, "*Poor little darlin…*"

"Who am I?" she asked.

"Victoria Farrington. You're my sis…"

"No," she said, her voice far away, "my real name." She looked at him, waiting for a reply. When he didn't speak, she continued, "I had a name. I had to have had a name other than Gamma. And a mom and a dad. What happened to my family? What happened to *me?*"

"Maybe this trip was too much for you," he said, still looking at the river, a grave edge in his voice. "I shouldn't have brought you. I thought it would do you some good, but…"

"No," she said, turning her whole body toward him. Her voice was a fierce whisper. "You can't shut me up that way this time! I have a right to know who I am!"

The muscles in his face pulsed as he gritted his teeth and his voice became hard, "Do you? You gave up those rights when we agreed to help you and you entered the organization. You knew what you were giving up, what you were leaving behind. You chose this. Your parents would have chosen this over the alternative. You are here because of a choice *you* made."

Lex's brow tightened as she absorbed the shock of his words. "I don't understand," she said. She groped for the memories that wouldn't come. "How could I have made a choice I don't remember?"

"It's the way it had to be," he said. His voice softened. "Now come back to the suite and get some rest. You look tired. It's too late to search the other suites tonight. If someone's in them, they'll be there now. We'll have to do it tomorrow. Besides that, I still haven't been able to locate Mr. Theodore Bailey. The Chief is," Ray winced, "anxious for results. I'm going to need your help after all."

Lex nodded and walked silently back to the hotel with Ray. She had a lot to sift through in her mind. And she knew that sometimes it was good to have secrets of her own.

Back in her room where bull and matador perpetually faced one another in a dance to the death on her wall, Lex couldn't sleep. After knowing so little for so long, she finally felt close to having answers to the mystery of her past. What did Mr. Bailey know?

She took the satin sheet from her bed and silently slipped out to the courtyard around the pool. It was a beautiful night. The air was cool and dry. The hushed sound of a mariachi band drifted on the still air as a wedding banquet at the hotel lasted way into the night. She tested each of the doors leading to the suites and the access door. They were locked and all was quiet and dark, so she slipped out of her clothes and slid fluidly into the pool for a swim.

The water cradled her in a warm embrace. She had never felt so free, so alive. Her body shimmered like an island in the moonlight. She lingered in the pool, floating on her back, as the moon dawdled its way across the sky. As the moon set and stars fought to be the brightest in the heavens, she climbed out of the pool and wrapped herself in her sheet. She lay on one of the plush lounge chairs and watched the stars until she drifted slowly in the sea of slumber.

As she wandered in the mists of dreams, she heard voices speaking quietly. They sounded vaguely familiar, and yet so far away she couldn't quite identify them.

"Mmm, she's sizzlin," said the first voice. "She's well worth the trouble."

"Yes. Well, like I said, it's just business," said the second.

"If she's just business, then I'm going to have to change careers," said the first.

"You can't. I need you exactly where you are," said the second. "No one else I know could possibly do 'the voodoo you do so well.' When can you deliver?"

"Just say the word. I'll need to extract the ARFID, but other than that a piece of cake."

"ARFID?"

"Autotronic Radio Frequency Identification Device. Hi tech stuff. Draws its electricity from the magnetic field of her own body. It has a special coating that makes it mesh with her flesh."

"She know about it?"

"I doubt it. Almost imperceptible unless you know what you're looking for. "

"And you do?"

"The payoff for my two days in hell, among other things. They may have caught me, albeit temporarily, but not before my team got what we were after."

"One week then. I'll meet you in Colorado Springs."

"One week it is."

19

FEARS REALIZED

When Lex opened her eyes, the sun had risen above the courtyard walls and was shining warmly on her face. A figure stood over her and she became acutely aware that she had not put on her clothes after her swim in the middle of the night. She squinted against the sun as she reached for her sheet to make sure it was still around her.

"If you wanted to party last night, you should've woken me up." It was Ray. His voice was strained and cruel. "Then again, I'm awake now."

Despite the warmth of the air, Lex shivered. The edge in his voice bothered her more than the crass remarks. "I couldn't sleep."

"Like I said, if you wanted to party…"

"Don't you ever give up?" She interrupted, sitting up and pulling the sheet more tightly around her. "It's *never* going to happen."

"Can't blame a guy for trying," Ray said, his voice lacking its usual mirth. Something in the way he looked at her, unflinching and without excuse, made her uncomfortable, fearful even, and she swung her legs over the edge of the chair away from him. He continued, "We've got work to do. I'll order room service while you get dressed, unless you'd rather drop that sheet and get back in the pool."

"*Never* going to happen," she repeated, and left the courtyard quickly. On her way through her room, she laid out an outfit for the day and grabbed a fresh towel. She needed a hot shower and time to think.

As water poured over her and steam rose around her, Lex ran her fingers over every inch of her body, searching for any sign that it had been invaded by a foreign object. She took a deep breath and let it out slowly. Strange dreams, but what did they mean? She didn't dare tell Ray. The way he'd acted the past few days made her nervous. In fact, he'd not looked at her the same way since her failed encounter with Andrew Mosby. Something had changed. Or maybe it was her imagination running wild after the strange discussion with Mr. Bailey. Still, it had started before that, and it wasn't just Ray. The Chief, and even Ophelia had looked at her differently, hadn't they? Or had that been her imagination? Had her fear risen from her failure?

Turning the water off, she pushed back the curtain and reached for a towel. Her hand met a bare towel rack, though she was sure that she had hung a towel there on her way in the shower. Then she saw Ray, leaning against the sink, towel in hand.

Lex pulled the curtain around her quickly and held her hand out. "May I please have my towel," she said coldly.

"Come and get it," he said, laying the towel on the sink behind him. His eyes held a wild combination of excitement and malevolence.

"What's wrong with you? Give me my towel!" Lex demanded.

"That's a question I've been asking myself. What's wrong with me? I've spent the last two years of my life watching over you, taking care of you, protecting your…interests."

"That's your job," Lex hissed, gauging the distance between the shower and the bathroom door and her chances of getting through it before Ray could catch her.

"Two years preparing you to take down one man, protecting your *virtue* for a mark that in a matter of minutes reduced you to a useless liability, a waste of Omega's time and money."

"Stop," Lex said. He knew just what buttons to press, and tears filled her eyes as she fought to stave off the panic that came with knowing she had been unable to fulfill her mission.

"Two years of work so you could fail in just one night," he said, twisting the words with sarcasm. "Do you think Omega has any use for a failure like you? They want you dead."

"I don't believe you," Lex said, but they had looked at her differently. She knew they had.

"You've been a mess since that night you met Mr. Mosby. Omega has people that can make messes disappear."

"Please," she whispered as the tears escaped her eyes and blended with the water on her face.

"I argued on your behalf, told them to give you another chance. I'm the only thing keeping you alive, and still, I'm not good enough for you." Ray walked toward her. "It's time you paid me back for all the devotion I've given you."

Lex's training took over. Modesty aside, she dropped the curtain and used his momentum to slam him into the shower wall. She ran from the bathroom, grabbing the towel as she went. In her room, she wrestled the clothes that she laid out on the bed onto her wet body.

Ray walked out of the bathroom, wiping blood from his nose. "You can't get away from me," he said, looking at the blood on his hand. "I always find you."

"Because of the tracking device on me?" she hissed, backing away from him into the living room of the suite. His eyes narrowed, and she knew she had his attention. "I'll get rid of it!"

"You don't know what you're saying," he said, maneuvering himself between her and the door of their suite.

"Don't I?" she asked. "Perhaps you should ask Mr. Bailey about it. That is if *you* could ever find him."

"What do you know about Mr. Bailey?" he asked, anger flickering in his eyes like embers bursting into new flames.

"I know enough."

The scorn in her voice made Ray's face red and ugly. The muscles in his jaw worked furiously. "You don't want to make me angry. You screw this up and you can never go back home, not that they want you back anyway. You need me." He took a step toward her, his eyes wild with anger and desire. "You'll do what I say, and you'll like it."

"No," she said and backed away to the glass door leading to the pool. Confusion crippled her senses. Omega was the only home, the only family, she could remember.

Ray smiled, his confidence growing. "You've nowhere to go. You might as well accept it."

Ray had changed since she first met him. He'd always had a hard, professional edge to him, but in the beginning, he'd never strayed from his dedication to her training and protection. Now she could hardly see any trace of that man in this one. "You don't know what you're doing."

Ray laughed. "Believe me. I've got skills that would make you scream." With a sweep of his hand, he ripped off his shirt and threw it on the floor.

Where could she go? Not into the arms of the enemy, surely, but how else could she find out about the tracking device? Perhaps she could still salvage this.

"Please, Ray."

"That's right, darlin'," Ray said, running his tongue across his upper lip. "Beg." He charged across the room toward her, and she fled into the courtyard. Unwilling to fight him, she backed away, keeping her eyes on him. But he was equally unwilling to let her go, and the violent dance began. They circled each other, Lex looking for a way out, Ray looking for a way in. Their movements were swift and fluid.

When Ray refused to relent, Lex attacked, launching herself at Ray's chest and knocking him to the ground. He sprang up angrily, surprised that his pupil had caught him off guard. He punched at her face with one hand and at the same time swung around, his foot connecting with her shoulder, knocking her off balance and across a lounge chair. She rolled off the chair and onto her feet. As Ray lunged across the chair, Lex thrust her feet into his chest and rolled backwards, letting momentum carry him over her head. He jumped to his feet quickly and came at her again, more carefully now. His eagerness had given her an edge, something she could not count on happening again.

Ray hammered at Lex with a volley of punches and kicks which she countered with her own. Occasional connections registered with soft thuds of flesh against flesh. Lex ignored the blood dripping from her lip and the throbbing pain in her side and swung her leg low, connecting with Ray's knee and knocking him off balance. He crashed to the tile of the courtyard, and she leaped on top of him. One heartbeat away from a final blow, Lex looked at the man, her guardian, her protector, her key to her home in Omega. If what he said about Omega was true, then what? What if the next person sent to find her didn't wait to find out if she would come back? What if Omega really wanted her dead?

Lex hesitated—wanted to believe she could still go home—and it cost her. He toppled her easily, her head striking the side of the pool; she lay dazed and disoriented on the edge of the pool.

Ray stood over her, looking down at her limp form. He laughed a low guttural laugh. "And that, darling, is why you never go swimming without a lifeguard." With one last grunt of disgust, Ray kicked her, knocking her body into the pool.

20

DEAD OR ALIVE

Lex awoke, rolled to her side, and retched water laced with chlorine. Her throat burned as if scalded with acid. Her head throbbed with each beat of her heart and her chest ached as if she'd been hit with a sledgehammer. She gasped, filling her aching lungs with air, and coughed.

She lay back on the bed, blinking her burning eyes, trying to focus on the room and wondering what happened. The familiar walls and light fixtures of the hotel suite slowly came into focus, though the colors seemed slightly darker than she remembered. She focused on the painting, the matador smiling, the bull wet with blood, its shoulders pierced with brightly colored banderillas. When had the painting changed?

"Ray?" Her throat ached from the effort of trying to speak, and she coughed again. Her fingers probed her aching head where a cut just above her hairline still oozed warm and sticky blood into her wet hair.

"I wouldn't touch that if I were you," a voice said through the haze that had invaded her brain, a voice not Ray's. She bolted upright and immediately regretted it as the room swirled into darkness. A strong but gentle hand pushed her back down onto the bed. "You may not want to do that either. You need to take it easy." She grabbed the hand that held her down. The voice continued, "Poor little darlin'. I told you to watch your back. Lucky for you, I was watching it, too, or you would have drowned."

Lex blinked her eyes and tried to focus on the man sitting on the bed leaning over her, "Mr. Bailey?" she croaked. Her voice strained above a whisper and her lungs felt like they were full of gravel. The acrid smell of vomit laced with chlorine assaulted her nose as she fought for breath. Then she remembered the fight with Ray.

"I told you to call me Theo," he said, his eyes focusing on something shiny in his hand. She heard a sharp clinking sound. The sound chilled her blood as she rolled again to her side, her body surging and protesting the water that had invaded her lungs. When she lay back again, she had almost forgotten the sound. Then a sharp prick on her arm brought the memory crashing back into her consciousness. *Syringe,* she thought helplessly, and the room blurred toward blackness. She felt herself wandering in that darkness, looking for herself, looking for memories that wouldn't come.

The voices returned. This time Lex knew one of them had been Mr. Bailey. She could see him in her mind as he talked. The other sounded familiar, but she couldn't find a face to match.

"You're sure you know what you're doing?" the familiar voice asked.

"Do you?" asked Mr. Bailey.

Lex sensed that they were close, that something important was happening, something involving her. She tried to open her eyes but couldn't.

Mr. Bailey continued, "I was a Navy Medic before I turned to a 'life of crime' for your father, remember? I think I can handle a few stitches, and the ARFID extraction is nothing. You, on the other hand, are dealing with a very dangerous, albeit very beautiful, weapon. Omega altered her genetically. She's a genomatrix, a targeted weapon, and right now you are her target. There's no hope of this going well."

The other voice dropped to a quiet whisper, "There's always hope."

Lex held on to those words as the drug carried her into restless dreams.

21

TIGER KITTEN

Andrew stood at the sliding glass door looking out over the pool in the courtyard from Theo's suite. His jaw pulsed as he ground his teeth in thought. The sun had passed beyond the west wall of the building and a shrinking triangle of sunlight reflected off the remaining walls. Lex moaned. Andrew turned away from the courtyard and his thoughts to look at her lying on the bed. Her hands and ankles were tied, a precaution Theo had insisted upon.

"How is she?" Andrew asked.

"She's coming around," Theo said taking an oxygen mask off her face. "I stitched up the cut on her head. She'll have some nasty bruises, and her lungs and throat will probably hurt for a few days from the chlorine, but she'll be ok."

Lex opened her eyes, her eyelids heavy with the drugs still in her system. She moaned again and her bound hands lifted towards her head, but Theo caught them gently and pulled them back down. "Still not a good idea to touch that. I wouldn't want you to mess up my beautiful stitches."

She forced her eyelids wide at his voice and struggled against the rope on her wrists. She sucked in a deep breath to scream, and Theo silenced her mouth with tape.

"Now is that any way to act?" Theo said. "We just saved your life."

"Is the tape necessary?" Andrew asked. He wanted her to trust them, and this wasn't the best beginning for that.

"It is until we get her somewhere no one can hear her scream."

Andrew watched her fight with what little strength she had, terror filling her eyes. He walked across the room to stand beside the bed and touched her cheek softly with the backs of his fingers. Her eyes jolted to his hand and followed his arm up to his face. His eyes, the only thing about his demeanor that betrayed any emotion, softened to a gentle hazel gray. She stopped struggling, her eyes searching his, pleading.

"Be gentle with her," Andrew said. "She's been through a lot today."

"She's still dangerous," Theo said, his voice low. "You read the files we took from the cattle ranch. God help us if they start cloning these women."

"There are many different kinds of dangerous," Andrew said. "She seems about as dangerous as a kitten." He took a lock of her hair in his fingers and toyed with it.

"A tiger kitten," Theo said. "With sharp fangs. Omega wanted you to think she was harmless so she could get closer to you."

"It's obvious whatever Omega intended failed."

"I never trust the obvious. It's too easy."

"Her handler tried to kill her."

"And he would have succeeded if we weren't there, but that doesn't change what she is." Theo pointed to a small tray of surgical tools and bloody gauze on the bedside table. "Hand me that tray. I need to sterilize my tools before I put them away."

Andrew picked up the small metal tray and handed it to Theo. "She must feel very alone right now." He couldn't help pitying her lying there like a captured wild animal.

Her eyes narrowed. She struggled uselessly for a few moments, and then sank back into her drug-induced exhaustion.

"It's a shame, about her *brother*," Theo said flatly as he threw away the gauze and doused his tools with alcohol. "Payne's efficient if nothing else."

"I was hoping we could have questioned him today." This wasn't how Andrew had wanted things to go. He had wanted a chance to study them a little longer, learn a little more about how they operated before they took them down.

"It was either take his time with that bastard, or let your tigress drown."

"What's going on in that head of hers?" Andrew's words were calm, as if completing a business transaction.

"Nothing you'd care to hear, I imagine," Theo said. "But what's done is done. We move forward. We keep our focus on what we can control, not what we can't."

Andrew nodded. Now that they had her, like Hector, he could control when she dreamed and when she didn't.

Andrew reached his hand into his pocket and pulled out a pocketknife. He slipped his hand into her hair. Lex twisted her head away from him, away from the knife that was moving closer to her face. Her eyes opened wide as panic surged over her feelings of helplessness. She struggled vainly to free herself.

The knife sliced through a lock of her hair with a quiet whoosh. "Can't hide from me anymore," he said, holding up the lock for her to see. Then he turned away from her. "You know what to do with her," Andrew said quietly to Theo.

"Yes. I know," Theo said, "though I wish you'd reconsider. I hate the idea of Faeder getting anywhere near the information we've found."

"We don't have to tell him everything. If he wants my cooperation, he'll let me run this my way."

"I'm not so sure. Your father might have gotten away with that…"

"He needs to see what we are capable of as a group. I need to leverage our success to keep the Mongrels together, and that means going back to the base. I can't do this without you."

"Your father would be proud of you."

"I'd rather have him back than his pride."

"We're getting closer," Theo said. "We're going to find his killer."

"Are you sure you removed the tracker?"

"Yeah. There was only one. Won't even leave a scar. Tucker's taking it in the opposite direction. Let Omega chase that for a while. But even with the ARFID out, they may have ways of keeping track of her. When her dirt bag handler doesn't return, Omega will want to verify she's dead."

"I trust you'll figure it out, Theo," Andrew said. "You always do." Andrew turned back to look at Lex one last time. He dropped the lock of hair into a small envelope and stuffed it into his pocket. "I'll see you in Colorado Springs in a week. Take good care of her for me." The edges of his mouth curled up ever so slightly.

"Don't be late," Theo said. He pulled a syringe from his bag and two medicine bottles. "You know how Faeder is when you aren't there."

"What are you giving her?"

"Just a little something to help her sleep and something to help her not dream."

"Good idea." Andrew reached his hand out and gently caressed the line of Lex's jaw with his knuckles. He smiled as the warmth welled up in her cheek. She may not have had the effect on him that Omega intended, but the effect he had on her did affect him.

He turned his head slightly Theo's direction, his eyes never leaving hers. "Be a good scout," he said.

Theo chuckled behind him, "Leave no trace. Got it."

22

UNCERTAINTY

Andrew turned away from the bed where Lex lay and walked toward the door. Lex's eyes, the only thing she had any control over, darted quickly from one man to the other, but Andrew never looked back at her. He opened the door and walked out without another word.

Theo flicked his finger lightly on the barrel of a syringe, carefully removing any air bubbles. That sound Lex had heard somewhere before, somewhen before she was Victoria or Lex or even Gamma. That sound made her panic. Terror grasped her in its jagged teeth and the very primal urge to flee overwhelmed her, flushing her veins with adrenaline.

Arching her back, she bucked against her captor to free herself, screaming against her gag in vain. She struggled against her bonds, pouring all of her energy into the hope of escaping the syringe, but Theo's hands were strong and practiced.

"Easy there, Miss Victoria, or whatever your name is. This is just a little travel medicine."

Lex watched helplessly through tear blurred eyes as the liquid went into her arm. Her heart thundered in her chest as panic took over. She couldn't help asking herself if the sound, the flicking of the syringe, had haunted her from her past, or if that sound had somehow reached her from her future—her now. She gasped and fought with all her strength even as she slid again toward the darkness of nightmare and the helplessness that had haunted her for all her memory.

She felt herself being lifted, folded carefully into a suitcase, and listened powerlessly as the zipper ripped its way around to close her in. Moments later she was rolling down the hallway of the San Christopher hotel toward uncertainty.

23

RUBIK'S RUBRIC

Andrew's flight from San Antonio to Bethesda had a short layover in Dallas. When the plane landed in Dallas, he checked his watch, grabbed his carry-on, and headed for the next terminal, to his quiet first-class seating. The sounds of the airport accosted him—loudspeakers announcing flight arrivals and departures, families separating or reuniting, businesspeople making deals between flights, the hum and whir of conveyor belts as luggage clunked through the chute seeking owners. He sidestepped a squealing young woman as she ran to meet a man in an Air Force uniform and took out his phone to check for messages from Theo.

There were no messages from Theo, but he had thirteen missed calls and seven text messages, all from Coretta.

I need you to call me when you get this message.

Call me or answer your phone.

Call me now.

Are you even getting my messages?

I know you are getting my messages. It
says they are being delivered.

Call me.

Stop acting like a petulant child and call
me.

DO NOT, UNDER ANY
CIRCUMSTANCES, GET ON THAT
PLANE.

Andrew sighed, ground his teeth, and stepped into a bagel shop
where it was a little quieter. He ordered an everything bagel with cream
cheese and a bottle of water, took a seat at a table, and took a deep,
steadying breath for the call he was about to make. Before he could
dial, an incoming call from Coretta popped up. He sighed and
answered.

"Little sis! How are you?" Andrew winced as she launched
herself at him through the phone.

"Little sis, is it? Seriously, Andrew, I thought you would be over
pouting by now. You've now officially avoided me longer than the time
I told dad that you and Zach Tatum were going to toilet paper Dean
Whittleby's house and get expelled from college as your last strike. I get
that I'm your personal killjoy, but when are you going to understand
that I'm trying to keep you out of trouble, at least enough so that your
regrets don't exceed your victories."

"It's so nice to hear your voice. How's the weather there?"

"Quit the sarcasm, Andrew. I have a meeting in five minutes.
Maybe if you would have answered my earlier calls..."

"I was on an airplane. My phone was on airplane mode. If you
know everything else, you should know that, too."

"You know that's not how this works for me," Coretta paused,
and Andrew waited. Finally, Coretta said, "If you'd answer my calls,

maybe I would have more than five minutes to talk. I know you don't understand my decisions, but it's not always about you, Andrew. I have a life, too, and my own dreams." She let the words hang in the air for an awkward moment as Andrew tried to think of something to say. Before he could, she began speaking again, more softly this time. "This job, well, it means a lot to me. At least you could have said congratulations or I'm proud of you or something."

"Is that why you called?"

"No. It's not. You know it's not. You can't get on that plane. You have to promise me."

"I was just on a plane. I'm fine."

"Not that plane. The plane to Bethesda that's leaving in a half hour from the Dallas airport."

"I have a busy schedule. Jon is expecting me."

"I'm sure by now Jon knows not to expect smooth sailing with you."

Andrew leaned back in his chair, trying to swallow his frustration. "Your premonitions aren't always right."

"I'm right about this. And you're not going to get on that plane, because somewhere deep down you know I'm right. I love you. I've got to go."

"Coretta?"

"Yes, what is it?"

He rubbed at a spot on the table in front of him. "Congratulations on the job. I'm proud of you."

"Thank you, Andrew." She sounded sincere. "That means more than you know. I...well, I love you. Come see me soon, so we can have a real conversation and catch up."

"I will. As soon as I have time."

"Make time."

"Ok. I love you, little sis."

"I love you, too, thick-head and all," Coretta said, and hung up.

Andrew took another deep breath. He ate his bagel quickly and then headed to the ticket counter to change his flight. When he had secured a ticket for a flight later that evening, Andrew decided just to stay in the airport until the time for the flight. He had plenty he could work on until then. He'd find a spot at the bar and pull out his laptop once he got through the security check a second time. Andrew joined the long serpentine line for the security check behind two elderly ladies wheeling their suitcases and carry-ons in the inching procession toward the counter. As they waited, they discussed the importance of compression socks on airplanes.

"Remember poor Ida, God rest her soul? She took a trip to Italy last year, got off the plane, and the next day, dead of a blood clot. And she was younger than us, Mae. She was only eighty."

"Oh, yes, Betty. I remember. Just like that. So sudden. At least she was doing what she loved."

"Like us?" She winked conspiratorially. "We'll be in Budapest tomorrow."

"Once we get through here, we'll find a place to sit. Then I'll go to the bathroom and put on my compression socks while you watch our carry-ons, and when I get back, you can go put yours on."

Andrew smiled at the women. He hoped when he was their age, he would have as much spunk. Right now, it felt like all he had was responsibility. He sent a text to Theo to let him know about his delay, and then pulled up his emails at Dream Simply to go through a few— no sense in wasting the time while standing in line. He had several messages from Helen about business, ending so often with *call your sister* that it might well have been her email signature. He had a few emails from clients that were evidently important enough to rate getting to him without going through Helen.

There was even an email from Nancy that read, "Hello Andrew, I heard you are going to see Jon. Tell Jon I said Hi. If it would be appropriate, could you please give him my contact information, in case he ever makes it back to Las Vegas and needs assistance, of course. - Nancy"

You sly dog, Andrew thought, and made a mental note to talk to Jon about Nancy as the line inched forward.

Someone joined the line behind Andrew bumping into him and jostling him from his musings.

"Oh! I'm so sorry!"

Andrew turned to acknowledge the apology and found a pair of girls not much younger than him with backpacks and rolling carry-ons. He gave a nod and started to turn back to his phone, but one of the girls launched into an explanation of her carelessness.

"We're just so excited," the girl said. "I'm Lizzie, and this is my friend Kait. It's her birthday."

"Happy birthday," Andrew said to Kait.

"Thank you," Kait said without turning to look at him. Her head whipped back and forth scanning the airport.

He nodded, but before he could turn back to his emails, Lizzie started talking to him again.

"We're being groupies for the weekend. We're going to find the next Effigia concert."

"Trying to find," Kaitlyn countered.

"Ok, trying. But we're going to do it. I just know it."

"Effigia?" Andrew asked.

"It's her favorite indie band."

Betty leaned around Andrew to address the girls. "Excuse me dear, but did you just say Effigia?"

"What's Effigia?" Mae asked.

"It's a band. It's all my great-granddaughter talks about."

Lizzie nodded. "Yes, ma'am. I have a friend who knows a guy whose girlfriend works at the hotel where Shane stayed last night. My friend said the guy's girlfriend said she overheard him saying his flight left this afternoon, like," she glanced at her cellphone, "in thirty minutes. The only flight leaving this afternoon at that specific time is the flight to Reagan Washington Airport."

"So, Shane is coming here? To this airport?" Betty asked. She dug in her purse and pulled out her cellphone as the line inched forward.

"We hope," Kait said.

"I believe!" Lizzie giggled excitedly and bounced on her tiptoes. "We're going to find the concert. I just know it!" She studied the airport with her friend.

"Find the concert?" Andrew asked.

"Yes! They never say where they are going next. They just appear at a new venue and give a concert."

"What does he look like?" Mae asked. "This Shane person?"

"Oh, he fancies himself a dandy," Betty said, also scanning the crowd for any sight of the mysterious man. "Dresses all in white and has long blond hair."

Lizzie pulled up a picture on her phone for Mae. "See? He even wears special contacts, so his irises are white, and his pupils are different shapes."

Andrew looked at the photo. Indeed, the man's irises were shaped like stars, and he had a knowing smirk on his face. His hair looked like a curtain of silk flowing down over his shoulders and out of the photo. He'd been so caught up in finding his father's killer that he'd lost track of pop culture.

Betty opened the camera on her phone. "I'll be ready, just in case," she said. "My great granddaughter would be so excited if I got a picture of him."

"So, no one knows where the next concert will be?" Andrew asked. "How do they make money if no one knows where they are going to be?"

"Some things are more important than money," Kait said. "They don't care about money. They're philanthropists."

"I imagine that translates to they have a patron or two who foots the bill," Betty said with a knowing nod.

"No, really," Kait said. "Every concert they take up money for DAV."

"Wait," Andrew said. "The what?"

"DAV. It's a charity for disabled veterans." Kait said.

Andrew knew well what DAV was from his father. It was the coincidence he questioned. He searched for Effigia on his phone. Nothing came up but some obscure dinosaur from New Mexico, effigia okeeffeae, which lived in the late Triassic period.

They scanned the sea of people waiting in line. On a hunch, Andrew turned the other direction and watched the VIP entrance where people could skip the insane line and move directly through a check station. He'd done that the first time but was so annoyed when he went through the ticket line to rebook his flight that he'd forgotten to request it this time.

It did not take long for Andrew's hunch to pay off. "Does he look like that guy?"

All four women turned to see where he was pointing Lizzie squealed, "Shane!"

The man dressed all in white stopped and looked in their direction!

"We love you!" Kait yelled. "Effigia rocks!"

The man smiled as the girls bounced jubilantly, Betty snapped photos with her phone, and Mae waved. Others turned to see what caused the commotion, some joining in the waving.

Then Shane's gaze fell on Andrew. He quirked a knowing smile not unlike the photo Lizzie had shown, and winked at Andrew, tipping his fedora and letting a waterfall of blonde hair cascade down his shoulders and over his back. Then he continued through the VIP lane toward his destination.

Andrew couldn't help glancing behind himself to see if Shane had winked at someone else, but that clearly had not been the case. The people behind him seemed as clueless as he had been. *Odd*, Andrew thought. *Very odd*.

He reached in his pocket and pulled out the lint that had gathered there. Then he ran his fingers through Lizzie's hair. She turned at the touch. He showed her the lint from his pocket. "You had a piece of fuzz in your hair," he said.

"Oh, no!" Lizzie's face fell. "Do you think Shane could see it?"

Andrew smiled what he hoped was his best reassuring smile. "No. I'm sure he couldn't."

"Oh, good!" she said with relief.

"How do you plan to find the concert if you don't know where it is?" Andrew asked.

"Kait has an algorithm."

Kait rolled her eyes. "I follow the subreddit. It's not rocket science. We just need to get close enough that we can go when it gets posted."

"It sounds cooler to say you have an algorithm," Lizzie said.

"Good luck," Andrew said. "I hope you find the band."

"Thank you," both girls said.

Andrew's phone buzzed as a new text came in from Theo, acknowledging his itinerary change. Turning back to face the flow of the line, Andrew sent a text to Helen. *Find all you can on a band called Effigia. Front man Shane.* Then he added a reminder to his calendar. Lizzie- Effigia- Shane- DAV." He would check later to see if they found the concert.

Tracking down elusive musicians sounded fun, but more than that, the way Shane had looked at him and the fact that the band benefited DAV felt a little too coincidental. He had imagined Coretta made him change his flight because he was in danger. Now, however, he wondered if this encounter with a ghost band that advocated DAV could be the reason Coretta made him miss his flight.

Then again, with her, she may have just felt he needed to relax and have a little fun and knew this would pique his interest. Either way, he would check out the band when he had time. For now, he turned his attention back to finding his father.

24

FLIGHT

Andrew's flight from Dallas International airport to Reagan Washington Airport had him cursing his sister under his breath. He'd lost his comfortable seat on an afternoon flight in first class and had to settle for economy seating late in the evening. He'd been angry with Coretta since his father's memorial service, and she had been letting him stew in that anger. Letting him sulk had always ended when she felt he was in danger. For her, blood had always been thicker than water.

Coretta and Andrew had both inherited dream abilities, though only a handful of people knew about Coretta's. Andrew had been a brash child, and his talents had been evident to those who knew the signs.

Coretta, on the other hand, was different. Where Andrew's dreams took him to people and places, her dreams took her to possibilities. She saw things not as they were, but as they might be. When they were little, she would get him in trouble for things he was 'about' to do that she had dreamed the night before. Looking back now, he could say that she probably saved his life at least a dozen times. The first dream she ever recounted to their parents, finding it unsettling enough that she felt compelled to do so, was also the first time she saved his life.

Coretta had gone down to breakfast before he woke up. She

told their parents that she had dreamed Andrew opened his bedroom window and climbed out onto the roof that covered the front porch to see if he could fly. Their mother had smiled at her imagination, but their father had simply climbed the stairs to their rooms. His great grandmother possessed the gift of prophetic dreams, and his father knew better than to take a dream at face value, at least in their family.

His father's calm but serious voice stopped Andrew just before he jumped off the roof of their house with a blue sheet from his twin bed tied around his neck like Superman's cape. That was the first time her dreams saved him, literally, since in her dream he broke his neck as the sheet caught on the gutter. But it hadn't been the last.

Their father's disappearance had been difficult for Coretta, even if she hadn't come to the memorial service. Unlike Andrew who was expected to carry on his father's legacy at Dream Simply enterprises, answering the unanswerable questions by finding the answers in other people's dreams, Coretta seemed to never have to carry any responsibility. But he knew that wasn't fair either. She had always been responsible.

Even though she was younger, she had doubled up on classes during the year and taken classes during the summer as well to graduate and get her master's degree in history when he graduated with his Bachelors. He knew, though he didn't like to admit it, that his irritation with his overachiever little sister had more to do with the fact that her constant successes made him look bad.

It was easy to be mad at her, when, after the news that their father's sailboat had been found, she said, *What good are the dreams if you can't save the ones you love*? When the Coast Guard gave up the search for their father, Coretta emptied her apartment of its meager furnishings and numerous books and left Las Vegas. *For good and good riddance*, she had said, though she and Helen talked regularly based on the number of notes he had received from Helen telling him to call his sister.

By the time Andrew accepted that their father wasn't coming back, she had already moved to southwestern Virginia and accepted an adjunct teaching position at a small university as a new start. In some ways, if he was completely honest, he had been jealous. Feelings aside, he knew she wouldn't tell him not to get on the flight if she didn't care.

So, unavoidably, Andrew took the only seat left on the late flight, squeezed between a plump man who smelled of bad cigars and sweat, and a young boy who hadn't stopped talking to him since he sat down. The boy talked, seemingly not pausing for breath, from the moment he plopped himself in the seat beside Andrew.

Andrew closed his eyes, feigning sleep, hoping the kid would take the hint and really let him sleep. Tired, and having missed supper standing in lines to reschedule his flight, Andrew wanted nothing more than to escape this reality for a short time in delicious sleep. However, when the boy realized Andrew wasn't listening, he grabbed his arm and shook it back and forth. Finally, exhausted, Andrew turned his head to look at the boy.

"My Mom says ignoring people is rude," the boy said in a haughty tone.

Andrew smiled at the boy, and leaning very close to his face he whispered quietly, "Stop talking to me and I won't have to ignore you,"

"Why should I," the boy said unfazed. "My Daddy says it's a free country, and I can do what I want."

"If you don't stop talking," Andrew said in a quiet hiss, "I'm going to sit on you."

"I'll tell my mom," the boy said, pointing to the woman in the seat in front of him, the same woman who had ignored his behavior for the last hour.

Andrew frowned angrily at the boy, "Let's do that."

Evidently bothering his mother's rest was the one thing the boy did fear. The flight was quiet after that, with just the hum of the powerful engines. However, Andrew's mind raced too quickly over the events of the past few days for him to doze. The information Theo recently acquired, most of which was just genetic gibberish to Andrew, needed to be deciphered. He needed help from someone other than Faeder who shot down all his ideas as useless. He needed help from a scientist not on Faeder's payroll, someone who could look at the data with fresh eyes. He needed to consult an expert, and his college roommate Jon, new assistant director of the National Genome

Research Institute in Bethesda, had more than enough knowledge to help him on this one.

Andrew considered what he did understand, and it was unbelievable. For years Omega had been funding its own independent laboratories to study the genetics and genomics of infertility, impotence, libido, and pheromones, all in the name of medical advances. Some of the work was even funded by government grants.

Separately, the research projects seemed innocuous. Combined, they made up the technology used to create a genomatrix, a woman genetically engineered to take down a specific target. Nicolette or Victoria, or whatever her real name was, had been altered by Omega, but for what purpose? It didn't make sense. While Andrew had heard of gene therapy before, he'd never considered its use as a weapon.

When the plane touched down in Baltimore, Andrew was beyond exhausted. He checked the flight information for his former flight. It had landed on time with no apparent difficulties. He shook his head. Coretta's dreams didn't always come true. They were possibilities, not probabilities, and perhaps another reason she wasn't groomed to be part of Dream Simply Enterprises.

His carry-on in hand, he stopped only to pick up his rental car and then drove to his hotel. He undressed and climbed into bed for some much-needed rest. He needed his mind to be fresh to understand the discussions that were about to take place. Besides, Andrew wanted to check on his newest acquisition.

He looked at his watch. Theo would have things set up for him by now. He pulled the envelope from his pocket that held the lock of hair he'd cut from the girl, Nicolette or Victoria. He closed his eyes, rubbed the lock of her hair like fine satin between his fingers, and thought of her smooth beautiful face on his bare knuckles. He concentrated on these things and slept.

25

GET OUT OF MY HEAD

Andrew plunged into the darkness between dreams with one objective—reaching his Nicolette, his Victoria, his newest piece of the puzzle for finding his father's killer. The physical distance between Andrew and the girl might be vast, but the metaphysical distance between his dream and hers was a short stroll for an experienced dream walker. Andrew traveled the dark, familiar paths, feeling his way toward his memory of her.

As he neared her dream, he could hear the dull clink of glass like a heartbeat. He pressed into her tortured vision just in time to stop her projection of Ray from hitting her. Andrew knocked the projection of Ray to the ground as his words still echoed, thick in the air. "You chose this," Ray said before his advance on her. The girl stood there, trembling beside the pool at the San Christopher. Her hands clenched defensively in front of her already bloody face. How long had she been experiencing this nightmare? A few seconds? A lifetime?

Andrew frowned at the mass at his feet, clapped his hands and said, "Be gone!" The crumpled figure of Ray disappeared, and Andrew turned his attention to the girl. "Are you okay?" As her projection of Ray disappeared, a panicked awe seized her visage. Too late, Andrew realized he had startled her into awareness.

She stepped back warily, and the dull clinking of glass grew louder and more insistent. "What do you want?"

"Nothing," Andrew said. He tried to make his voice calm and gentle. "I'm just making sure you're safe."

"Why do you care?" she asked, her fear and anger mingling in a dangerous cocktail.

"You don't deserve to be treated this way," Andrew said. He was torn by her vulnerability, not wanting to frighten her by his presence, and yet not wanting to leave her like this.

"Maybe I do," she said. The sunlight faded from the courtyard and the pool blurred out of existence. Drab gray walls of a small room began to take shape. Details took shape: a cot, a small table and chair, and a stand mirror. She grabbed the doorknob and yanked on it, but it was locked from the inside.

"I don't believe that," Andrew said, shaking his head. "Did they lock you in here?"

Tears welled up in her eyes. She pulled harder on the locked door, trying to force it open. "They said I deserve this. They said I chose this."

"Did you?" Andrew asked. "What could you have possibly done to deserve this?"

Her breathing quickened and her eyes darted around the room. Like a wild animal suddenly aware of its cage, she screamed as primal fear gripped her, "Get out of my head!"

Andrew retreated, but not quickly enough. Her screams hit him like he was the only ball at batting practice, beating him back until he was knocked out of her dream.

He awoke with a gasp, his head pounding. *What the hell was that?* he thought. He put his hands to his head to rub the ache out of his temples and found that he was covered in sweat. He opened his eyes, wincing at the pain.

Sunlight peeked around the edges of the curtains, barely illuminating the basic furnishings of his room. He sat up in the bed, throwing the covers off, and looked at his watch. The entire day was nearly gone. He had slept much longer than he had anticipated. Jon would be getting off work soon, leaving just enough time for Andrew to take a shower.

Andrew stood under the shower head allowing the water to strip away the sweat, but it did very little for the pounding in his head. As many dreams as he'd entered in the past, he'd never been violently, painfully thrown out before. He made a mental note to be less conspicuous next time, which would not be any time soon. He had a lot to accomplish in a very short time if he was to meet Theo in Colorado Springs in less than a week. He couldn't afford to waste time with a headache like Nicolette had given him.

A question occurred to him. Ray had said she *chose this. Chose what?* What part of the girl's life had she chosen? Certainly not to be beaten by the likes of her handler Ray. Andrew shook his head, trying to make sense of her dream, without success.

Andrew toweled off and got dressed. Then he phoned Jon, asking if they could meet over dinner. He was starving. Jon suggested a Chinese restaurant just around the corner from his office at the NHGRI. On his way out of the hotel, Andrew bought some extra strength analgesics and a bottle of water at the gift shop, swallowing a couple of the capsules before he started his rental car. As he drove, his thoughts wandered to his friendship with Jon.

After Andrew's freshman year, his father had strongly suggested he move off campus where he might be able to concentrate more on his grades and less on the female population of the campus. He'd finished his suggestion with his famous, "caught in a cycle of the stupids" speech. His father had a particularly motivating way with words, and the speech, although tailored for the situation, ended with the statement, *One of man's greatest strengths is being able to understand his weaknesses and rise above them.* Andrew had answered his father's suggestion the only way he could, by searching the want ads for people seeking roommates.

The only thing available at the time he was moving out of the dorm for the summer was an apartment a few miles from the college with Jon, a graduate student working on his doctorate whose former roommate had just graduated. Though Andrew had been reluctant at first to cramp his style with what he saw as a socially awkward science nerd, they became fast friends, balancing out each other's foibles. Andrew's grades improved and Jon enjoyed the female attention that came with being Andrew's friend. Andrew, the athletic ladies' man, and Jon, the shy and insecure genius, broke down the social barriers on campus, pulling the two groups together in what Jon termed symbiotic mutualism. Andrew just called it friendship.

26

AN INTERESTING THOUGHT

Jon leaned against a lamp post outside the restaurant, his attention absorbed by the paperback novel in his hand. His hair, obviously untrimmed since his forced makeover with Nancy, sprouted in a dozen gravity defying directions. He tucked the paperback in his coat pocket when he saw Andrew. He was still the socially awkward, gangly man Andrew remembered, bubbling with excitement over the thought of discussing genetics, genomics, and the human double helix.

The idea of genetically engineering a hunter fascinated Jon, and he was even more curious about the breakdown of her relationship with her handler. Had he become unable to control himself around her? The idea that the latest targets were Andrew and the government's scientist, a geneticist at that, concerned him.

He brimmed with questions—questions that would have to wait because Andrew hadn't eaten since long before he boarded the plane for Baltimore yesterday. Andrew handed Jon a manila folder from his briefcase instead and tore into his food. Before leaving the hotel, Andrew printed off the initial DNA profile that Theo had sent from the samples he had taken. He'd also brought samples for Jon, knowing he would want to do his own tests. But for now, this was a start.

"Amazing," Jon said when he was done reading. "The idea of a genomatrix, a woman genetically altered to be uncontrollably irresistible—like a heat-seeking missile. How could they miss?" He shook his head slowly back and forth, still staring at the file. "But who would do this to someone? And how many more targets do you think there are?"

Suddenly Andrew's attention lost its focus on his plate. He considered the possibility that there were more. *How many more?* He shuddered at the thought. And if they truly were target specific, *who else might be a target and why?*

Jon's words broke into his thoughts, "Odd. It looks like you might have been her ultimate target. She seems to have been specifically designed for you, except..." he ran his finger over the squiggles on the paper. He read the DNA profile like someone else might read a newspaper.

"Except what?" Andrew asked.

"See this," Jon asked, pointing to a set of lines on the paper. Jon looked over his glasses at him, waiting for a response. He was farsighted, and his glasses, whether by design or poor fit, had always perched closer to the end of his nose.

Andrew paused his chewing long enough to shoot him an incredulous look.

Jon sighed, "This specific set complements yours as if she were created for you."

"Why do you say that?" Andrew asked.

"You were my doctoral thesis, remember?" He pointed again at the squiggles. "While you were getting your degree in *revelry* with a minor in *women's studies*, I was studying your DNA. I know your DNA by heart, and this was designed specifically around you, except..." he paused again.

Andrew ignored the allusion to his social life in college. "Except what?" he asked again, this time with less patience.

"These are reversed. It's almost like you could be *her* genomatrix, or whatever the male version would be called. Everything about a genomatrix is designed to take down a man, and yet it seems her genomic programming might also have a specific emphasis on a single target. I think she was intended for you, but you may be the only man who is immune."

"I've never met anyone quite like her. She's fierce and vulnerable all at the same time." Andrew shook his head in thought. "I assure you, I'm not immune."

"Maybe, but it's like you are her kryptonite. She'll fall for you, and fall hard, if I understand the theory correctly. Seems like a rather odd mistake to make."

Jon paused to take a sip of his green tea, and then frowned when the cool liquid hit his mouth. So consumed by the file in front of him, he had allowed his food to get cold as well and as the waitress passed, he asked her if she could heat it up again before turning back to the file. "What's she like?"

"Gorgeous. Fragile. Intelligent. Very fit. Legs of a runner. A smile you could get lost in." Andrew cleared his throat, as he noticed Jon's amused expression. "Packs one hell of a punch metaphysically," Andrew continued, rubbing his temples unconsciously. "She threw me out of her dream today."

"A talent I wish I'd had when we were roommates," Jon laughed. "You were constantly intruding on my dreams."

"Hey, I needed a study buddy to get my grades up after my first year, and you were always too busy with your labs during the day." Andrew grinned. "Besides, it wasn't just my grades that improved. In fact, you should thank me, Mr. Assistant Director, for all the extra research and study time you had. It seems to have paid off."

Jon laughed, "Now, if you could only do the same for my social life." He accepted his plate from the waitress and took several large bites before studying the file further.

"I noticed you're not wearing the clothes Nancy helped you pick out," Andrew scolded.

"I'm saving them for special occasions."

"Every day should be a special occasion when you're looking to make a good impression," Andrew said.

Jon looked at Andrew and grinned. "You always did have good taste in clothes. I think it takes a little more than that though."

"It's the whole package, Jon. You don't expect to find pearls in a flounder. You need to dress the part, although you seem to have made an impression on Nancy. She asked me to give you her regards."

Jon blushed and glanced around as if expecting to see her. He ran a hand through his hair as if trying to tame it. "Really?"

"Yes, really," Andrew chuckled. "But, back to what you were saying, just to make sure I understood," Andrew said, "you think this girl was supposed to be irresistible to me, but it seems to be the other way around?"

Jon nodded and took another bite. "Bizarre, isn't it?"

"Why would the Omega scientists make such a huge mistake?"

Several quiet moments passed when a thought occurred to Jon. He paused studying the profile and looked at Andrew. "Hey, she really threw you out of her dream?" he asked.

Andrew laughed quietly, "Yeah, I guess she did."

"Has that ever happened before?"

Andrew's thoughts ran through the dream again, his hazel grey eyes darkening to brown with his concentration. "No. I don't remember that ever happening before," he said finally. "But until I started working for Sojourner, I didn't really dream walk on a regular basis with people I didn't know. Even at Dream Simply Enterprises, I tended to do the leg work while Dad did the dream walking. Not until recently have I been focusing on strangers. Before, it was mainly you, Dad, Coretta, and a couple of other friends. And a few girls I dated."

"Just a few?" Jon asked, laughing.

"I found, quite misfortunately, that it gave me an unfair advantage. Relationships shouldn't be based on what can be found in dreams."

Jon nodded sagely. "I remember your brutal breakup with your senior year romance. What was her name?"

"Talia," Andrew said. He rubbed his napkin absently at a smudge on the table. "She left me right after I told her about my abilities. She thought I was taking liberties in her dreams. She wouldn't believe me that I hadn't. I was going to ask her to marry me."

"That breakup was epic," Jon said, and he seemed to shiver at the memory. "I guess even the pretty people sometimes aren't accepted for who they are."

Andrew frowned. He didn't want to think about that chapter of his life. "What else do those little black lines tell you?"

"You know, they say opposites attract, but there are some pretty major studies out there that tend to favor the narcissistic view of love. People choose mates that have a similar genetic makeup—people that look like them. Some even focused on the right smell. The gene therapies they use affect specifics, but not the whole. They would have looked for a subject that was close to what they wanted. And even then, what she would have gone through!" Jon shook his head. "Who would do something like this?"

The question reminded Andrew of Hector's Rubik's cube. Who indeed?

"So, what happened with your girl?" Jon asked. "Why did she throw you out?"

"I think I scared her," Andrew said, thinking about her in the dream. "I rushed in too quickly, trying to save her from a nightmare. And she doesn't trust me yet. She mentally shoved me out of her dream faster than I could get out."

"Humph." Jon mused. "That's interesting…"

Andrew took another bite and waited. He knew there was no use hurrying this line of thought. He'd spent enough time with Jon to know when he had that look of quiet concentration you just had to let it run its course. Jon was likely considering dozens of lines of thought at one time. He never seemed to stop thinking and could carry on multiple conversations at one time. It made Andrew wonder if all great minds weren't somewhat attention deficit, allowing them to think on so many different tangents at once.

"I wonder if your dad knew it was possible to throw a dream walker out of a dream," Jon finally said.

Andrew winced at the mention of his dad. "I don't know," he said, thinking of all the lessons he'd ever had with his dad. His dad had taught him how to keep things out of his dreams that he didn't want to come in, building the walls, holding the gateway shut while they circled just outside. He shivered at the thought. But throwing them out once they're already there? He wasn't sure.

"I'm just wondering how much power one has in dreams and in dimensional space."

"In your own dream, I'd have to say unlimited," Andrew said. "If you can learn how to channel your energy, and focus on your surroundings, almost anything would be possible in your own dreams."

"So, possibly, you could hide whole dreams from other people, if they were your own?"

Andrew thought about it for a moment. "I guess it's possible, but I've never had any reason to do it." Then Andrew thought about his father's dream visits when he was a teenager. It would have been a useful skill then. "Where are you going with this anyway?" Andrew asked.

"Just that, if I remember correctly, I came to a memorial service for your father, not a funeral," Jon said.

"Yes," Andrew said tensely. "And…"

Jon either ignored his tone or was so deep in thought that he didn't hear it. "Well, if it was a memorial service, I'm guessing you never found a body. I suppose you tried to find him, afterwards I mean, in his dreams. Without success I'm guessing, which is why he was presumed dead."

"Yes. Of course," Andrew said.

"Hmmm…" Jon was still deep in thought, reading the file while chasing stray ideas.

Andrew gritted his teeth and stared at Jon. Jon's thought progression sometimes wound around in circles for hours until they brought him to a conclusion. None of what Jon asked was new to him. Jon knew that Samuel Mosby's sailboat had been found after a storm in the ocean, empty. No body had been found. He was presumed dead, and as the waters where he had been sailing were known for sharks, they didn't expect a body. Jon had to know that he would search the dream realm for his father. Andrew had searched, with no success. The hope, which only Andrew had held on to, dwindled as time plodded forward, until he'd finally had to accept that his father wasn't coming back.

As if suddenly remembering that Andrew was there, Jon looked up at him and asked, "What if your dad knew? What if he knew you could throw someone out of a dream? What if he could take it a step farther? What if he could 'keep you out' instead of 'throw you out'?"

Andrew let this sink in. "Why would he do that?" he finally asked.

"I don't know. It's just an interesting thought," Jon said, turning his attention back to the thick file in front of him. "You know, your father may have also put the idea into the minds of the scientists, to confuse the genetics. It wouldn't have been that difficult to switch the two pairs, make you dominant, and her recessive, so to speak." Then he was silent, reading again.

Leave it to Jon to think outside the box, Andrew thought. For the first time in many months, there was a spark of hope. Andrew forgot about the problem at hand and pondered again the last time he saw his father.

As usual, his father's infectious smile greeted him and invited him to enter his office, the office at Dream Simply Enterprises that Andrew had been using as his own in hopes of feeling closer to his dad. Andrew sat in the leather wingback chair across from his father, idle conversation filling the space between them. They discussed the weather, the local baseball team's record losing streak, the overcooked chicken at Coretta's apartment the previous Saturday and their attempts to eat it so as not to hurt her feelings.

Suddenly his father became very serious. "There will be a time when you will need to step up," he'd said. "A time when things might not make sense, and you won't have me around to give you the answers."

"Dad," Andrew tried to interrupt.

Samuel Mosby raised one hand, stopping his argument.

"You'll be the only one who can restore things to the way they should be. Look for the answer. You will find her. Or she will find you."

He'd thought at the time his father had given 'the answer' a gender, like you would a boat, or a favorite truck. But now he wondered. Was this what his father meant? Was the girl Nicolette, or Victoria—neither name seemed quite right for her—was she the answer? And, if so, how had he known about her? Certainly, his father was a much more talented dream walker than even Andrew could fathom, and with Coretta's prophetic dreams, what else might his father have arranged?

Suddenly even Andrew's friendship with Jon seemed like a very strong coincidence considering his knowledge of genetics. Perhaps his father had nudged him toward moving off campus at just the right moment, with only one option available for a roommate. Perhaps he was indeed the reason that Andrew had not succumbed to the girl's wiles.

Unbidden, the strange words of Dr. Polk popped into his mind: *I rather thought your father invincible.* Was he? Had his father seen something so terrible that he couldn't share it with Andrew, something that made him do something desperate, like disappear without telling his family? If so, how had he fooled even Coretta? Perhaps he could cut his visit with Jon a little short and make time to go see Coretta.

The sound of Jon chuckling softly to himself interrupted Andrew's thoughts. "Andrew Mosby. Ladies' Man." He chuckled again, still reviewing the file that Andrew had given him. "Can't even *make* the woman that can take him down…"

27

SEX ON THE BEACH

The stay with Jon proved productive, more so than Andrew could have imagined. After dinner, Andrew retrieved his things from the hotel in favor of staying with Jon. They worked late into the night discussing different theories and applications of genomatrixes and woke early to take the samples Theo prepared to Jon's lab. Even when they took a break to play a game of racquetball, their discussions led back to the probability of others like Nicolette.

They even discussed possible reasons why someone from Omega might be interested in Hector's research. Andrew had the feeling he was finally beginning to understand Hector's dreams. Someone in Omega had messed with the patterns—her DNA patterns—and maybe other girls', too. However, Hector's research didn't seem to have anything to do with genetic manipulation, but rather genomic cataloguing similar to the work Jon did for the NHGRI. Whatever Omega wanted, Andrew hoped they had failed to extract it.

During the next few days, Andrew tried to walk the dreams of the mysterious Nicolette, but without success. The fact that she recognized him so quickly as not belonging in her dream was amazing in itself, but her ability to block him and literally throw him out of her dreams intrigued him the most. If he could learn to get past her defenses, maybe, just maybe, if his father really was out there somewhere, he could reach him, too. Still, every attempt he made to get closer to her made her more and more wary.

Unable to access her dreams, Andrew turned to Jon's. If someone could get to Hector, someone could also get to Jon. Andrew slid into Jon's dream just as Jon sat down at his desk at work.

"I swear Jon, do you ever do anything for fun?"

Jon peered over his glasses at Andrew. "What do you mean?"

"Even in your dreams, you're still working."

"Dreams?" Jon asked.

"Yes, dreams. The people we're dealing with…they're dangerous. You need to learn to protect yourself—recognize when you're dreaming."

Jon smiled ruefully. Then he stood and walked around his desk. "It's not as if you didn't just bring me a ton of information for my subconscious to work through."

Andrew thought for a moment and then smiled to himself. "Do you remember that little cabana bar by the pool in the Bahamas during spring break my senior year?"

Jon grinned. "Do I? Best time of our lives…or, at least mine."

Andrew laughed. "Good. I want you to think about that place. We're going to play a little game."

"Am I defending myself, or playing a game?"

"Both. What do you remember about it?"

Jon closed his eyes for a moment, a dangerous thing to do in a dream if you wanted to stay there, but just what Andrew had in mind. The drab grey of the office walls began to soften as a warm breeze blew into the room. Jon opened his eyes, looking for where the breeze might have originated.

"Let go of the office," Andrew said, encouraging him to continue. "The sun was hot, and the rum was cold…"

A blazing sun appeared in the office ceiling.

Jon took a slow deep breath and relaxed his mind. The edges of the dream became crisp as he settled back in, techniques he'd learned from Andrew when they were roommates. The walls faded as if the sun was melting them away. The russet thatch roof that covered the bar appeared before them. The cacophony of tropical birds fought to overpower the gentle beat of the waterfall in the pool. Jon's lab coat faded away and he was wearing the blue and white bathing suit Andrew insisted he buy for the trip.

"Now," Andrew said, "I'm going to make changes in the dream, things that didn't happen, or aren't real. You try to figure out what doesn't belong without shocking yourself awake. Got it?"

"Sounds easy enough," Jon said. "In theory."

"OK," Andrew said. "What do you notice? Don't just look. Feel."

Jon looked around the pool. "I don't know." The edges of the dream blurred, and the colors started to fade.

"You're thinking too hard," Andrew said. "It's more of a fluid concentration. Open your mind and just let things impress on you. Feel it. If you have to think about it, then you're doing it wrong. Like an orgasm."

Jon blushed, but he relaxed his shoulders and looked around the pool again. "The flowers. The flowers were orange, not purple."

The colors changed.

"Good," Andrew said. "What else?"

"The bartender was a guy with a mustache, not a girl."

"Very good."

Jon and Andrew sat on driftwood bar stools, both with a cold beer in their hands.

Jon shook his head. "We didn't drink beer. You ordered a Sex on the Beach for both of us. You laughed and said, 'It's probably the closest we'll get to it on this trip,' though I'm pretty sure you just meant me. I was sure you and what's-her-name would get back together." The beer bottles changed to fruity hurricane glasses and Jon took a long sip as he scanned the dream for more anomalies.

"Talia." Andrew said. "Her name was Talia." Andrew set his drink down on the bar and stared across the pool where a group of girls dangled their legs in the water near the waterfall. A beautiful girl in a satiny black bathing suit grimaced and turned her back to him. When he'd told Talia about his dream abilities and that he had visited her dreams, she'd felt violated and hadn't forgiven him. He hadn't forgiven himself, either. "I haven't dated anyone seriously since that trip."

"I'm sorry, man." Jon took another sip of his Sex on the Beach. "I never thought she was your type, anyway."

"I think this is enough for one night." Andrew stood up and walked toward the edge of Jon's dream.

"I never did get the nerve to talk to Persephone on that trip." Jon said looking at one particular girl who dangled her legs in the pool by the waterfall.

Andrew turned back. "Why not?"

He looked at Andrew nervously. "Too shy, I guess. Besides. I was your wingman. You needed me."

Andrew ran his hand through his hair, leaving rows of black waves falling across his head. He'd been so blind in his pain at losing Talia. "I'm sorry, Jon. I should have been your wingman."

Persephone's eyes traveled across the water to the bar where Jon sat, and then glanced away again as she was drawn back into conversation with her friends.

Jon drained his glass and set it on the bar, face resolute. "This is a dream, right?"

Andrew laughed, "Go for it man!"

Jon jumped into the pool and started swimming toward the girls, but before he could get halfway across the pool, a loud alarm started blaring from somewhere. Jon looked back at Andrew and cursed as he disappeared along with his dream.

Andrew woke to his cell phone ringing and lighting up Jon's modest studio apartment. He glanced at his phone long enough to register that it was Theo, and then answered. "Yeah?"

"Pack your things and get to the airport," Theo said. "I've chartered a plane. I'm sending the information to your phone."

"What's wrong?" Andrew asked.

"Faeder," Theo said, and hung up.

Andrew looked at his watch and then at the flight information on his phone. He dumped his carry-on bag onto the couch where he'd been sleeping. He dressed quickly. "Sorry, Jon. I've got to go."

"It's the middle of the night." Jon fished his glasses off his nightstand and put them on his face.

"Can't be helped." Instead of his clothes, Andrew filled his carry-on with the documents he and Jon had compiled that might be useful when he got back to Colorado.

"You owe me a dream," Jon said.

"I owe you more than that," Andrew said scooping the keys to the rental car off the table.

"When will I see you again?"

"Thanksgiving with Coretta?" Andrew asked as he grasped the doorknob to leave.

Jon laughed, "Is Coretta cooking?"

"Probably," Andrew conceded. This had felt like the first quasi-normal time he'd had since his father's disappearance. He somehow wasn't ready to leave his best friend.

Jon nodded, like he knew what Andrew needed to hear. "I'll be there. We'll order Chinese after she goes to bed."

28

A PURPOSE

This time, as soon as the airplane launched itself into the air, Andrew slept, dream walking with Theo for answers. Through Theo's eyes he saw her crouched in a corner of a cell, wild eyes narrowed and angry, crazed from a self-inflicted deficiency of sleep. Even in her disheveled state, the girl was beautiful and alluring. A wearied whisper echoed from her lips as her eyes drooped, a mantra to keep from sleeping: *Do not go gentle... Do not go gentle...*

Andrew didn't understand Nicolette's panic any more than she could control it. Her tortured eyes and the terror on her face turned his blood to ice in his veins. Had he done this to her? He woke, alert and with a purpose.

The remainder of the flight seemed long, a tedious necessity. The girl's tormented appearance haunted Andrew. He could not get past the feeling that he had caused her misery. Most people never even knew that he walked into their dreams to spy, to break into the very secret of secret places and steal knowledge.

She saw or felt his presence every time he drew close to her. He might enter a dream to steal information, but he was not a torturer. Had he become so unsympathetic in his search for his father?

When the plane landed in Colorado, Andrew rushed through the airport to where Theo waited with a limo.

"How is she?" Andrew asked as he slid into the back seat and closed the door, carry-on case still in his hands.

"Put these on," Theo said, tossing a pair of blue jeans, a jade polo shirt, and hiking boots to Andrew as the limo started moving.

"I'm fine in what I have on," Andrew said.

"The girl needs to feel comfortable around you. Casual clothes might make that easier."

Andrew kicked off his shoes and his dress slacks and stuffed his legs down into his blue jeans, arching his back to pull them up and button them. "What happened? I thought the plan was to keep her sedated until I got back."

"Faeder, that pencil-pushing inconvenience, insisted. Since we let her wake up, she's refused to sleep, which isn't helping with her disposition."

"Faeder." Andrew swore. "I should have known."

"The ambulance drive to Colorado Springs was uneventful," Theo said and pulled out a half-empty pack of cigarettes and tamped them down on his knee. "Allowing the girl to wake up, on the other hand... She's angry and confused. Frightened." Andrew frowned at the pack of cigarettes and Theo shoved them back into the breast pocket of his uniform. "Call me crazy, but I think she's doing it to bring you back here. It's a dangerous game she's playing."

"Game?" Andrew asked, remembering the tortured look on her face.

"She's flirting with sanity. Sleep's as necessary as food and water. But I think she knew, or at least suspected, that we'd send for you if she wasn't doing well. She wants to finish what she started. And she keeps asking for Ray."

Andrew paused mid-button on his dress shirt. "Even though he tried to kill her?"

"I don't think she sees it that way." Theo fingered the box of cigarettes in his pocket unconsciously. "She thinks this is some kind of test. She thinks if she can pass, they'll take her back."

"To kill her, maybe," Andrew said. He stripped off his dress shirt, pulled the polo shirt over his head, and settled back into his seat.

He needed to find out what the girl knew about Omega. And about his father. To do that, he needed to earn her trust. Yet, how could he gain her trust without using the same weakness against her that her architects intended to use against him? He couldn't take that advantage. He wouldn't.

"I've only used my own men to guard her, rotating them on six-hour shifts in an exterior room, monitoring her on closed circuit, debriefing them after every shift. Even in her state, she's still got a way about her. Whatever Omega did to her…"

Theo took a bottle of Kentucky bourbon from the bar in the limo and poured himself a tumblerful. He offered some to Andrew, but Andrew shook his head. "No, thank you. I need to have a clear head when I see her."

Theo nodded and put the bottle back in the minibar. "She's really messed up. Total sleep deprivation can be an especially ugly descent into psychosis. I've seen Payne use the technique before when questioning a prisoner. I'm not used to seeing it self-inflicted though."

Andrew's lips tightened into a thin line, but he didn't speak. He looked out the window through the tiny droplets of water that formed on the tinted glass as the rain began to fall. They danced upwards and toward the back of the limo as it gained speed and headed for the highway.

The smell of bourbon floated on the air. Theo took a sip of his drink and then swirled the glass slowly, watching the liquid spin. "I have to admit, it's odd to have you show up and poke around my head while I'm sleeping. But I think it's more than that for her. She thinks she's being haunted by her failure to bring you down. She sees you as the reason that prick agent turned on her. Why all of Omega turned on her."

Andrew turned his gaze back to Theo. "She came after me, not the other way around."

Setting his drink down, Theo leaned toward Andrew. "So, are we assigning blame now, or trying to help her? Because this would go a lot more quickly if I just gave her over to Payne."

Andrew felt the slap of Theo's tone, so unlike his father's gentle guidance, but just as effective. "No. This is not her fault. We should exhaust all hope before we do something we can't take back."

"Good. As long as we know," Theo said. "If you're going to do this, you need to keep your head on straight, 'cause the girl definitely doesn't. Staff shrink I consulted said it sounds like Stockholm syndrome; said she doesn't understand what's been done to her and she feels some allegiance to them. Whatever happened to her, she's not talking. We've been…" He cleared his throat, and his voice lowered, "handling her gently…"

Andrew's eyes narrowed. "You questioned her?"

"Only trying to calm her down," Theo assured, "that and to keep that cue-ball-head Faeder away from her."

"She wouldn't be there at all if it wasn't for us," Andrew said, the fingers of his right hand curling into a fist. He bounced the fist on his thigh a couple of times hoping he wouldn't have to deal with Faeder when he arrived, but he imagined Theo would have taken care of that, too.

"Faeder's more of a possession-is-nine-tenths-of-the-law kind of guy. Andrew, I don't want to put too much pressure on you," Theo said, taking a sip of his bourbon, "but Faeder's losing patience. If you can't get through to her, and fairly soon, it's going to be really hard to keep Faeder from taking over her, shall we say, *care*."

Andrew frowned. "He won't if he wants me to keep working for him."

Theo laughed dryly. "You already know how he feels about me and my team. You get in the way of what he wants, he may not be as fond of you anymore either. This is more than he's had in almost a year. Tangible stuff. He may not care if he loses you."

"Point taken. What do you suggest?"

"If you can't calm her down, we're going to have to shoot her with a tranquilizer dart. She's like a trapped wild animal, and it's only been getting worse since she refuses to sleep. Bring her back to humanity first, then work with her."

Andrew stared out the window again. He would do what he could to avoid such harsh handling. He didn't want to see her hurt or mistreated, though if she was as messed up as Theo said, she might not leave them any alternative. He thought about Theo's words, *Whatever Omega did to her…*

"Make sure my suitcase gets to Hector." Andrew patted the carry-on case that rested on the floor of the limo beside him.

"Shouldn't be a problem," Theo said. "He keeps coming to the monitoring room, like he thinks if he stares at her on the monitor long enough, he'll remember something."

Andrew thought about the girl. Was she the key, the beginning of understanding, the edge pieces of a puzzle? Could understanding her mean all the other pieces would begin to fall into place? Andrew needed information and he needed it quickly.

The idea of using whatever power he might have over her repulsed him. He would not let himself go there, even if it meant getting what he needed faster. He would take his time with her. And he would find the people who did this to her and make them pay.

29

LOST

Lex squatted in the corner of the cell rocking back and forth on the balls of her feet. With her back to the ever-watchful eyes of her captors, she fought sleep with the tenacity of a pit bull. Her entire world had dissolved in a matter of days because of a man who could invade her dreams. She never wanted to sleep again.

Everything she remembered had been ripped away from her by one failed assignment. Her home, her room, her closet, her safety, everyone she had known in the past three years—for her entire memory—gone. When she'd returned from that first encounter with Andrew Mosby, the people she thought she knew had changed. The Chief, who rarely even looked at her when he spoke, had stopped speaking. Her nurse Ophelia questioned her about the night and the mysterious Andrew Mosby, and insisted she tell her the story again and again, asking new questions as if she might find some answer to help her. But now, even that seemed skewed. Had Lex seen a new sadness in the depths of Ophelia's eyes? Or had it been there all along?

A tortured whisper escaped her lips, a plea for Ray to help her. He didn't come. The ache in her chest made it difficult to breathe. Had everyone known that her first failure would be her last? She tried to grasp the meaning that had been hidden in their averted eyes, the rigidness of their bodies, and the hushed voices as she prepared to leave for Texas with Ray. The life she knew had slipped away, like sand through her fingers.

Her body trembled as her emotions raced from confusion, to anger, to fear, to longing, to hate, and cycled through again, but it all came back to one thought: she had lost everything because of one man.

"Hello, Nicolette."

Mr. Andrew Mosby's voice behind her sent an angry torrent of ice down her spine. She stopped rocking and arched her back as if his tongue had lashed her like a whip. She turned her head slowly until she could see him through the bars of her cell. Wild with exhaustion, she peered through the tangled hair that fell over her bloodshot eyes. A low growl curled up from the pit of her stomach.

"You!"

"Or should I call you Victoria, though that doesn't seem right either," he said as he took a step closer to the bars. "I hear you aren't cooperating with Theo."

"You did this to me." Still crouched like a cornered animal, she twisted her body to face him.

"I'd really hate to have to sedate you again," Andrew continued, his voice sincere. "But if you refuse to take care of yourself, you force my hand."

Her eyes narrowed to thin slits of hate. "I'm going to kill you, Mr. Mosby."

"I do wish you'd call me Andrew," he said gently, and took another step closer to the bars. "It's unhealthy to avoid sleep. Let me help you."

An angry hiss escaped her. The moment had come to prove her worth to Omega.

Like a spring uncoiling, Lex lunged at Andrew through the bars, her fingers intent on breaking his neck. Andrew took a quick step backward and grabbed her wrists, pulling her body tightly against the cool steel bars. She struggled to get away, but Andrew held her wrists in a firm but almost tender grasp.

"I'm sorry," Andrew said as Theo stepped up quickly and pushed the contents of a syringe into her arm. "You leave me no other choice."

An agonized scream burst through her lips and then a few exhausted sobs. Her body slumped against the bars as the drugs began to work.

"Have a medical team check her and clean her up," Andrew said, lowering her to the floor of the cell with Theo's help. "When she's feeling better, we'll try again."

Yes, she thought as the drug lulled her to sleep. *I will try again.*

30

SAFE

Convinced the girl would be safe under Theo's supervision, Andrew retired to his room to walk the perimeter of her unconsciousness, seeing to her recovery in his own way, though reluctant to approach her. He heard her dream before he saw her. Always the quiet clink of glass poured from her nightmares. She lay curled in the fetal position in the blackness of empty dream, her hands covering her ears. Her rich brown hair covered her face as sobs shook her body. "You're safe now," Andrew whispered quietly into her darkness, and the sobs eased. "You're in a safe place."

The sound faded, and bright colors began to swirl around her slowly taking the shape of shoes scattered on the floor, then blouses and skirts, shorts and pants dangling above her head. She lay in the floor of a small walk-in closet which housed pair after pair of fuzzy slippers in every color. Nicolette's sobs ceased and her shoulders relaxed a little. Her hand slid into the pile of fuzzy slippers and pulled a multicolored assortment of them to her chest, hugging them tightly.

Andrew smiled in amusement, so childlike she was, her safe place tucked away on the floor of a closet surrounded by her clothes and shoes. He turned his eyes away from her, unwilling to disturb her and self-conscious of invading her retreat, her refuge from her pain and fears. "Sleep now," he whispered and left her dreams in search of Jon's.

31

DREAMERS

Jon sat behind his desk in his laboratory office, pouring over stacks of paper covered with numbers and graphs. "You're so predictable," Andrew said, leaning in the doorway. "Even in your dreams, you're working."

Jon looked up from his research over the top of his glasses and grinned. A wave of recognition, not of Andrew, but of his own dream, rippled across his face. "I'm glad you're here!" Jon said, standing up to walk around his desk. "I've been thinking about your girl. How's she doing?"

"Well, she's sleeping peacefully now," Andrew said. "That's a step in the right direction." He explained how he had found her when he arrived at the base in Colorado. "There was no way any rational conversation was going to take place. The only thing we could do was sedate her and hope she wakes up in a better mood."

Jon nodded soberly, "She's been through a lot. The process of engineering her genome had to be hard in and of itself. What she must have been through! Genetically engineering an embryo is one thing, but to make changes beyond that, would involve modified viruses infecting all her cells."

Andrew held his hand up and a three-dimensional image of Nicolette in the cell hovered above it. "She's so fragile—so vulnerable… And yet so fierce."

Jon looked at the image for a moment, then took his glasses off and cleaned them on his shirt. Forever Jon, even in his dreams when he could have cast his glasses away, he perched them precariously at the end of his nose again. "She's protecting herself. It might not be so easy to get through her self-preservation armor. But maybe for you…"

Andrew cut him off, "I will not take advantage of her through some genetic alteration."

"Even if it's for her own good?"

"Even if," Andrew said. "I need to show her that I'm different. That Sojourner is different."

"Show her? Or show yourself?" Jon asked, his eyebrow cocking up slightly.

Andrew closed his hand, and the image of the girl disappeared. "We're trying to help her."

"There must be a mouse in your pocket, because I doubt anyone there besides you really gives a damn what happens to her. I'd be careful if I were you."

Andrew wanted to be angry, but he couldn't. Jon was right. "Point taken," he said, thinking of Faeder's desire to assume her *care*. "But I'm trying to help her whether she knows it or not."

"What if she won't let you?"

Andrew sighed. "I have some ideas. It's going to take time. But that's not why I'm here. I need your help to do a little research. You up for it?"

"Always available for research," Jon said grinning.

"Excellent," Andrew said. He took a slow calming breath. He needed to be calm to work. "I've been thinking about some of the things we discussed while I was here, about what they might have wanted with Hector's research."

"So, where do we start?"

"I was thinking. What if I could recreate parts of Hector's dream for you? Maybe you could make sense of it."

"I can try."

"You'll have to relax your grip on your dream, like our dream walk to the Bahamas when I stayed with you. Not think too hard so I can show you things." Andrew held his hand out in front of him and a scrambled Rubik's cube appeared on his palm.

"Oh," Jon said. The dream began to fade as Jon's concentration pulled him toward consciousness.

"Relax," Andrew said softly, letting the cube disappear. "Stay with me. Stabilize the dream."

Jon had practiced staying in dreams with Andrew in college, one of his unofficial studies of Andrew's abilities. He certainly couldn't have put that information in any thesis; his peers would have laughed at him, his professors would have failed him, and Andrew would have denied it anyway had Jon tried. Still, explaining covalent bonds and calculus calculations was very different from the mystery and excitement of genetic modification. Andrew would have to take it slowly.

Jon relaxed and the dream's solidity improved. "What now?"

"Try to open your mind and let this happen." Andrew held out his palm and the Rubik's cube hovered above it again. Then he concentrated and the balloon hat he had seen Hector wearing appeared on his head.

"Nice look for you," Jon said. "Not your usual tailor, I see."

"Funny," Andrew said. "When Hector took it off his head, it spiraled into this." Andrew removed the hat, and it morphed into a complicated double helix.

Jon gaped in awe and the dream wavered. "Are you sure this is exactly what you saw?"

"Stay with me," Andrew said.

Jon relaxed and stopped fighting the dream with reality. The dream strengthened again as he allowed his subconscious to suspend disbelief. "I'm ok."

"Good. And yes, I'm sure. He said someone was messing with him. He said someone had scrambled the colors. Do you know what it means?"

"Remarkable." Jon stretched out his hands and the double helix expanded until it was big enough for a man to stand inside it, surrounded by the pattern of colors. "To start with, these sections—they're slightly larger than the rest."

"So?"

"So, they shouldn't be. It should be uniform. These are probably the sections Hector was concerned with."

"How does that help us?"

"These portions here, I know. Or at least I know what my research suggests. It's all very complicated and intertwined, but I believe this is the part that controls your libido and continence. Your desire and your ability to constrain that desire. Your senses, smell, taste, touch, work together—receive signals that a potential mate gives off. How your particular physiology interprets those signals—and how other people interpret your signals.... sexual selection. How we communicate on a sexual level."

"You mean like pheromones?" Andrew asked.

Jon pushed his glasses up on his nose. "There are a lot of factors that work together besides our biochemical responses, but yes, that's part of it."

"What about the other areas on this thing? What do they control?"

"Hold on," Jon said, rubbing his hands on his polyester slacks. He went to his desk and picked up a stack of papers. He studied the papers intently, and as he did, a second double helix formed beside the first, starting at the bottom, like a Lego structure building itself. When it was done, he picked up a second stack of papers and a third double helix formed. Then he lined them up to study the corresponding sections.

"Whose DNA are these?" Andrew poked at one on the strands and it buckled like gelatin.

"I told you I knew your DNA like the back of my hand," Jon said. "And I've studied the girl's for days."

"And?"

"Whatever Hector was worried about, you both have it. For him to have an understanding of this area, he needed to study it, have a sample group with the trait and narrow it down, like blue eyes or being able to roll your tongue, or a certain type of cancer."

"When I joined Sojourner, a lab tech took a DNA sample. He said it was routine for one of their scientists." Andrew said. "I hadn't thought about it, but that scientist was probably Hector."

"Which means Hector probably had a sample from all the dream walkers in the program," Jon said, a look of horror spreading across his face. The edges of Jon's dream began to fade.

"Could dream walking have a genetic link?" Andrew asked.

"Good Lord." Jon said, taking a step back. "Dream walking genomatrixes. There'd be nowhere you could escape them." Jon and his dream disappeared as he woke, leaving Andrew in the void between dreams.

JUST KRIS

32

DISPOSABLE

Late the next evening, Lex awoke from a deep, restful sleep to find Andrew Mosby sitting on the edge of her cot, watching her attentively as she found her way to consciousness. The wildness had drained from her psyche, and only the exhaustion from her mixed-up sleep cycle remained, at least until her eyes met his. She tried to sit up and found sturdy straps fastened her securely to the bed.

Her face twisted into a scowl and a furious snarl escaped her. "Let me go!" she said, fighting her panic. She struggled against the leather straps that held her.

"I'd like to release you, sincerely I would," Andrew Mosby began calmly, "but I don't think that would be such a good idea right now."

"I'm going to kill you," Lex growled. She had been hasty in her first attempt. He'd seen her coming, been waiting, counted on her weakness even.

"Now, see?" he said, leaning closer to her. "We're going to have to work on your attitude a little if I'm going to trust you."

"My attitude, Mr. Mosby, would be greatly improved if you untied me," she said, struggling against the restraints. His nearness made her shiver, and she turned that feeling to hate. She would destroy the man in whom her weakness resided. She forced her eyes away from him, around the bare cell, but the drab battleship grey did little to distract her from his nearness.

Then her eyes fell on Theo who watched from the other side of the locked cell door. His hand rested comfortably on his sidearm. Theo didn't trust her, even if Andrew professed a desire to. She glared at the man who had succeeded in selling her to her target. She would kill him, too. Her head sank back into her pillow, and she focused on the wall beside her bed, trying to hide her tears.

"It's not my intention to hurt you," Andrew said softly. He lifted his hand toward her face, then pulled it back again, as if fighting the urge to brush a stray strand of hair from her face. "I want to help you."

"By taking everything away from me that I know?" Lex blinked away the tears and turned to look at him, clinching her fists. She swallowed thickly at the lump that grew in her throat the longer she looked at him. "Because of you I have nothing."

"Perhaps you see it that way now, but your handler Ray tried to kill you. The way I see it, you already had nothing." He leaned closer to her and whispered, "In time, you'll realize that I'm trying to help you."

"By drugging me and tying me to a bed?"

"Until we can come to some sort of truce that involves you not killing me, yes."

"Why would you want to help me?" She turned her suspicion over and over, like laundry tumbling in a dryer. "You must want something."

"I propose we make a deal. You give me something I want, and in that spirit, I will give you something you want."

Her eyes narrowed in mistrust.

He continued, staring into her eyes, "Now perhaps we can start with your name. I'd like it very much if you would call me Andrew. And I'd like to call you by your real name. I don't think Nicolette or Victoria really fits."

She frowned, his nearness making her heart race, and she again turned this feeling to anger. "Call me whatever you like. I'll still kill you."

Andrew nodded once, and then turned and walked to the cell door. There was a clink as Theo opened the door, and Andrew was gone.

"You really should learn to listen to him," Theo said as he locked the cell door securely.

Lex thought of their conversation at The Iron Cactus in San Antonio. "Why? So you get a better return on your investment?" she hissed angrily.

"No," Theo said, putting the keys in his pocket. "Because he's the only chance you've got. And you're blowing it."

33

CHERRY PIE

On his way to the dining facility far below the solid granite of Cheyenne Mountain, Andrew marveled again at the size of the underground base. The bunker, originally constructed as a Command Operations Center in the event of a nuclear war, housed top secret operations like the Sojourner project. Andrew occupied a small office space in a building dedicated to paranormal abilities.

Individuals who possessed the talent to dream walk were employed, tracked, and studied there. Given their abilities were not generally location specific, most of the dream walkers lived normal lives, often working from home until called upon to serve, but they had all started out here. They had all given DNA samples when they arrived. Was Jon right? Had Omega targeted Hector to find the perfect combination of genes to create a dream walker?

For the past few months when he wasn't in the field, Andrew did what he thought his father would do. He learned the protocol of the organization and got to know as many people as he could while looking for clues to his father's death. Now the stakes seemed much higher.

So, after a ferocious game of racquetball with Theo's right-hand, Payne, Andrew showered and headed to the mess hall to eat, and more importantly, talk with a few men he held in confidence. He considered Hector one of the good ones, and perhaps because he'd spent so much time in his head, Andrew trusted Hector despite Faeder's warnings.

As he walked, Andrew considered how to use the dream skills he had practiced with Jon, zeroing in on specifics rather than waiting for the dreamer to wander across details. Focused suggestive thoughts to dreamers, if done right, could produce actual visions of places, things, and people that could be helpful. He risked waking the dreamer by moving too quickly, but if Jon was right and the girl had what it took to be a dream walker, perhaps when she'd learned to trust him, and more importantly when he could trust her... should he dare dream walking with her to see what she knew about Omega and his father?

Theo and Payne met Andrew at the door to the mess hall, eager to discuss what they had learned on their separate errands. Several people were already seated at one of the tables when they arrived, including Hector and Wendle, Hector's colleague. Wendle looked like he should still be in high school, pimples and all, but he had a particular interest in microelectronics that interested Andrew, and Payne had vetted him.

"We're ready," Theo said. He gestured toward the table with his coffee mug.

"Any trouble getting them to come?"

"Are you kidding?" Theo asked. "Your capture of the girl made believers out of any dream walk doubters. It raised your status among the men on base."

"It's not them you'll have to worry about," Payne interjected. "When Faeder finds out he wasn't invited, he'll have your ass."

"Then we'd better talk quickly." Andrew grabbed a wilted Cobb salad and a slice of cherry pie and joined the group at the table. Theo and Payne followed. Conversation almost always started with the meal choices of the day and the weather outside the mountain. Today was different.

Hector hadn't touched his food. He played with his fork nervously as he waited for Andrew to sit down. "I still can't remember her. Are you sure she's the one?" he asked.

"We think so," Andrew answered. "But it's one of the things I intend to find out for sure."

"Perhaps you can figure out why they targeted me while you're at it," Hector poked at a tomato on his plate with his fork.

"I have a theory about that," Andrew said, frowning at his salad. "When I came here, some guy in a lab coat took a cheek swab. Was that for you?"

"Yeah. I take a sample of everyone's DNA who comes on base. It's a basic protocol. But it's not like it's active. It's just data. It's not like I have high profile DNA, like the president. I mean, the data you brought back from your trip suggested that this girl was supposed to be tailored to you, but I haven't had your DNA information long enough for them to genetically alter that girl. That would take time."

"But with that collection of data, one could make inferences, right? Like, say, comparing all the dream walkers in Sojourner to see if dream walking was genetic?"

Hector's face paled. "You think they targeted me so they could use the DNA data I've collected to make more dream walkers?"

"Could they?"

"I guess hypothetically it's possible, if they could attach the right information to a viral vector. But why would someone do that?"

"Are you kidding?" Theo asked. "An army of dream walkers with the power to control their enemies in and out of their dreams? There would be nowhere to hide. They'd be unstoppable."

Payne stabbed sliced carrots with his knife and plucked them from the end of his knife with his teeth. "So, the girl—she's a dream walker?"

"I don't think so," Andrew said. "Not yet. She shows a lot of promise, though."

"Promise," Theo snorted. He fingered the pack of cigarettes in his uniform shirt pocket. "Let's hope she never learns how. She's dangerous enough already."

"You still can't remember anything from when you were in a coma?" Andrew asked Hector.

"No," Hector said, but his face was now pale. "I hope you're wrong about the DNA. I have no idea what, if anything, I gave them. I do have a theory about why I can't remember what happened though."

"Let's hear it," Theo said.

"Whatever could be derived from my dreams has been repressed or erased somehow. I can't remember anything, and there's simply nothing left that Andrew could find. So, I started thinking, what makes people forget"

"Drugs," Payne said with a sudden seriousness, making Andrew remember Payne's specialty with a mild revulsion.

"Trauma?" Wendle suggested.

"Both are possibilities," Hector said. "But since there were no known drugs found in my body at the time, and no physical evidence of trauma, I was thinking in a different direction."

"What direction would that be?" Theo asked.

"We forget things all the time, and research suggests that people dream every night, but lots of people never remember their dreams. I was thinking if Omega is interested in dream walkers..."

"Go on," Andrew said.

"Dreams," Hector said slowly, smoothing his paper napkin on the table in front of him, "are like hypnosis in a way. They both deal with the subconscious mind. A hypnotist can say, 'When you wake, you will feel refreshed and have no memory of what just happened' and the brain accepts that and promptly forgets. I think it might be possible for a dream walker to do the same thing. While I was still out, or under, or whatever, I still had a convoluted understanding of what had happened. But when I woke, it was all gone."

"So, you're saying that if Andrew wanted to, he could dream walk with me and make me quack like a duck when I woke up?" Theo asked.

"Cool," Payne said. Bits of food showed behind his wide grin. The calculating seriousness that surfaced a moment ago once again submerged behind his boyish mirth.

Theo fixed Andrew with a hard look. "Don't even think about it. If I wake up quacking, I'll know it was you."

Andrew laughed and just shook his head. "I wouldn't even

know how. Besides, dreams visited by a dream walker are usually more vivid and memorable. People tend to remember them more, not forget them altogether." Still, Andrew made a mental note to research hypnosis techniques.

Hector shrugged and looked down at the table. "It was just a theory."

"I'm glad you're thinking outside the box," Andrew said. "We need to investigate every possibility. Research it further and get back to me."

Hector smiled his appreciation. His earnest need to prove himself showed. His credibility on base had been compromised by the attack that left him in a coma. If Andrew hadn't brought him on as a Mongrel, Faeder would have shipped him to Alaska.

"Payne," Andrew said, watching him stab another carrot with his knife, "how's the girl's handler?"

"He'll live, but he's in rough shape. He thinks he succeeded in killing the girl," Payne said, chagrinned. "I'm sorry, Andrew. I should have been watching her closer. I had no idea he'd try to kill her."

"She's alive. That's what matters. And considering what Ray was trying to do to her, he didn't deserve better," Andrew felt the edge to his words and wondered if hunting criminals for Faeder had made him hard, or if his feelings for the girl were clouding his judgment. If he spent too much time with her, would she drive him crazy with desire as well? "Is his mind still intact?"

"He's miserable. But yeah, he's lucid enough," Payne said, punctuating his words with a carrot tipped knife. "I haven't been letting him sleep. It's quite effective for questioning."

"When you're done, it might be effective for me to question him, too. My way. Have you questioned Ray about Hector's lapse?"

"Not yet. I've been asking him about the girl, and the compound where she was trained." Payne grinned, as if fueled by Andrew's absolution. "But I'd be happy to."

Remembering the disappointment in Payne's eyes when he told him where Theo was being held in Texas, Andrew smiled uneasily. Payne had wanted to *make* someone tell him, not float the answer out of Theo's head during a dream. Theo referred to Payne as "the man with the answers" because he could make anyone tell him what he wanted to know. Ray was no exception, regardless of his condition. Payne explained what he had been able to get out of Ray so far with a sort of wild excitement in his eyes, as if reliving the interrogation.

"According to Ray," Payne said, "he was specially trained by Omega to be this girl's handler, but there were nine other operatives being trained with him. He only ever saw one other girl, and I think that was by accident."

"You figure we're looking for nine different women?" Andrew asked.

"I'd guess at least four or five. It's possible some of those were backups in case they lost a handler. He remembered that some were reassigned to the base in other capacities at the end of training. But that's also assuming this was the only compound. There are no guarantees that there aren't other women out there somewhere being altered and trained. Omega's holdings are expansive. It would make sense to spread your assets around."

The group sat in silence for a moment while they assimilated the new information. Andrew shuddered to think of the women, like the girl in the holding cell, as assets going through the painful genetic transformation so someone sick with power could use them as a weapon to attack an unsuspecting victim with delusions of love. Andrew would have to be careful with the girl. Even if she did seem to eventually trust him, could he ever trust her?

Payne continued, an uncharacteristic seriousness possessing him. "The necessity to eliminate the women at the end of their usefulness was part of the handlers' training. Ray was pissed when his genomatrix failed to control you, Andrew, essentially putting him out of the program unless he could be reassigned, which wasn't likely."

"Unfortunately," Theo said gravely, "the compound where they operated was already abandoned when Faeder's men raided it. There was nothing useful left."

"Everything had either been destroyed or taken with them, possibly due to Ray falling off their radar," Payne said. "I would have waited until he made the call saying she was dead, but by that time, she would have drowned."

Theo nodded. "More likely, they moved after our little reconnaissance mission at the cattle ranch when they realized security had been breached. That's when we discovered their location."

"Your difficulty in Texas," Andrew said. "They have to know that we have their research now."

"Which, by the way, was also how we acquired the data on the genomic therapies used to alter the woman," Theo said.

"Don't forget the ARFID device they used to track her," Payne said. He loved gadgets.

"Either way, everyone at the compound is gone now," Theo said.

"The ranch in Texas," Payne said, nodding. "The compound in Colorado. Spreading around assets and pieces of the puzzle."

"Speaking of the ARFID device, I examined the one you removed from the girl," Wendle said. In the center of the table, he set a tablet with a photograph of what looked like a tiny circuit board so everyone could see. He looked at Andrew as if asking permission to go on. When Andrew nodded, he continued. "It's an amazing piece of technology used to track the individual's movements. However, due to the low amount of energy that is produced by the body, the tracker would have to be within a mile to pick up the weak signal."

"Certainly, an important bit of information, but not very practical for locating others like her—unless you know how and where to look," Theo said.

"The *how* I can do," Wendle said, tapping the tablet screen to reveal a complicated diagram. "Finding the right frequencies—I can rig a randomizer to search for them, then follow the ping."

"Like a police scanner?" Theo asked.

"Sort of. Maybe not on a large scale, but with some reverse engineering I can make you a short-range detection device," Wendle said.

"Good," Andrew said. "You'll work on that for us?"

Wendle nodded, his eyes sparkling excitedly. "Absolutely."

"Anything else?" Andrew forked a hunk of chicken from his salad.

"Well, what I can tell you about the genetic manipulation," Hector said hesitantly, "might give you some insight into their modus operandi."

"I'm listening," Andrew said, shoving the chicken into his mouth.

"Consider making a drink, say a Tequila Sunrise. You take a glass, add ice, tequila, grenadine, and orange juice. The drink would be a lot easier to make if the glass was filled with ice and tequila rather than rum and coke, right?"

Andrew smiled and nodded. Hector knew how to explain things so that everyone could understand, whether they spoke science or not. In not abandoning Hector to the dream realm, Andrew had acquired a friend. He knew Hector would give it to him straight.

Hector continued. "So how do you find the best glass to work with? They have to have access to a large number of young girls and their DNA profiles. Considering that the process of reordering DNA is likely to kill, I'm guessing, about seventy percent of the subjects, you're looking at a very large pool of girls, that unfortunately, won't be missed if they disappear."

Andrew set his fork down. "Let me just make sure I understand you," he said, shaking his head skeptically. "The people doing this, they are expecting to kill about seventy percent of the girls they do this to?"

Hector looked at Andrew grimly. "Give or take. Just the fact that it's a very new science implies there will be a lot of trial and error, and this is not a simple procedure. They're using a live virus to infect the cells with new DNA patterns. It's tricky." The room was silent as the import of his supposition sank in. This was no longer just a search for answers to what happened to Andrew's father, or an investigation of how Omega might be involved.

"Omega has to be stopped," Andrew said. Having lost his appetite, he pushed his tray back. The girl in the holding cell, who professed her desire to kill him at every opportunity—what she must have gone through just to what? Kill him? Andrew would find the people responsible and make sure they paid for their crimes.

Theo looked at his hands as one rubbed absently across the other, as if his thoughts might materialize into an answer there. "Omega has large holdings in hospitals, but I can't imagine a large number of girls could go missing without someone noticing."

"So...what? We're looking for a large population of expendable girls?" Payne asked. Andrew winced as he said *expendable*. "Girls no one would miss?"

"I'd focus on any holdings Omega has that service homeless shelters or free clinics...even juvenile homes or prisons," Hector suggested. He'd obviously given this a lot of thought. "Look at places that require a physical, or some other means of acquiring sterile DNA samples. The larger the number screened, the easier it would be to find matches to the desired genome."

"They'll be more careful, that's for sure," Payne said. "It still doesn't make sense that they would target Andrew. But the real question is who's next?"

"Who's next, indeed? If we are looking for more than one girl," Theo said, "we must consider the tactical probabilities. Were the girls released on their missions at the same time or one at a time? If they were released one at a time, they might be less noticeable by people watching, like us. But if Omega thought they were already exposed, they would prefer a blitz, hoping that it would spread their enemies' resources too thin, and at least some of their genomatrixes would reach their targets. Unfortunately, we have no way of knowing their strategy. And you're right, Payne, it would help if we knew specific targets."

"It's doubtful we'll get any additional information from the girl since it seems her handler Ray informed her of things strictly on a need-to-know basis," Payne said. "And he doesn't know as much as he pretends to."

"Payne?" Andrew asked. "Could you see about getting me some hair from Ray's head?"

Payne grinned wickedly, more than eager to fulfill his request. "That would be my pleasure."

"And when you get a chance, I need you to go into Colorado

Springs for me. I need some fuzzy slippers," Andrew said, remembering the girl's dream, curled up in the bottom of her closet hugging the bedroom shoes tightly. Perhaps if he could give her some of her comfort things, she would relax—give him what he needed.

"What size do you wear?" Payne asked with a smirk on his face.

"For the girl," Andrew qualified. "You figure it out."

"One other thing," Theo said. "It seems the girls are carefully tailored to their marks in every detail. Payne learned something else from Ray that I think will interest you. You'd think a girl like this had been educated in every skill needed to take down a mark. There's one thing we know she didn't have firsthand experience with."

"And?" Andrew asked. "What is that?"

Payne chuckled. "She's still got..." He stabbed a cherry from Andrew's pie with his knife and waved it around suggestively.

Theo frowned at Payne. "It seems Omega had the impression that you have a reputation with the girls, Andrew. A preference, shall we say? Specifically," he cleared his throat, "nice girls."

Andrew's back stiffened as he placed his palms on the table to steady his irritation. "What are you talking about?"

Theo picked up his coffee and took a sip, studying Andrew's reaction over the lip of his mug. "Social media from when you were in college had some particular things to say about your...preferences."

"College? What social media?" Andrew said incredulously, trying to think what might be out there.

"We did an internet search for your name," Payne interjected. Practically the only thing we could find was posts by a girl calling herself Cinders Valentine."

Theo continued. "She indicated you had a thing for deflowering girls."

"I've never heard of a Cinders Valentine, and sure as hell never dated one. And I swear I never took anything that wasn't offered. By senior year I was dating one girl exclusively," he flinched as he thought of Talia, "and I haven't dated anyone seriously since she broke up with me." He shook his head. *This is ludicrous*, he thought. "I know I made a few mistakes in college, maybe more than a few, but I never... I wouldn't... I swear I don't know a Cinders Valentine."

Payne looked at Theo expectantly, and Theo nodded. "No one does," Payne said. "She was AI generated."

"Your proclivities toward something matter a whole lot less than the perception of your proclivities."

Andrew looked at Payne incredulously. Sometimes the words that came out of his mouth were shocking when taken in with the rest of him.

"What I mean to say is, they used what they could find to tailor this girl to you," Payne said through a mouthful of food. "And if that's all we could find, then it's probably all they could find, too."

So much had changed since Andrew's graduation and his father's death. "So why would this Cinders Valentine, or someone pretending to be Cinders Valentine, depict me as a..."

"Don Juan of the Vestal Virgins?" Payne asked, punctuating the words with his knife.

"This girl, Nicollette or whatever, seems, what, twenty at the most?" Theo asked.

"Her alterations may have taken several years," Hector said.

"She was a child when they took her?" Andrew watched Payne devour his cherry pie with his knife.

Hector shrugged as he thought about the question. "Probably. It seems they would have had to be planning this for a while. They would have had plenty of time to, well, research you."

Andrew clenched his teeth together, his lips a white line of anger. Now he understood his father's devotion to his work, a devotion that he now claimed as his own.

"Unfortunately, the website wasn't that difficult to find either," Theo added. "When Payne gave me the heads up, I had him obliterate everything about you on the web and set up a virus program to monitor and take down future posting. Should have done it a lot sooner."

"I haven't even had so much as a date since Dad died," Andrew said bitterly. "I've been blindly trying to fulfill my responsibilities, not even noticing that they were the wrong ones. I've been too busy picking up the pieces..."

"Too busy maturing," Theo said matter-of-factly. "You're not a kid anymore, Andrew. You're a man. That only strengthens the argument for making her pure."

"Pure man-eater," Payne laughed. Then pointing at Andrew's dessert plate, "You gonna eat that?"

Andrew shook his head and pushed his cherry pie toward Payne who took it hungrily. Andrew had lost his appetite. He thought about beautiful, refined, intelligent Talia he'd fallen for in college. Knowing her had changed him, in a good way. He respected her, loved her, saw her as an equal. She'd been a transfer student and hadn't heard the party boy gossip, or at least hadn't believed it. She'd chosen to see the good in him, and he'd willingly released the bad, for her. But he'd broken her trust, because deep within him he'd been unable to believe she could really love him. He'd invaded her dreams, but not the way she imagined.

"Your tigress may be a ball of fire," Theo said, bringing Andrew out of his thoughts, "but she's still naïve in some respects. That was for your benefit. The people we're dealing with do their research and do it thoroughly."

"It's probably the only thing that kept that tool Ray off of her," Payne said through a mouthful of pie, punctuating his words with his fork. "As long as she was useful to Omega, she was off limits to him. He's a real piece of work."

"Once they slated her for disposal, she was fair game," Theo agreed. "Her refusal of him sent him over the edge. She's lucky we were there."

"Now we just have to convince her of that," Andrew said. He tried to fathom the evil that would steal a child, use her until she was no longer useful, and then dispose of her as if she were a broken toy. Anger boiled in the pit of Andrew's stomach.

"It's interesting," Hector said. "Did you say that the only media they could find about Andrew was from Cinders Valentine?"

"Yeah," Payne said. "What are you thinking?"

"Well," Hector adjusted his glasses and looked up for the first time. "In today's day and age, it doesn't seem like that would be possible. It seems like someone else would have had to scrub the rest of his web presence for there to be nothing."

Andrew thought about it. He didn't use social media that much, but he knew a lot of people that did. It couldn't have been the only thing about him on the web, could it?

"And," Hector continued, "if you are fishing in a stream that only has trout, you're bound to catch trout. It's just interesting."

One of Theo's men arrived, interrupting their discussions with a report on the girl. She was ready to talk. After a few hours of stewing and trying to free herself from her restraints, she'd started yelling for Andrew. That had been going on for about a half hour.

"If you will excuse me," Andrew said to the group assembled. "Looks like I'm on."

34

BABY STEPS

The underground complex was an amazing feat of engineering; the tunnels and massive caverns that held the buildings had been cut from the granite of the mountain. Several buildings inside were three stories tall, and all the structures sat on massive metal coils to minimize damage from shaking during a nuclear explosion or earthquake.

Like a small city, the underground base had everything needed to survive for months in the event of a disaster. Besides the research and development buildings, the brig, dining facility, and the fitness center, they also had a medical facility, a pharmacy, a small base store for essentials, and berthing quarters for both officers and enlisted. They even had a barber shop which Andrew had visited that morning to tame his raven hair.

Hector's words nagged at the back of his mind as he walked to the building that housed the brig where the girl clamored for his attention. If someone had scrubbed his presence from the internet, why would they have left those lies about him there? Lost in thought, Andrew didn't notice Theo following him until he reached the cell door and Theo reached in front of him to unlock it. Andrew smiled his thanks to Theo, and stepped through the door, waiting until he heard it lock behind him.

The girl heard it, too, and lifted her head to see him.

"I understand you want to speak with me," Andrew said, his voice calm and gentle as if talking to a stranger in a supermarket about the freshness of the broccoli. "Ready to tell me your name perhaps?" he asked.

She frowned, "I'm hungry, and thirsty, and…I need to…you know…use the ladies room."

Andrew stood waiting for a few moments, trying not to smile at her attempt at modesty. He let the silence between them settle like snowflakes in a snow globe. His placid demeanor showed nothing of the urgency he felt. When she didn't answer his question, he nodded. "I'll have the nurse bring a bed pan," he said, and turned as if to leave.

She released an angry, exasperated growl. "Wait," she pleaded, struggling vainly against the restraints.

Andrew paused, and then pivoted where he stood, his face expectant.

"I don't know what my name is," she admitted.

Andrew turned again toward the cell door.

"I swear! I don't know! Please!"

Andrew walked to the side of her bed. "Explain."

"If I do, will you untie me before you need to change the sheets?" Her voice was desperate.

Andrew smiled, "If you are honest with me…And if you promise to behave…"

"Fine," she said, her voice quivering with anger. "I don't remember anything from before I woke up in the compound at Omega three years ago. They called me Gamma, at least until I got tired of it and started insisting they call me Lex. I got that name from a book I read while I was there."

"Gamma, as in the third letter of the Greek alphabet?"

"I guess. I don't know. But would you please let me up?"

"You promise?"

"I promise, I promise! Just let me off this bed!" She was close to hysterics, and he was sure her bladder must be about to burst from the pained look on her face. He unbuckled the restraints on her wrists and ankles and then stood back. She jumped from the bed and circled to the toilet behind a half wall in the cell. "A little privacy would be nice," she said angrily.

"That wasn't part of the deal," Andrew said, but he retreated to the cell door anyway. Theo waited there for him, key in hand, but Andrew motioned to him not to unlock the door. "Some food," he whispered.

Theo nodded and motioned for one of his men to come near.

"You should come out," Theo said as the sound of running water from the sink echoed in the cell. "You're not safe in there."

"Not yet," Andrew said.

"Never turn your back on her," Theo said, nodding toward the girl. He placed one hand on his sidearm. "It's bad for your health."

Andrew turned back to the cell and the girl who had no name. She stood in the middle of the room, her eyes sizing him up as if she had changed her mind about her promise, but she didn't move. The nurses had dressed her in military issue grey shorts and t-shirt. Her golden-brown hair fell softly about the curves of her face and down over her shoulders. Her bare feet gripped the floor in a defensive stance as she waited for his next move.

They regarded one another for a few minutes until Andrew finally filled the space between them with the sound of his voice. "Victoria and Nicolette don't seem to suit you, and certainly not Gamma. And Lex, while it may be your preferred name, is perhaps a little too close to your old life. May I call you Lexie, for new beginnings?"

She shrugged, "Whatever."

Andrew nodded. He didn't want her to hold onto personas from her life with Omega. If Lex felt right to her, he would use it, but in his own way. "Lexie it is. Good. This is progress."

"What do you want?" she asked.

It was Andrew's turn to shrug. An amused grin skipped across his face, "I'd kind of like to know why you'd rather kill me than talk to me. I mean, we'd never met before that night at the bar, had we? You don't even know me."

"You destroyed my life," she said, each word an accusation

tipped with anger. "Because of you I have nothing."

"You came after me, remember?"

The girl's eyes narrowed, but she said nothing.

"I hardly think it's fair to blame me for something *you* did. But…if you are looking for someone to blame, maybe you should blame Omega. It was Omega that stole your life from you, and their scientists who reprogrammed your genome."

Her eyes momentarily lost their anger as his words piqued her interest, but she didn't take them off of Andrew. "What do you mean?"

"You don't know?" Andrew asked, genuinely surprised.

"Know what?"

Theo cleared his throat. Andrew backed to the door, his hand extended, but he didn't take his eyes off the girl—Lexie. Theo passed a bag of food and a diet soda through the bars. "Hungry?" Andrew asked, carrying the food and drink toward the small table and bench seats that were bolted to the floor. In fact, everything in the cell was bolted securely to the floor or to the wall. He set the food out, careful not to take his eyes off her, and sat on one of the bench seats. "Sit down," he said, motioning to the other seat.

Warily she approached and sat down. "Know what?" she repeated, picking up the bag of food and looking inside. She pulled out a turkey club sandwich wrapped in wax paper and carefully examined the contents before she took a dainty bite.

Andrew could see she was being careful to be decorous, even though she must be starving. "You were genetically…altered," he said, choosing his words carefully. "It wasn't so much that *you* failed to have the effect Omega wanted, as *they* failed to program your genome correctly to make it happen."

Lexie shook her head carefully as if considering what he was saying. "That's crazy," she said. "You make me sound like some kind of computer."

Andrew laughed dryly. "That's what I thought when they told me. But the intel is good. We stole it directly from one of Omega's newest acquisitions. And your genome *has* been altered. I had my own scientists examine your DNA structures and they had quite a lot of interesting comments about it."

Even with her dainty bites, Lexie finished the sandwich quickly, but she turned up her nose at the soda that had been offered. Andrew called back over his shoulder, "Bottled water?"

"Yes, sir," a voice answered, and footsteps hurried away behind him.

"Now," Andrew said, "your turn. Just what were you supposed to accomplish that night you infiltrated our party?"

She smiled a wicked smile and leaned closer to him across the table, "Would you like for me to show you?"

"No," Andrew said firmly, forcing his words to remain calm and his face indifferent despite her nearness. "Tell me."

She frowned. "You're no fun."

"Never pretended I was," Andrew said, amusement dancing in his eyes.

"I could teach you to be," she tried again.

"No," Andrew said, his demeanor becoming serious again, his voice calm but firm. "Tell me."

Anger flashed in her eyes, but she acquiesced. "You were supposed to like me. You were supposed to want me. You were supposed to give me everything I wanted."

"And what did you want?" Andrew asked. He thought he saw a slight blush in her cheeks.

She leaned even closer to him, her eyes dancing, and whispered in a thick, husky voice, "You."

Andrew felt the muscles in his jaw tightening and realized that it wasn't just his jaw that was responding to her words. She might not have achieved what her designers had hoped, but she was still a genomatrix, and she had been trained well. He could not allow her to act this way around him; she would have to learn that this behavior was unacceptable. If Omega could train her to seduce him, then surely, he could train her not to.

"Your water, sir," the voice said behind him.

He nodded his head, stood, and walked to the door. Theo opened it and Andrew was through before she knew that he was doing anything besides getting her water.

"Wait," she pleaded, her lip trembling, but he left without looking back and Theo locked the door behind him, shaking his head at the girl as if disappointed.

35

PAIN

The terrified scream of a woman ripped through the air and echoed off the close, dank walls of a cement cell. Ray was sure he had heard that scream before. But when? When he killed Gamma? No, she'd been unconscious when he pushed her into the pool with his foot, hadn't she? Someone else then. Perhaps from a horror movie, or perhaps from hearing it repeated over and over as he stood helplessly in the center of his cell. The sound was only one in an arsenal of horrific sound bites being used to keep him awake.

A pale orange light illuminated the six foot by six foot battleship grey room and its single occupant who stood in the center, his hands dangling heavily in the cold steel manacles attached to a thick chain that emerged from the darkness overhead. A small bead of water slipped its way, link by link, down the chain, descending like the slow, monotonous drip of an I.V. The cold, wet cuffs cut mercilessly into his flesh. Ray, feeling less human with each passing moment, had stood almost ceaselessly in this room since arriving at the underground base. Against one wall and out of reach, the wooden frame of a cot covered with taut army green canvas mocked him.

The chain allowed Ray some movement within the confines of his cement cell, but it was still cruelly short. The length appeared long enough to let him kneel, get off his aching feet, but in reality, the cold, damp floor avoided his knees by mere inches, refusing him refuge. He was forced to stand or hang hopelessly close to relief. Ray's feet were so cold that he marveled that they could feel anything at all, but the lacerating pain never dulled, and the water never stopped dripping. Often Ray's maddened screams added to the horrific sounds or broke the battered silence, for his torturer had no mercy for a man who would kill one of his own.

In the center of the cell, a small cistern allowed the trickle of water to escape from the bare room. It afforded Ray no such luxury, only the constant reminder that his life, his position at Omega, and his hopes of escape had, like the cruel water, slipped silently down the drain. Sometimes Ray counted the drips as if they might be minutes in the timelessness of his despair. Occasionally, and by no regular schedule that Ray could discern, a man entered the room and placed a metal chair within Ray's reach. He gladly sank into the icy grip of the folding chair and rested his legs as he was bombarded with questions. At first, the conversations had been brief.

"My name is Payne," the man would say.

"I have nothing to say to you," Ray would answer.

"It's unfortunate that you killed the girl. Very unfortunate."

"Leave me alone, Pain," Ray would say.

Payne would smile wickedly. "It won't be long before you're begging me to stay." Payne would then wrest the chair from under Ray and leave the room, taking the chair with him.

Payne was right. The longer Ray stood in the cold dripping cell, the more he longed for the man who evidenced his name to bring the chair, for just a short respite from standing. The longer Ray went without sleep, the harder it was to focus on the words Payne spoke to him. As hours wore into days without proper sleep, Ray's confusion grew. Then Payne would turn up the heat in the room and stop the dripping of water long enough for more questions. Ray slid so close to sleep, that when Payne shouted questions at him, words would tumble from his parched mouth that he didn't know were hiding there. Sometimes he wondered if they escaped to help him, so that he could sit and sleep for just a few moments.

Sleep.

"Were there others?"

"Yes."

Precious seconds of sleep.

"What was her name?"

"Beta."

The deceptiveness of sleep.

"Why did you kill the girl?"

"She was a liability," and tears of regret wouldn't come because he was so thirsty. If only he'd controlled himself, made sure Mr. Theodore Bailey wasn't a threat before he'd tried to kill her. If only he'd never met Payne.

When Payne left, the dripping water returned and the cold air chilled Ray's bones. Loud, twittering screeches of bats tore through the cell, and Ray knew the chilling sound bites had started anew. A cold bead of water slipped from his manacles down his forearm. His dry tongue sought the salty, metallic tasting drops of water before they could escape to the cistern. He shifted from ache to ache, and bit down on the urge to ask for Payne.

Ray closed his eyes in the exhausted darkness, tired enough to sleep standing up. But he wasn't allowed. The second his eyes closed and the draw of sweet sleep approached, the sound of a revving chainsaw shredded his nerves and a strobe light wrenched itself into action, bathing the room in quick bursts of white light. Burnt orange circles danced before his open eyes. He stared through the hazy circles at the two-way mirror on one wall of the room. Ray imagined Payne standing behind the glass, a wicked grin consuming his face.

Defiantly, or perhaps unable to stop himself, Ray closed his eyes again, giving in to exhaustion. More strobe lights flashed, and the guttural whine and hiss of an angry cat forced Ray's eyes open. Payne's arsenal of sound bites triggered youthful memories of Halloween, horror movies, and haunted houses in Ray's already tortured mind. Then the terror had been fun, dodging masked ghouls with chainsaws or watching an executioner lop off a fake head with a guillotine and then ask the crowd who was next. Now the terror was not so aloof, and the heads were not fake. The terror wasn't imagined. It was real, and Payne enjoyed it.

Ray winced as he shifted his weight from one foot to the other and sharp spikes of pain shot through both feet and into his calves. He licked at a new bead of water that raced gravity for the quickest way out. "*Water, water, everywhere, And the boards did shrink; Water, water, everywhere, Nor any drop to drink,*" he said quietly, quoting *Rhyme of the Ancient Mariner* that he'd tried to memorize in high school, and the weak laughter of a madman escaped his lips.

Ray's own words, teased like splinters from his mind had been added to Payne's sound bite artillery. His own cruelty accosted him. "And that, darling, is why you never go swimming without a lifeguard."

36

SICK SON OF A BITCH

Theo walked into the small control room full of Payne's computers and gadgets as Payne set off another volley of sensory stimuli. "How's our guest?" Theo asked dryly.

"Enjoying his stay in the House of Payne," Payne answered. His face was serious as his eyes flitted over the many screens and monitors. He twisted knobs and dials and tapped touch screens as he made adjustments to the living nightmare that Ray endured. "Is Andrew ready for Ray to sleep?"

"That's why I'm here. He said to give him about thirty minutes, and he'd be ready."

Payne looked at his watch and began making minor adjustments. He turned off the slow drip of the water and turned the dial to raise the temperature in the cell. As the cold air stopped blowing on Ray's crumpled figure on the other side of the two-way mirror, he raised his head and spoke to his reflection. "I know you're coming Pain, you sick son of a bitch."

Payne grinned balefully. "He doesn't know as much as he thinks." He twisted another dial and pale blue lights dappled serenely on the walls like sunlight streaming through water. On one screen Payne pulled up a list of sound bites he had been saving, ones he had recorded of the genomatrix since her arrival. Recordings of her saying things like, *Do not go gentle* over and over again, or screaming Ray's name, and sweeter things, like her entreaties to Andrew not to leave her. Payne fed the voice samples into the program and spoke into the microphone. The result was eerie. He flipped a switch, and his voice echoed around Ray in the cell. Only it wasn't Payne's voice; it was Lexie's.

"Why did you kill me, Ray?"

Ray's head snapped up, twisting from left to right searching for the source of the voice. Hopeful suspicion swirled in his eyes as he tried to gaze through the two-way mirror. "Gamma?" Ray asked.

"Why didn't you tell me there were others like me? Other genomatrixes?"

"I didn't know."

"Don't lie to me, Ray. The dead see everything." Payne touched a screen, and the sound of splashing water filled the room, followed by the quiet hum of a swimming pool pump.

"I'm sorry," Ray sobbed.

"You knew about Beta. You had to know about others."

"No. I swear. Seeing Beta was an accident. Keeping us separated meant if one person was compromised, the whole group wasn't."

"You were supposed to help me, Ray. Protect me."

"I tried. But the way you felt with Mr. Mosby. You were too dangerous."

"You didn't trust me."

"How could we? You couldn't trust *yourself*? That's when they knew. They knew you couldn't resist him."

"Who gave the order, Ray?"

"When I told the Chief how you were acting in San Antonio, he said it was time. I tried to argue, but he said it wasn't up to me—or him."

"Then who, Ray? Who did the Chief report to?" Payne touched a button and the sounds of waves lapping against the side of a pool joined the hum of the pump.

"I'm not sure. I never met anyone higher than the Chief," Ray said as terror mounted in his eyes.

"But there was someone. Who was it Ray? A name."

Ray searched around his muddy mind for something to give and came up with a single word. "Quin."

"Beg, Ray. Beg for me to help you."

"Please," Ray whined. "Please help me." Then his body convulsed with sobs punctuated by a raspy, whispered, "Please."

Payne flipped the switch to turn off the headset. He touched a few buttons and tapped the touch screen a few times and the sounds ceased and the light returned to the dull orange glow. "Now to crush the illusion," Payne said, grinning at Theo. "He ought to be just about primed for Andrew. I'll have him in the infirmary within the half hour." Picking up a dart pistol, Payne loaded a silver syringe dart with yellow fletching.

"You could just use a syringe," Theo said.

"This is more fun," Payne said. Then he flipped the switch to turn on the head set and left the room. A moment later he appeared on the other side of the glass.

Payne stood facing Ray, his eyes hard as diamonds, and just as brilliant. "If you wanted me to help you," Payne said slowly, his voice mingling with the one piped through the machine, the one that sounded like Lexie, "you shouldn't have killed the girl. Pity you did. She might have been stronger than you thought."

Hope faded to anguish and fear as Ray realized the voice of his savior was only that of Payne through the headset. He slumped forward, pitifully resigned to his fate as Payne raised the gun and fired the tiny silver dart into Ray's neck.

"You *are* a sick son of a bitch," Theo said admiringly, and left to inform Andrew that Ray was being prepared for his particular form of questioning.

37

CANDIRU ASU

Andrew lay restlessly on his back in his bunk, thinking about Lexie, the genomatrix, the girl who must have at some point been someone's daughter, even if she couldn't remember. Could that little girl somehow still be reached? Or, as Faeder believed, was there nothing left except a dangerous weapon. He wondered if Jon was wrong about her genetic programming, and if she somehow did have power to control him. She was beautiful, but he'd known many beautiful women. There was something more to her, something he couldn't put his finger on, something that he needed to figure out before he faced her again.

He couldn't let her get to him if he was going to help her, and right now, leaving her when she slipped into that seductress persona seemed the best way to teach her that that behavior was not acceptable. If he could train her to control that part of herself, perhaps something good could come of his influence on her.

He pushed the thoughts of her from his mind and turned his attention to questioning Ray. For the second time in his investigations, the name Quin had come up, first with Hector's dream, now more concretely as someone who might be high up in Omega, if not at the top. The name felt familiar, tangible almost, but when Andrew considered it, no new revelations came.

Andrew opened the envelope containing a sandy clump of hair. He pulled the hair from the envelope and ran his fingers over the wavy wisps, recalling the wicked grin that stretched across the whole of Payne's face when Andrew requested some of Ray's hair. Payne still wore that grin when Andrew returned from his visit with Lexie. *There* was a man who *really* enjoyed his job.

Though Andrew didn't need to feel someone's hair to walk with them, it helped him to concentrate, to focus on that person as he drifted to sleep. Other walkers used similar devices, tangible items that reminded them of the person they were seeking. His father used stones of different shapes and colors and sizes; the feel of them as he drifted to sleep reminded him of his errand. Other walkers liked to have an article of clothing that the person had recently worn or pieces of their jewelry.

Andrew rubbed his fingers again through the small lock of Ray's hair that Payne had brought him. He imagined the straight razor that must have come so close to scalping Ray. He also knew that this was the first night Ray would be allowed to sleep deeply in days. He would be an easy mark for Andrew, and hopefully easy to manipulate into revealing the other genomatrix Ray had once seen. Andrew closed his eyes and took a walk.

Night never seemed so dark as the space between dreams. Andrew traveled the inky pathways with ease, like a blind man sensing objects and doorways by the change in air pressure. Ray's dream was just forming as Andrew approached. Ray sat in a puddle of blood staring dumbly at his legs, or what should have been legs. From the knees down, his legs were shattered, his dingy pants in tatters about the remains as if he'd stepped on a land mine. Andrew wondered what would cause Ray to dream this dismal existence, or more precisely, what Payne might have done to cause this. These details he would leave for another night — another dream walk. Tonight, he pushed the thoughts from his mind and got to work.

With a few suggestion-laden whispers, the face of Beta appeared, forming out of the grayness of pre-dream, followed by the rest of her faultless body. Invisibly Andrew circled the projection, carefully noting every detail. A torrential blaze of red hair framed her ginger face and a fire as fierce as her hair smoldered behind her eyes. Every voluptuous curve of her body seemed to have been sculpted by Michelangelo, but she moved as fluidly as a waterfall. Andrew wondered if she was really that perfect, or if Ray's genomatrix-jaded memory made her that way.

Satisfied that he could remember her for the sketch artist, Andrew moved on to other subjects, particularly Quin. Whispering Quin into the dream brought no projected memories, just a pitiful, terrified expression on Ray's face.

"Please," Ray whispered.

This approach took Andrew nowhere toward the identity of Quin, so he changed his tactics. Andrew revealed himself in the dream, facing Ray and letting his presence sink into his weary eyes. "Who is Quin?" Andrew asked.

Ray snarled his lip at one corner. "I'm not telling you anything, dream walker."

"Perhaps you'd rather tell Gamma?" Andrew said, taking a step closer to the wounded Ray. "Oh, that's right. You killed her. Though perhaps for you, she'd make an appearance."

The suggestion worked. Beside Andrew, a projection of Lexie stood facing Ray. "Why did you kill me, Ray?" Lexie's voice quavered with accusation.

Ray flinched and looked away, back at his legs as if he might be able to figure out how to put them back together if he just thought hard enough.

Andrew didn't give him the chance to think about it. "Amazing what drowning does to a body, isn't it? The first signs to appear make the body look like someone spent too long in the pool: soft, wrinkled hands and feet. But it doesn't stay like that. The body and face start to bloat and take on an unholy color. Bloody froth comes from the nose and mouth."

The beautiful projection of Lexie began to change, slowly adopting the horrific description. Andrew focused on Ray, avoiding the gruesome figure of the apparition, but Ray couldn't help looking at her, watching the putrid transformation. "My Zombie Queen," he whispered, swallowing thickly.

"You did this to me," Lexie hissed.

"Drowning in a pool is nothing like drowning in a lake or river though," Andrew continued. "Did you know in the Amazon there is a tiny fish called the candiru asu that bores holes the size of bullet wounds into its victims and eats them from the inside out?"

The suggestion worked, and thin slivers of writhing fish began chewing holes into the decomposing girl and swimming in and out of the holes.

"Why Ray?" the corpse asked.

"I didn't want to," Ray shouted. "The order came from Quin!"

"Who is Quin?" Andrew demanded.

Ray shook his head frantically. "Quin is everyone and no one!"

"Where Ray?" Andrew asked. "Where can I find him?"

"Everywhere and nowhere," Ray sobbed, his eyes fixed pleadingly on the corpse.

There were no latent memories from which to draw an identity or location. If Ray had ever seen Quin, he didn't know who he was at the time. His reputation, though, was enough to make Ray tremble at the mention of his name.

"How can he be everywhere and nowhere?"

"Aren't you?" Ray asked, his blood-covered hands trembling.

"Is Quin a dream walker?"

But Ray's attention was consumed by the projection of the girl Ray had known as Lex, Gamma, Nicollette, Victoria and possibly other names. She stepped closer to Ray and pointed a finger at him accusingly. The words lisped angrily from her mouth as a tiny candiru asu swam out a hole in her cheek and back into her mouth. "You were supposed to protect me, Ray."

Andrew abandoned Ray to the horrific scene, leaving Ray to a night of torture of his own creation, and followed the dark pathways toward his own dream. Andrew could question him again later if he found the need. Tonight, he'd lost the stomach for it.

38

EVERYONE AND NO ONE

Ray hardly noticed as Andrew left his dream, so focused was he on the twisted projection of the girl that Omega had labeled Gamma. Candiru asu riddled her pale blue skin with bullet sized holes and silver slivers of wiggly fish swam through her skin chewing on her insides. Black circles drooped beneath her eyes like obsidian half-moons and bloody froth escaped one corner of her mouth as she pleaded, "Why, Ray?"

Ray tried to turn his head away, but he found himself frozen by the sight of the ghastly apparition. Stuck in a nightmare of his own construction, he felt compelled to look at her, at what he had wrought, the writhing, rotting corpse of someone who had once trusted him with her life. *What have I done?* he thought. "It's not my fault, Lex," he said, trying to reason with her, trying to vindicate himself of his crime. "You drove me insane. I couldn't help myself."

"Really, Ray?" the corpse sneered. "I'm sure that defense would hold up in court." Sarcasm filled the chasm between them.

Ray flinched at her words. He knew she was right. Regardless of how she had been altered, she was still human and what he had done was murder. He also knew that lately he hadn't avoided staring at her, had imagined what it would be like to be with her. He was guilty, and his own conscience convicted him. "You wouldn't listen to me anymore. You stopped respecting me."

The corpse laughed without humor, and as it did, fingers of writhing silver fell from her mouth and bored into her distended blue stomach. "Respect is earned, Ray."

"Hello, Ray." A voice spoke from the blackness behind his zombie queen. For the first time since his dialogue with her began, he forced his gaze away from her and toward the darkness. A towering figure dressed in a tailored suit walked casually out of the darkness and stopped beside Ray's projection of Gamma. "You wouldn't be feeling a little remorse, would you?"

"Who are you?" Ray asked. He searched his memory for the aged face with the prominent aquiline nose and came up empty.

"Come on, Ray. I think you know who I am. I'm everyone and no one." The man's eyes hardened to gleaming black marbles of wickedness.

"Quin," Ray whispered, the color draining from his face. He sat helplessly in the pool of his own blood as tears fled from his eyes as if they were too afraid to be associated with him.

"You killed the girl then?" Quin asked, pointing at bloated, rotting Lexie.

The ground in front of Ray shimmered, and golden sunlight reflected off the chlorinated water at the San Chritopher hotel. Ray watched as once again Lexie's lifeless body toppled into the water and lay at the bottom of the pool.

"Good, Ray. At least you got something right. However, you shouldn't leave the door to your dreams open. You never know what might wander into them," The corners of Quin's mouth twitched upward slightly. From the darkness surrounding them, unholy growls as deep as earthquakes erupted, drowning out Ray's helpless screams that only everyone and no one heard.

39

NOT CONVINCED

When he woke, Andrew called the base sketch artist to his office to try to capture Ray's memory of Beta before it dissipated. Andrew watched as the pencil slowly brought the genomatrix to life in grayscale. Like the battleship gray walls, everything seemed pale and wan compared to the Technicolor of dreams.

Andrew pointed to the sketch. "The eyes were a little rounder and more penetrating. The lips a little fuller."

The artist nodded and made adjustments. When he finished, the artist presented Andrew with the sketch. It was amazingly similar to the beautiful face he'd seen in Ray's dream, but the artist had failed to capture the charismatic glow that surrounded her.

As the artist left, Theo strode into Andrew's office, pulled up a chair, and eased into it. Andrew didn't like the look on Theo's face, pinched and hard, like he had bad news.

"You look like you pulled the short straw for cleaning the latrine," Andrew said.

"Almost as bad," Theo said sourly. "Is there anything about your walk last night that you'd like to tell me about?"

Andrew handed Theo the sketch. "We now know what Beta looks like."

"You sure?"

"It looks almost exactly like Ray's memory of her," Andrew said. "Just add a little more fire. And if there's a Beta, I guarantee there's an Alpha out there somewhere. But this isn't why you came."

Theo shook his head as if still trying to wrap his mind around something, but his eyes rested squarely on Andrew. "Ray's dead."

"Dead?" Andrew rose from his desk, closed the door of his office, and returned to his seat. "How?"

"We don't know yet," Theo said. "Heart attack maybe. According to the guys in the infirmary, he was still dreaming. His heart rate shot through the ceiling and then it just stopped. They tried for a long time to revive him, but with no luck. They're taking his body now for an autopsy. You sure there's nothing you'd like to talk about?"

"He was fine when I left him." Andrew swallowed, forcing the bile back down his throat. "A little screwed up, but fine. He was having a hell of a nightmare, but that shouldn't have caused his death. How was he physically?"

"Physically?" Theo asked.

"Just…he didn't have legs in his dream. He looked like he'd stepped on a land mine."

Theo grunted his understanding. "He still had all his appendages. So, he was fine when you left, and you have no idea how this could have happened?" Theo asked.

Andrew scowled at Theo. "I got what I wanted and left him dreaming…or nightmaring. But he was alive."

Theo held his hands up defensively. "You think Faeder's not going to ask you the same thing? The main reason I came was to warn you that Faeder's looking for you and he's all kinds of pissed. I don't think I have to tell you what capturing Ray meant to him. He's like a dog that's lost its bone."

"I appreciate the heads up," Andrew said.

"If you did have something to do with it, then that would be helpful to know before Faeder figures out that you didn't leave the base early this morning for a hike."

"I didn't kill Ray," Andrew said. "But it's good to know you'd have my back."

"I lost one Mosby. I don't intend to lose two."

"Do you think something like this happened to my father?" Andrew asked.

"You're the dreamer. You tell me."

What could cause someone to die in a dream? Andrew wondered. *If Lexie could throw him out of a dream, could she do this?* Andrew's jaw tightened, fearing the answer. "Was the girl..." Andrew shook his head, refusing to finish his thought.

"Was the girl what?" Theo asked, the edge in his voice sharp enough to pull the rest of Andrew's thought from him.

"Asleep?"

"No," Theo said, his thoughts shrouded behind eyes that carefully observed Andrew. "She was pacing in her cell like a caged animal, asking for you. You think she could do this?"

Andrew relaxed back in his chair, relieved that it couldn't be her. "I don't think she's aware of her dreams enough right now, but she's strong. Maybe there are others like her who have been trained to do it somehow...but I still don't know how a dream walker could kill someone."

Stroking the scruff on his chin with his fingers, Andrew replayed the events of Ray's dream in his mind. Nothing he'd done last night had been unusual—a little cruel maybe, but not without precedent. Andrew had let Ray's own mind create the horrors in his dream, with a little guidance perhaps. Ray seemed remorseful, sad even, not terrified to the point of death. Andrew carefully considered everything that had happened in his dream. It couldn't have been something Andrew had done. Or could it? A thought occurred to Andrew, a memory of a dark nightmare he'd had as a child, and he shivered with disgust and fear. "Unless..."

"Unless what?"

"Did Dad ever tell you about the dark ones?" Andrew asked, his voice barely audible.

"No," Theo said. "Not that I recall."

Andrew shook his head slowly. "They exist somewhere in the space between dreams. I had a close encounter with one when I was about eight, not long after Mom died. It followed me home, so to speak. As I was trying to settle back into my body, return to myself, it grabbed my ankles and began dragging me toward the end of my bed. I can't even describe the terror. It felt like pure hate and anger had seized me. I thought I was going to die. I fought to hold onto my bed, convinced that if it could drag me off, it would drag me away forever. I screamed and kicked, but it was so strong."

"What did you do?"

"I kept fighting. I'm not sure exactly how I escaped. The dark one was over me like a humanoid form made of deep shadows, and I could see its red eyes, like smoldering embers staring into mine. I felt like it was sucking my life out. While I was fighting it, I was also fighting to get home, to wake up. When I finally woke up, my heart was pounding so loud in my head that I couldn't hear myself screaming. I was covered in sweat, like I'd just gotten out of the shower. Then Dad was in the room with me, trying to calm me down.

"It was a long time after that before I dared dream walk again. Dad said that a dark one probably followed me back to my dream without me noticing it, and I was too inexperienced to know how to close the doors to keep it out. He started coming to my dreams, drilling me on how to keep dream doors closed after that. During the day he taught me about the dark ones. He said they feed off our fear. If anything could kill someone in a dream, I think a dark one could."

"So, you don't just think you were having a regular nightmare? Losing your mom so young would have been very traumatic."

"It's more than that. It's like they're the embodiment of nightmares. Some might even call them demons."

"So, you think one followed you to Ray's dream last night?"

Andrew shook his head again. "I don't know. They've never followed me to someone else's dream before, not that I know of anyway, and I would think by now I'd notice something like that. But they're the only thing I can think of that could really do that kind of damage to someone in a dream. If someone could harness that kind of power, or unleash it..."

"There'd be no stopping them," Theo finished. "How could

you catch them? There's no evidence to leave behind. No proof that they were ever there."

"They'd be the perfect assassins," Andrew agreed with a shudder. "Just the idea..."

"If I didn't live this stuff on a daily basis, first with your father and now with you," Theo said, "I wouldn't believe it. I'd still like to see what the autopsy reveals, but I'd be inclined to believe that anything is possible at this point."

"I wish Dad was here. There are so many questions I'd like to ask him."

Theo grunted his understanding. He sighed and rubbed his palms against the legs of his pants. "What are you going to do about Faeder."

Andrew put the sketch of Beta in his copy scanner and punched the copy button. The scanner hummed to life and spit out a stack of copies. "I'm going to face him. No sense prolonging the inevitable." He handed several copies of the sketch of Beta to Theo. "See that everyone on your team gets a copy of this. Make finding her the top priority."

Theo took the sketches and clapped Andrew on the shoulder. "Your father would have been very proud of the way you've stepped up."

"Thank you," Andrew said. "I'd like to think so, but I couldn't do this without you."

"You don't give yourself enough credit." Theo gave the stack of sketches a shake and left.

Andrew spent the rest of the morning trying to convince Faeder that he and the mongrels had nothing to do with Ray's death. At least Andrew had something to give Faeder. The sketch of the girl that Ray remembered only as Beta did little to assuage Faeder's anger. Though they knew what she looked like, they had no idea where to start looking for her. They didn't know her target or her handler. As far as Faeder was concerned, it was another dead end.

Given the dead end with the name Quin and the absence of leads about his father, finding Beta, or any others like her, was Andrew's only hope. Andrew was sure there must be an Alpha out there somewhere, too. He shuddered as he considered the possibility of a Delta, or an Epsilon, or more. There was a lot to consider. Besides what part Admiral Mosby might have had in sabotaging Omega's plans to control Andrew, and whether he might still be alive, Andrew believed now, without a doubt, that other girls were in danger.

Despite finding the courage to face Faeder and his wrath, Andrew devoted considerable time to avoiding the brig. While he grew bolder in his job and his abilities, he trusted himself less and less around the girl. Theo doubted him, too. Andrew could see the unease in Theo's eyes. What lengths would Theo be willing to go to in order to protect him from Lexie? And did he really need protecting, or was Lexie the victim?

Andrew launched himself into the search for Beta, avoiding Lexie as much to see if he was strong enough as for any other reason. By the end of the day, Lexie forced him to visit her by threatening to bash her head into the wall until her skull cracked if he didn't come. He grabbed the brown paper bag Payne had brought him from Colorado Springs with the fuzzy slippers and a copy of the sketch of Beta and walked to the holding cell where Lexie waited.

"A little dramatic, don't you think?" Andrew asked, as he approached the bars that separated him from Lexie.

Lexie smiled mischievously. "It worked." She walked to the bars and wrapped her hands around them.

He smiled. He couldn't help smiling. When he smiled, she glowed like the full moon just cresting the horizon. He set the paper bag on the floor and handed her the sketch. "Do you recognize this woman?"

Lexie's eyes lingered on the paper bag for a moment, then slid to the sketch. She took her time studying the details. "She's beautiful."

"Do you know her?"

"Am I not enough for you? Caught your prey and now you're moving on to the next quarry?"

Ignoring her taunt, Andrew tapped the top edge of the paper drawing her attention back to the sketch. "Your handler Ray remembered this woman as Beta, another genomatrix. I believe her life might be in danger. I want to find her. Help her, like I'm trying to help you."

Lexie tossed her head disdainfully. "Help? Is that what you tell yourself so you can sleep at night?"

Andrew took the sketch from her. "If you're not going to cooperate then I have to get back to work."

"Just like that?" she demanded, anger in her voice, but she shifted her tone to repentant silk when he turned to leave. "Don't you want to see me?"

"If you think of anything else that could help us find Beta, or perhaps others like you…"

Her eyes hit the floor, and her lower lip protruded in a pout. "Is that all I am to you? A genetic experiment to interrogate?" She spat the words at him like they were bitter.

"No," Andrew said firmly. He fought the urge to approach the cell, to comfort her through the bars. "You're a girl…"

"Woman," Lexie corrected.

"…woman" Andrew acknowledged, "that needs my help. You've suffered a lot."

"I'm suffering now. What am I supposed to do when you're not here? No one else will talk to me, and there's nothing to do."

She had a point. Everyone else had been given orders not to talk to her. She was like a siren, her sweet voice calling the young sailors to crash their ships into the rocks. More than beautiful, she was enchanting. Even with Andrew's strong resolve, he had trouble spending much time in her presence without wanting to give her what she wanted, within reason.

"Perhaps I could spend a little time with you each night," Andrew suggested. He put his hand through the bars and moved a stray lock of hair behind her ear. She closed her eyes at his touch, her breath quickening.

"You could spend a lot of time with me if you wanted."

Andrew couldn't deny he wanted to be with her, but he needed to stay focused. He needed her to accept him as an authority rather than a conquest. "I could come to you in your dreams."

Lexie laughed a combination of amusement and wickedness, "Give me a chance. and I could make your dreams come true."

Andrew shook his head disapprovingly and dropped his hand to his side. "Stop."

"Why?" she asked. Her gaze met his directly, curiosity and chagrin mingling in her eyes. "Why don't you like me?"

"I never said I didn't like you," Andrew chided. "But I'm not sure I've met the real you yet. In fact, I'm not sure you know who that is either. What kind of man would I be if I took advantage of your offer before you could figure that out?"

Lexie released the bars and turned her back to him, leaning against the cool metal. *That question got to her*, Andrew thought. *That's the crack in her armor.* And it got to him, too. How long could he avoid the feelings she stirred in him? How could he use her feelings against her and still respect himself?

40

FUZZY SLIPPERS

Lexie's heart raced. Andrew Mosby's words sliced straight to the truth. She didn't know who she was now, and who she used to be at Omega didn't seem like an option either. She thought about the night in San Antonio on the river walk with Ray. He said that she chose life under the strict rule of Omega. Why would she choose a life where one failure would require her death? And what had she lost in the process? Committing herself to Omega must have been important. Perhaps it still held a significance she could no longer see.

"Lexie." Andrew's voice, as gentle as a soft rain, washed over her. No one had ever spoken to her the way he did—like she mattered—at least not that she remembered.

She faced him again, unable to deny him. He stood just out of her reach on the other side of the bars. His hazel grey eyes met hers with a kindness she'd never experienced either. Even Ophelia's friendship had been tempered, knowing it existed only so long as she adhered to Ophelia's expectations. For a moment as Lex stood there looking into Andrew's eyes, she felt safe.

Andrew smiled warmly at her and handed her the paper bag he'd brought with him. "If I didn't care about you, would I bring you a gift?"

Cautiously Lexie pulled the brown paper bag through the bars and peeked into it. "Fuzzy slippers!" She pulled them out of the bag and hugged them to her. Had he known her affection for them or guessed? "You do love me."

Andrew laughed, and she soaked up his laughter like the desert sand craves the rain.

"I'm still not convinced that you don't want to kill me. So, until then, look for me in your dreams. I'll see you there." He reached through the bars and tapped her nose with his index finger, "And in the meantime, I'll send you some books."

Lexie smiled at him as he left, but as he disappeared into the maze of tunnels, the hope in her faded and the foundation on which she'd built her strength returned—her training. A few kind words and a pair of fuzzy slippers would not win her over so easily, but he didn't have to know that. She would reserve judgment, draw him closer, learn his secrets. She would fight the way he made her heart thunder in her chest, ignore the way his touch made her resolve melt, and she would prove Omega was wrong to doubt her.

41

CAT AND MOUSE

Lexie sat cross-legged on her cot brushing her hair as Andrew walked into the brig. On the bed beside her lay some of the gifts he'd brought, including his last gift of a composition notebook and crayons. She'd asked for a pen and spiral notebook. He'd brought the safer alternative, but still, she recognized the attempt to please her.

She watched him exchange nods and speak briefly with Payne in a voice too low for her to hear. They laughed as if Andrew said something funny before Payne unlocked the outer door with a key card and passed Andrew through. Lexie hated that Andrew could enter a room and not look for her eyes immediately, making her wait for his acknowledgement. Despite her best efforts to win him over, she still felt like a spurned mistress, fighting to earn precious moments of his attention while he held her at arm's length, literally.

Lexie studied him as she waited, anticipating the polite game of cat and mouse that ensued whenever Andrew deigned to visit her. Using the barest of supplies she'd gleaned from Andrew's visits, she tried to make herself more appealing every time he saw her. However, pretending to trust him was what lowered his defenses the most. The more she allowed him to feel in control of her reactions to him, the more he gave in to her. The more she pretended to trust him, the easier it became, as if perhaps, just perhaps, he was sincere, and it might really be possible to trust someone.

Still, she wasn't stupid. She knew he was manipulating her. But why? Why would Andrew invest so much energy into trying to make her avoid what she was feeling? He had the upper hand. Why not use it?

Lexie slid off her cot and took calculated steps toward the door of her cell. She wrapped her hands around the bars, smiling at Andrew as he came to a stop just out of her reach, a distance Andrew repeated with precision on each visit. Beneath her smile, suspicion stalked Andrew's every movement. He smiled, that sincere, amused smile that made Lexie's heart race.

"This is hardly fair," Andrew said.

"What?" Lexie asked innocently. She loved his smile, almost as much as she loved the feeling of electricity that coursed through her body at his touch. Lexie's hair cascaded down her shoulders in soft waves of burnished gold, inviting him to indulge himself. She tilted her head so that her hair fell across her face.

"It's not fair that you are so beautiful," he said, bringing a blush to her cheeks. He reached through the bars and pushed her hair behind her ear, the one touch Lexie had learned she could elicit with ease.

Andrew's white polo shirt hugged his muscular chest and squeezed his biceps slightly as his arm lingered to toy with her hair. Lexie forced her eyes away from the sculpted curves of his body and held tightly to the bars of her cell, lest she forget and reach for him. She longed to touch him, his arms, his chest, his face. She didn't dare lose control, having learned from experience that reaching for him would cut his visit short. She was determined to win this battle of wills, make him long for her the way she longed for him.

"Oh. I thought you were referring to locking me in here and never coming to see me," Lexie accused playfully.

Andrew laughed and crossed his arms as if to pin them across his chest as a physical reminder not to indulge too much in toying with her hair and thereby find himself falling for her. At least that's what she liked to imagine when she was alone in the cell awaiting his next visit.

"I can't spend all my time here. I do have to work," Andrew

said.

"I've heard that before. I don't think I've ever met anyone who works quite as much as you do, or at least as much as you would have me believe."

"The government never sleeps."

"And yet you do, dream walker," Lexie said ruefully. As crazy as it sounded, she felt him at night, so close to her dreams, and yet she could never find him.

Andrew glanced over his shoulder at Payne. "True enough."

"When will you let me out of here?" Lexie asked. Her patience waned as her days of incarceration waxed. Yet, as long as he continued to give her audience each night, she felt she had accomplished something.

"You know I can't. Not while you're still loyal to Omega. Not while you don't trust me."

"Perhaps if you gave me more reason to trust you than because you said so."

"And yet that seemed enough for you when Omega demanded it."

How easily he turned her own doubts upon her. It had all been there and she hadn't seen it. She'd never thought to look for treachery in her own family, the only family she could remember. They'd taught her that the bad existed outside the Omega compound; the bad was where they told her to find it. They told her the bad originated from her target, Mr. Andrew Mosby. Yet, how was he different from Omega? She struggled to regain her focus, to remember her mission, to not let him win.

She frowned and looked at his empty hands. She bit her lower lip and her eyes fell to the pockets of his black tailored slacks, searching for any irregular lumps in his pockets that might indicate he brought her something. "Perhaps there's something else you could give me now?" she asked sweetly. "Did you bring me a gift? The key, perhaps?"

"Answer my questions first," Andrew said, shoving his hands into his pockets. "Then we'll see about gifts."

42

SLIPPING

The way Lexie's eyes glowed with excitement when she caught sight of Andrew entering the room made his heart thunder in his ears. There was something intoxicating about being adored, and he did his best to hide those feelings when he visited her. Whether from her dreams at night, or in her cell in the evening, he found himself more and more drawn to her.

Andrew had exhausted most of the questions that Lexie could answer. As Theo and Payne suggested, she had been told as little as possible. In the short time that they had Ray for questioning, they had gotten far more out of him than Lexie knew. But the questions and answers had become a game between Andrew and Lexie, and he indulged in it, drawing out the time with her, keeping her mind occupied on the gift rather than on him.

Lexie's lips tightened into a thin frown like a child who had just been told she had to eat her spinach before she could get dessert. "What could you possibly ask me that you haven't already?"

He nodded and wrapped his hands gently around hers on the bars, causing her to gasp adorably. She was right about the questions. What could he ask that he hadn't already? He knew this, and yet he drew out the time, avoided leaving her, just the same. "Why me?" he asked, probing the depths of her eyes with his.

She glanced at his lips, trembling with want. "I don't know," she said slowly. "They didn't tell me."

"What did they tell you?" he asked, moving closer.

She closed her eyes and took a deep breath, letting it out slowly. When she opened her eyes, she shook her head. "A couple of years ago, Chief Jones, our fearless figurehead, called me into his office."

"Figurehead?" Andrew asked.

Lexie smiled wanly and shrugged. "He doled out the orders, but he didn't make the decisions. I asked him once who he was always talking to on the phone. He glared at me and told me I needed to remember my place. I never asked again. The Chief wasn't the kind of guy you wanted to cross."

"They can't hurt you anymore," Andrew said.

"No. I suppose that's *your* job now," Lexie said, her words cold as steel. Her haughty, accusatory tone was immediately replaced by her perfected sweetness, the momentary lapse only a blip on Andrew's radar. "How can you be sure they can't find me?"

"We took out the tracking device, and even if we hadn't, it wouldn't work this deep inside the mountain."

Relief flitted across Lexie's face. *Could her desire to return to Omega be weakening?* Andrew wondered.

"Anyway, that's when I first heard your name. The Chief said you were the key to the end. I wasn't sure what he meant at the time."

Andrew nodded his encouragement. "And now?"

Lexie shrugged. "Now, I see a long list of possibilities."

Just as he dragged out the questions with the promise of a gift, she too seemed to drag out the encounters by making the memories sparse and embellishing a little more on them each time they spoke. Lexie pressed her face into the bars, looking at him longingly. Andrew wondered if it was his attention or his slow, painful death that she longed to have more. Lexie was right in a way. She had gone from the proverbial frying pan to the fire. She was no better off as a prisoner of Sojourner than the property of Omega.

"Right before I left to meet you that first time, the Chief called me into his office one more time." Her eyes were drawn again to

Andrew's lips. Biting her lower lip between her teeth, she swallowed hard and continued. "He told me that controlling you would take out the final obstacle in Omega's way."

"Their way to what?" Andrew asked.

"I don't know," Lexie said. Tears began building up in her eyes, threatening to spill down her face. "He told me not to fail." The tears broke free and coursed down her cheeks.

Andrew broke his own rule, leaning in and pressing his lips gently on her forehead, and then resting his chin against it. They stood there for a long time, his hands over hers, his chin on her forehead. Each drew strength from the other as they stood as if their hearts were touching instead of their hands. Finally, he pushed back, smiling at her with a touch of sorrow. "I don't like it when you're sad," he said.

She slipped a hand from under his and stuck it through the bars towards him. He took a step back. She dropped her hand and looked at the floor. "If that were true, you would never leave me," she said quietly.

The space between them was a chasm dug by circumstance. "You know I can't stay," Andrew said.

"You could visit me more often," she said hopefully, looking up to see his response.

Andrew looked at the floor. He smiled when he saw her feet snuggly tucked into the pink, fuzzy slippers he brought her just a few weeks ago. His plan to guide her away from her training had worked, perhaps too well. He watched with amusement as she probed for things that would make him break his own rule of ten minutes and became skilled at them. The time he spent with her had stretched from ten minutes, to fifteen, to twenty.

"And Quin?" Andrew asked.

Lexie shook her head. "I've already told you I don't remember a Quin. Just Ray, and Chief Jones, and my nurse Ophelia. The others didn't talk to me."

He glanced at his watch and then stuck his hands into his pants pockets. "I couldn't bring you bottles of fingernail polish and nail files like you wanted." He pulled emery boards and a four-way nail buffer out of one pocket and a small tube of lotion from the other. "But I'm told that you can make your nails shine like they are painted with these things."

"Thank you," she said. As she took them from him, tears escaped her eyes and eased down her face. "Please don't leave."

Perhaps a couple more questions then," Andrew said, wanting to soothe her sadness. He searched his brain for what to ask. "Tell me about your parents."

Lexie shook her head. "I can't remember anything before Omega. I've told you that before."

Although he walked the perimeter of her unconsciousness every night before forcing himself into his work, he was loath to truly enter her dreams. So desperately she searched for him that it somehow seemed like an inexcusable invasion to enter her subconscious, especially after what happened with Talia. Lexie wasn't like other people. His clients invited him into their dreams, and other people were unsuspecting. Lexie could sense him and knew he was there, and he was convinced she wasn't at fault. He thought perhaps a few nights Lexie caught sight of him through the mists, perhaps even pushing the envelope of her dream, but if it was a good dream, he didn't stay long enough to find out.

He thought about the dreams he had glimpsed. Sometimes he watched her from a distance, learning about her likes and dislikes, her fears, and her passions. His favorite discovery was that she played classical piano, and he often suggested this diversion to her through the mists. Then there were the nightmares, always accompanied by that sound. Maybe, if he could access the source of that sound, it would be some clue.

"You may not remember, but you do have a memory, one that torments you. There's a sound of clinking glass in your nightmares. Do you know what it is?"

Lexie pulled back from the bars and wrapped her arms around herself. "I didn't for a long time."

"Something changed?"

Lexie stared at the floor and spat the words, "I heard it again in

San Antonio."

Andrew could see her withdrawing from him as brick by brick she built her wall of defenses. He had touched something very raw. Andrew wasn't particularly excited about the possibility of being violently thrown out of her dreams again, but perhaps a dream walk with the girl would help them both.

"Lexie," Andrew said softly. "Help me understand. If we can find the memory that caused the sound, maybe we can make it stop." Andrew could see the battle raging in her eyes, to trust or not to trust, to accept help or not. She was again the fierce girl he first met staring him down from the other side of cell bars.

Lexie trembled and shook her head slowly.

"Don't you want to know why you're having this nightmare? Don't you want to remember more of your past?"

"Of course, I do," she hissed, a tear running down her cheeks.

Andrew held his hand out to her through the bars. He was crossing a line, even for himself, but trust had to come from somewhere, and perhaps it started with him. "Let me try to help you unlock the memories."

She stepped closer, staring at his hand as if it held the answer to her fears, and then took it in hers. "Why?'

"Because I care about you. Because I believe my father cared about you and others like you. And because I believe Omega used a girl like you to get to my father. I just want to know what happened to him."

"And I'd like to know what happened to me."

"Then let me try. I won't do it without your permission."

"A syringe," Lexie said. "The sound was someone flicking the air bubbles to the top of syringe."

With what Lexie had been through, it was no wonder that sound held meaning for her. But it was something. It was more of a lead than he had had in a long time. Maybe it would give him some understanding of Omega that he hadn't seen before, and maybe it was nothing. Because he knew Lexie craved validation, Andrew gave her a smile and a nod. "It's something. We won't know what until we unlock the memory. It might not be easy, but I'll be there with you."

Lexie sank into the bars, her other hand reaching through to rest on his chest. Andrew didn't pull away. "Do you think my parents cared about me?"

"They would have been fools not to." Andrew wiped her tears away with his thumb. He kissed her softly on the forehead. "Look for me in your dreams." His fingers lingered under her chin a moment before he turned and left.

43

DO NOT GO GENTLE

After Andrew left, Lexie paced in her cell until her training took over. She sought calm in her routines. She breathed deeply, feeling the air flowing in and out of her body, filling her lungs and holding the air there, counting it out again to complete emptiness, then filling her lungs again. She moved from breathing into her yoga poses, muscle memory carrying her from one soothing stretch to another until she lay on the floor, a light sheen of sweat covering her body. Sleep would come. She would will it to come.

She got up, took a discreet sponge bath in the sink, drank a bottle of water, and lay down on the bed. She covered herself with the sheet, drew her pillow over her head to block out the light, and closed her eyes, controlling her breathing until she was completely relaxed in the floor of her closet. Picking up an armful of fuzzy slippers, she hugged them tightly to her and wondered how long she would be safe from an intrusion from Ray.

Then the clinking sound came, quiet at first, and then louder. She blocked her ears with her hands, but the sound only became more insistent. She rocked back and forth a whisper escaping her lips, "Please stop. Please stop. Please stop."

A light tap came at her closet door.

"Go away, Ray," she said.

"It's not Ray. He can't hurt you anymore," a voice from the other side of the door said. She knew that voice. A shiver crept up her spine.

"The dream can't hurt you either. You are safe. You've opened the door to your dream, but now that you are aware, you control what comes through it. You are in control."

She opened the door, but there was nothing there, not her room in the compound, nothing. She shrank back into her closet, under her clothes, and into the fuzzy slippers.

"Don't be afraid," the voice said.

"Andrew?" She felt panic growing, and the edges of the dream began to fuzz.

"Focus. You are brave and strong and fierce. A syringe can't hurt you. Look at it. Where did it come from?"

Lexie blinked, and she was no longer in her closet. She was in a hospital bed in a room with windows, a chair that turned into a bed, and a television on the wall. An army of stuffed animals lined the broad windowsill watching over her, and beyond them, a heap of fuzzy slippers. On a bulletin board on one wall there were cards and a giant poster that looked like it had been made by little hands with magic markers. In one corner, brightly colored mylar balloons rustled in the air blowing from the vent overhead. One said, "Get well soon!"

She tried to get out of bed, but she had tubes running from an iv-machine taped to her arm and one in her nose blowing air that burned a little. Suddenly her legs felt like they were being squeezed, and she pulled back the covers to see that her legs were encased in plastic sleeves that were inflating and deflating.

She blinked, and she was standing in front of the bulletin board, looking at all the cards. She looked back at the bed, and her body lay there, looking so young, so small. Her body looked so weak and sick that it had a gray pallor to it. She wanted to go to the little version of herself, hold her hand, and tell her it would be ok. She wanted to ask where her parents were, but the sun winked out and the lights in the room dimmed. Night now, she stared helplessly at herself, wishing she could do something. And then, again, she was in the bed, inside the body her younger self, the cool burning air pushing into her nose, the air socks squeezing her legs, the pain in her arm from the IV, and she remembered.

Lexie heard a whisper in the darkness of her hospital room.

"Do you want to live?"

Did she really hear the voice, or did she simply think it? She had considered that question over the past year and a half of doctors, needles, and false hopes. She had asked herself, over and over, what it would take to stay alive. How long she could endure the pain and nausea that had accompanied the onset of a disease that no doctor had been able to name? Always she had answered, *thirteen short years are not enough.*

"Yes," Lexie said without opening her eyes. "I want to live." She would fight for the chance to live, however small it might be.

She heard a faint clinking sound, one she'd heard hundreds, maybe even thousands of times since her worried parents first pleaded with doctors in the emergency room to help her. A fingernail flicked a syringe, bringing air bubbles to the top to expel them before injecting the liquid into her IV. Then a burning unlike anything she'd felt before entered her hand where the IV poured its contents into her vein. She didn't have the strength to flinch.

"I'm sorry, Alexandra. But I'm afraid you're not going to make it."

Did she hear the whisper correctly? Did she just hear someone herald her death? The pain in her hand told her this wasn't a dream. With supreme effort, she opened her eyes and stared at the shadow standing above her in the darkness. Yes, there was someone there. He was thin and tall, but beyond that, she could see nothing but the outline, backlit by the dim light from the hallway. Fear poured adrenalin into Lexie's body. With every tendril of strength she could muster, she reached for the IV where it entered her hand. Her killer's thin, icy fingers entangled hers, almost lovingly, and trapped them mere inches from the tubing until her strength ebbed and she could no longer struggle.

Too weak to remove the IV, and knowing the medicine was

already working its way through her body, she allowed panic to ease into her mind like a familiar friend.

Lexie forced out a hoarse whisper. "I said I want to live." Tears escaped the corners of her eyes and ran down her cheeks as the drug continued its work.

"It's a real shame too," the voice said. "Your parents are such nice people. They're going to take it really hard. But I have my own claim on you, perhaps even more than they do. What did Shakespeare say about medicine? *Poison has residence and medicine power?* It all comes down to patience and timing really. If Romeo had waited just a few minutes, perhaps his happily ever after would have come true. That's the thing about teenagers. They haven't learned patience yet. But I—I have the patience of a saint."

"Why are you doing this?" Lexie asked. Or thought she asked. The shadow didn't answer, just turned and left her lying there in the hospital bed, alone in the darkness.

As consciousness slowly faded, she heard the screams of machines warning of her impending death and broadcasting the exploit of the intruder that had come in the night. Surely they would see that she had not given up—that she was still fighting.

The pounding of feet running to her side shattered the night. Light flooded the room, shining through her eyelids, burning her eyes. She wanted to speak, to tell them what happened, to tell them she did not give up.

"I will not go gentle," she thought as she felt herself slipping away, ripped from life by the cold, skeletal hands of a shadow.

Lexie woke in her cell, a scream of anguish tearing through her lips and her heart. She curled into a tight ball in her bed and sobbed as the horror and the terror of what had happened to her now lived in her mind, not just her nightmares.

44

WHY?

Andrew woke, threw off his covers, and sat up on the side of his bed, trembling with emotions. He was angry—angry at a man whose face he couldn't see, at the evil that could steal a child from her parents. And he hurt, a deep throbbing ache for a girl who had been stolen and tortured, and for what? To target Andrew? And for what purpose?

In what God forsaken world could it be possible that someone would do such a heinous thing to a child? And if Theo and Payne and the others were right, were there others like her?

He grabbed a bottle of water from his nightstand and drained it. Then he woke Theo up and filled him in on what he had learned. This man, these cowards that hid under the name of Omega, had to be stopped.

45

CATNIP AND KRYPTONITE

A week had passed since Lexie's dream in the hospital room, but she still seemed haunted by the memory of it. She, like Hector, had not been able to return to the dreams that held the answers they wanted. The scene of the hospital in her dreams, despite her desire to learn more, and Andrew's attempts to whisper her there, was gone. Unlike Hector, however, she did remember the dream after she woke. Andrew could see that it haunted her every waking and sleeping moment.

He plunged his face under the torrent cascading from the showerhead. Having long since washed away the grime and sweat of the day, he now waited for the tension to dissolve and trickle down the smooth tiles into the drain as well. The effort was useless. He could stand there for a decade with no relief. His muscles trembled from abuse on the racquetball court with Payne, true, but the tension he could not escape arose from thoughts of Lexie.

Since his first encounter with her under the mountain, Andrew had taken Lexie the books he'd promised, curious how she would react to each and hoping she might find some hidden meaning within the ones he chose. From the first book, *Wuthering Heights*, he hoped she might come to some understanding about the danger of loving too intensely, though in all reality, it had been the first book he could find without leaving the mountain.

He'd given her other books after that, and magazines, and she had read them all eagerly. The last book he had given her was a collection of Dylan Thomas poems. Lexie read through it until she got to the page with *Do not go gentle into that good night*—the poem she had quoted so feverishly before he returned from his visit with Jon and more recently quoted in her dream. She ripped out the page with that poem and tossed the rest of the book in a corner. She read that poem over and over, sometimes even aloud to herself in her cell as if it were a puzzle to figure out.

To Andrew, Lexie was the puzzle to decode. Even without rouge and skin-tight silk, she was like catnip and kryptonite. Behind the façade of sauciness and sex, vulnerability lurked that made her more alluring than she had ever been as Nicolette or Diana. He wanted to help her remember, but he didn't dare enter her dreams all the way, not since being painfully thrown out the first time.

Andrew punched the faucet with the palm of his hand and the water slowed to a residual drip. He stood for a moment in the shower stall letting the beads of water travel down his taunt skin, across the grey tiles, and into the drain where his stress refused to go. Then he grabbed a towel from the rack, dried his hair and the beads of moisture still clinging to him, and dressed in slacks and pullover shirt.

As he entered his bedroom, Andrew flinched, sensing Theo before he saw him, feet propped up on the table in one corner of the room. In the palm of Theo's hand sat the square jewelry box with the ring that Andrew had procured from Colorado Springs that morning, his latest acquisition for Lexie.

"I understood the books. And the chocolates and strawberries and other trifles did wonders for her disposition. Hell, I should thank you for keeping her busy and in a good mood. But this? Don't you think this is a bit much?"

"How long have you been here?" Andrew asked, taking the box from Theo and shoving it into the pocket of his slacks.

"Long enough to know you're trying to wash away more than dirt. She's getting to you."

"I can handle it," Andrew said with more conviction than he felt. For the past few weeks, Andrew had focused on finding Beta or more information about Omega, but his mind always returned to Lexie and how he might reach her. He avoided the brig until nightfall, and then, with some minor trinket in hand, approached the genomatrix who prowled like a proud lioness just beyond the steel bars that separated them, never quite sure if he was taming her, or she was simply luring him in for the kill.

Theo hadn't moved. He watched with keen eyes as if searching for the cracks in Andrew's armor. "She's doing exactly what she's designed to do. If you won't protect yourself, then I will."

Andrew's temper flared. "It's just a ring."

Theo snorted his disbelief. "I couldn't protect your father, but I'll be damned if I let anything happen to you. You act like you've forgotten what she is. I haven't. I can't." Theo took the pack of cigarettes from his pocket and tamped them on the table.

"And what is she, Theo? She was just a kid when Omega took her."

"She's not a child now. She never will be again, no matter how many leather-bound copies of Peter Pan you give her." Theo tapped the pack of cigarettes across his palm and one thin, white tube slid out.

"Do you have any good news, or are you just here to bust my chops?"

"Nothing good. No new leads and we're stuck here babysitting a dead-end that wants to kill you."

"She's not a dead end. I just haven't figured out yet where she fits into the puzzle."

Theo tucked the cigarette into the corner of his lips, spun the flint on his lighter, and brought the orange flame within a breath of the tip.

"Don't light that in here," Andrew snapped.

Theo raised an eyebrow, his eyes locking with Andrew's.

Andrew sighed, his voice softening. "You know how I feel about cigarettes."

Theo released the lever, and the flame sputtered out. He took the cigarette out of his mouth and held it gently between his fingers. "Funny thing about these. I keep them in the box, and nobody cares. They can't hurt me or anyone else as long as they are tucked away inside. The second I let one out of the box, people start telling me about all the dangers involved. I know the warnings. They're printed right on the side of the box. I just can't help myself."

"That's different."

"Is it? This girl is your nicotine. Tell me you don't want to take her out of her box, wrap your lips around her, and set her on fire."

Andrew's muscles tightened. He wondered if Theo was right, that the girl was winning. The gifts Andrew brought her had at first been a way of making her feel comfortable enough to trust him. The delight she exuded with each presentation made him want to please her. Besides the fuzzy slippers, he'd taken chocolates and fresh strawberries, and when Lexie asked for strawberry jellybeans, thinking she had a particular sweet tooth for them, Andrew had brought her a bag. The next time he visited, her cleverness was apparent in her slightly pinked lips where she wet a jellybean and rubbed it on her lips like a child trying to look grownup. She was dangerous and fierce, but also adorable and naïve. Surely the girl she had once been still existed somewhere buried deeply in her psyche. But could he reach her before she won?

"I'm not giving up on her."

"Do you hear yourself? You've been working yourself to death, day after day, chasing endless dead ends looking for your father. Then you wear yourself out on the racquetball court with Payne. Do you think I don't know what you're doing? Chipping away at the energy built up inside. But it's not enough, is it? You know this has gotten out of control, and you can't even admit it. Why can't you get your head out of your ass long enough to see she's dangerous? You can't fix everyone."

"I don't believe that," Andrew said. He wanted—no, he needed—to give her the childhood that had been stolen from her, memories she seemed so desperate to remember. He believed he could help her, just like he believed he could help Hector, and just like his father had believed in every one of Mosby's Mongrels before rescuing them from their own personal cycle of the stupids. Why couldn't Theo see that? "Dad didn't give up on you. There's a reason you're one of Mosby's Mongrels. Where would you be if Dad hadn't believed in your potential?"

Theo dropped the unlit cigarette on Andrew's table and stood up. His eyes, hard and unreadable, held Andrew in place. "Just…take a break. Get out of here for a while—away from her. Go back to Las Vegas and check on your business, visit your sister, something."

"I'll consider it," Andrew said. "But I can't stop trying to reach Lexie."

"I hope you know what you're doing."

"If I don't, I'm glad you've got my back."

"It'd be a hell of a lot easier to watch if you listened."

When Theo left, Andrew picked up the cigarette and rolled it between his fingers. Such an unassuming little tube—just white paper, a filter, and tobacco. But it was more than that, because someone had added chemicals to make it more addictive, just like someone had tampered with Lexie's DNA to make her irresistible. Was she really Andrew's nicotine? He felt his control slipping away, and so the wisps of a plan began solidifying in his mind.

46

RING TRUE

After Theo left, Andrew steeled himself for his last visit to Lexie. He'd put off leaving Colorado, walking the knife edge of temptation with each visit he made to her cell, but Theo's words had hit their mark like wisdom-tipped arrows. He needed to put some distance between himself and the growing feelings Lexie evoked in him.

Andrew fingered the ring box in his pocket as his thoughts raced ahead of him to the cell where Lexie waited. He had traveled alone to Colorado Springs to buy the final token he would give her: a dainty blue topaz mined at Pikes Peak in Colorado, accented with a circle of tiny marcasites, and set in a white gold ring—the ring Theo found in his desk. Despite challenging Payne to a long, exhausting game on the racquetball court, showering, and the lecture from Theo, Andrew thrummed with excitement as he walked to Lexie's cell, his heart aching with the decision he'd made. He had fallen for her, and that was not acceptable.

When Andrew entered the enclosed area before her cell, Lexie rose from her cot and walked to the cell door. He stopped just out of her reach.

"Good evening, Lexie."

"You kept me waiting a long time tonight," Lexie said. "You give a girl a complex."

"I came as soon as I could," Andrew said, though he knew that wasn't true. "I have a lot of responsibilities."

"Right." Lexie returned to her bed, sitting cross-legged on it and leaning her back against the wall. "I forgot you were too important to visit your prisoner." She picked up a book and thumbed through it like she was looking for a certain page.

"That's not true. I'm not important. Finding out what happened to my father is. I would think you could understand that."

Lexie closed her book, but she still didn't look at him. Her voice sounded flat and distant as she asked, "What are you questions tonight?"

Andrew took a deep breath and let it out slowly. He wanted to plant thoughts in her mind tonight, not pluck them from her. "Have you ever thought what you'd like to do if you weren't part of Omega?"

She looked at him then, as if caught off guard by the question. "No one I can remember ever cared about my wants."

"I do."

She dropped the book beside her on the cot and walked back to the cell door. She wrapped her hands around the bars and looked at him for a long time, perhaps trying to decide if he was telling the truth. "I guess I want what I always wanted. To remember who I am. To find my parents. How about you? What would you do if you weren't trying to forget about me?"

Andrew held his hands in his pockets by sheer force of will. Her words hit too close to the truth. "I could never forget about you, even if I tried."

Lexie smiled, a sad doubtful smile. "I would have thought the same thing about my parents, but it's like my life began with Omega until the night I heard your voice in my dream."

Andrew nodded understanding. "So, you haven't remembered anything else since the dream?"

Lexie shook her head, her hair bobbing around her face in soft waves. "I can barely remember the dream now. Is that part of your magic? Showing people what you know they want to see? Giving them dreams that aren't real?"

"It doesn't work that way. I didn't give you anything you didn't already have. I just urged your subconscious self to go looking for the memory."

"If it's my memory, then where did it go? It's like it never happened. The dream suggested I had parents that loved me. And then, like a vicious joke, it was gone again. Just a photograph when I need the whole movie. Why can't I remember?"

"I have some theories, but I need to do some research."

"Tell me." Her eyes pleaded with his, and he didn't want to keep secrets from her. He wanted to give her what she wanted.

He shook his head a little, trying to dispel the fog that had gathered there, the fog that told him she wasn't dangerous. "They're just theories…"

"Please," Lexie said, and the power behind that one pleading word crashed over him.

"I think Omega did something to you to make you forget, to make you easier to control. I just haven't figured out what yet."

"Memory thieves? Sounds as ludicrous as dream walkers, and yet you're standing here. You are standing here, aren't you? This place…no windows, the lights always on."

"I'm real."

"It's horrid here. I could be trapped in a nightmare and not even know it."

Andrew pulled the small ring box from his pocket and handed it to her. "This is real."

Lexie eyed the box suspiciously before taking it.

"I hope you like it," Andrew said. "I picked it out myself."

Lexie opened the box. "It's beautiful," she breathed, slipping it onto the ring finger of her right hand.

"So are you," he said.

She dipped her head adorably, hiding her blush behind her falling hair. He waited for her to give him her full attention. While she admired the ring, he committed every curve of her face to his memory. It would be so natural to take her in his arms and kiss her, which was why he'd made his decision.

When she finally gave him her attention, he blurted out before he could change his mind, "I have to go."

"So soon," she said, her eyes pleading for him to stay. "But you just got here."

"No. I mean I have to leave. Here," Andrew said. "The base."

Anger and panic battled across her face and her body went rigid. "Why?" she demanded.

"I can't do my work from here anymore. I need to go where the answers are."

"What answers?" Lexie asked. The fierceness that had slowly ebbed over the weeks of visits flowed once again in her veins. Andrew wondered if all the work he had accomplished in taming the girl's ferociousness had been a waste of time. Lexie began pacing the short distance in front of her cell door, no longer tame, but a caged wild animal.

Andrew mentally measured the floor between himself and the cell bars. There was just enough space to keep Lexie from reaching him, a distance he had memorized long ago for safety's sake. It had begun to seem unnecessary, but now, her fingers twitched as if they longed to wrap around his throat and squelch the arguments that lodged there.

"I have to find out what happened to my father," Andrew said, repeating the words he had rehearsed, words with which she couldn't argue. Surely someone who also didn't know what had happened to her parents would understand. Andrew glanced at the guard desk. Theo was there, pretending not to listen. "We thought he was dead. I'm not so sure anymore. If there's even a chance he's out there, I have try to find him."

"You think Omega had something to do with it?" Lexie asked rhetorically.

"They came after me with you. It's not a huge leap to think they came after Dad, too."

"Just one more reason why you'll never trust me," Lexie said. She stopped pacing suddenly, turned her back to Andrew and leaned against the bars. Pouting, she was like a child drawing an imaginary line and sitting on the other side of it, daring everyone present to cross it and praying someone would.

"I have to find the truth," Andrew said gently. "You can understand that, can't you?"

"What happens to me? Done with me and moving on? Will you dispose of me too?"

Images of her handler Ray, how he had turned on her, flitted through Andrew's mind. She lost not only that relationship, but all the people at Omega she had known, and before that, the family she couldn't remember. "No, Lexie," Andrew said. "I'm coming back."

"You're the only reason they don't dissect me. When you leave there will be no one to stop them."

Andrew shook his head. "I wouldn't leave if I believed that." His words were gentle, sincere.

Lexie turned abruptly, her eyes accusing. "Then you are a fool!"

Andrew nodded sadly. "Perhaps. But what would you do if you were in my place?"

A tear escaped the corner of Lexie's eye, and she brushed it away. "I'm not in your place. I'm in my place, trapped behind these bars."

"I'll tell them to leave you alone."

"And how long do you think that will last? I'm not a person to them. I'm a science project."

"You're not a science project."

Lexie reached a trembling hand through the bars. "Please, don't leave me."

Her hand seemed frail as she reached for him. Before he would have walked away when she crossed the line of the cell bars, letting her know his expectations, but now, his hand came up to meet hers. His fingers wrapped gently around hers. Stroking her palm with his thumb he said, "I have to."

"I can't stay here without you. *I won't.*" The last words were no more than a threatening hiss, a last attempt to sway him.

He couldn't look her in her eyes; his resolve to leave might fail. He stood regarding her hand for another minute, then lifted it carefully to his lips and placed a whisper of a kiss on the inside of her wrist. Then he dropped her hand and backed away from her. She reached for him again, her hand small and innocent in the empty air between them, but he turned away. He felt a thickness growing in his throat at the thought of leaving her this way.

"I'll be back as soon as I can," he said, and left before she could change his mind.

47

SEEDS

Andrew's first destination after leaving the base was his father's last, at least the last one Andrew knew—the hotel in Los Angeles near the marina where he kept his sailboat before his disappearance. This search had been done before, but not sure where else to start, Andrew decided to give it another try. This time, however, he had a new weapon in his dream closet—the power of suggestion and Beta.

Andrew made a point of shaking the hand of every hotel employee that he questioned, as well as the hands of every employee at the marina where his father had charted the boat the night he disappeared. He spoke with anyone who might have some glimmer of information that hadn't been drawn out the last time. He even took the liberty to flirt a little with the female employees so he could touch their hair, get to know them better. Then he showed them a sketch of Beta, planting the seeds in their minds for him to cultivate in their dreams.

From the dozens of people to whom he whispered quiet words in the mists of their dreams, he found no new information at the hotel or marina about his father. However, he did find two people that remembered seeing Beta around the time that his father disappeared, even though neither was willing to admit it during their waking hours. Beta used the name Beth Atwell while staying at the hotel, stayed about a week, and tipped well with instructions that she was never there. This was all information that Theo and Payne would find very useful in the morning.

Traveling the dream world, Andrew found everyone that he wanted to question, except the bartender from the hotel bar on the main level. Given his occupation, he was probably just having a late night. He would make it a point to talk to him again tomorrow. Otherwise, he would let Theo handle the bartender, which would probably mean giving Payne free rein to interrogate him.

Tired from the mental exertion, his thoughts drifted to Lexie. He left the hotel employees far behind and let his mind travel to the feel of her satin hair between his fingers, the warmth of the blush in her cheeks, the strong warm pulse of her wrist under his lips. He had avoided these thoughts since he left Colorado Springs three days ago. But tonight, he was too tired to fight his longing to see her again.

As her dream came into focus through the mists, he could see her sitting in the floor of her closet on the Omega base, her knees hugged tightly to her chest, her head down. Quiet sobs shook her body. He was not prepared to find her like this, broken, hurting, and thinking of her life with Omega again. It hurt him to know that he had, at least in part, caused her pain. Wanting to warn her about the danger that Omega posed, he walked into her dream and knelt beside her, easing his hand on her shoulder. "Don't cry, Lexie," Andrew said. "I'm here."

Confusion swept over Lexie's face as she saw Andrew kneeling beside her in the closet, deep inside the Omega compound. "You can't be in here," Lexie whispered frantically. "Ray will find you."

Andrew laughed lightly. "So, you do love me," he said smiling, using the words Lexie had spoken when he gave her the fuzzy slippers. Then seeing this did not calm her, he continued. "Ray can never hurt you again. He'll never hurt anyone again."

The words slowly sank in, and her eyes widened. "He's...? Did you...?"

Andrew hesitated. How much should he tell her? Still, he couldn't stand watching her suffer. "He is, but I didn't. We didn't. He had a heart attack."

Lexie held perfectly still and for a moment, the edges of her dream fuzzed. "He's gone?"

"You're safe. He can't hurt you. No one can see me but you. I'm perfectly safe."

She looked at him skeptically but ceased her protests. The edges of her dream became more solid as she let the thoughts go and allowed his presence to harmonize with her dream.

"You left me," Lexie pouted.

"But I promised to come back." He took her hand and looked down at her long, elegant fingers. Every inch of her was beautiful from her French tipped nails to her dainty feet. Andrew wondered again if Jon had been wrong about her genome restructuring, if she really was fulfilling her purpose to gain control of his emotions, of his thoughts…of him. "Still, I'm not convinced you don't want to kill me," he laughed tapping her nose with his index finger.

The action seemed to wake up part of Lexie's subconscious, drawing her into the dream and out of it at the same time. She pounced, knocking him into a flurry of brightly colored fuzzy slippers, her body on top of his, her lips mere inches from his mouth, she whispered, "I'm a lover, not a killer."

Andrew couldn't help but laugh. Encircling Lexie's small waist with his arms, he rolled them both until his body pinned her to the floor. How sweet those lips; how easy they would be for him to kiss. He closed his eyes and rolled away and contemplated the mountain of fuzzy slippers.

"I'd better go," Andrew said.

Lexie sat up and put her hand on his arm. "Take me with you," she said with quiet desperation.

Andrew laughed at the thought, and then paused. He traced the curves of her face with the back of his hand, and she closed her eyes, leaning into the caress.

"Perhaps another time," Andrew said. "My alarm will be going off soon, and I could leave you stranded. It's not easy finding your way home, trapping yourself back into your body, once you've found the freedom of the dream."

She looked at him, confused, and he realized, even at this

heightened state of lucidity, she still didn't know she was dreaming. He smiled at her innocence, and lifted her delicate hand to his lips, bringing a warm red glow to her cheeks. "Perhaps another time," he said again. "Until then, promise me you won't cry. It's hard enough worrying about your safety without thinking that I've caused you pain."

"You worry about me?" She seemed pleased by the idea.

"Just promise."

"I promise," she said, still looking confused. She glanced around her closet as if she knew she had forgotten something but couldn't remember what.

Andrew leaned toward Lexie, wrapped his arms around her, and kissed her forehead; the confusion and misgivings seemed to drain from her in his embrace. Andrew stroked Lexie's hair, glad that she hadn't realized she was dreaming. The fact that she, for the moment at least, had forgotten to be angry with him was promising. Maybe she really was learning to trust him.

"Sleep now," Andrew whispered. "I'll stay as long as I can."

"I don't want to sleep," Lexie said. "I don't want to waste a moment that you're here." She laid her head against his chest and held onto him tightly. Eventually though, she closed her eyes, and the edges of her dream dissipated as she slipped deeper into sleep.

48

AWAKENING

Lexie awoke to the hard reality of an uncomfortable military bunk in the brig under a mountain. She plucked at the hole she had made in the pillowcase, a hole she had put there when it became clear that Andrew really had left her there at the mercy of Faeder. She tugged at the individual threads, teasing them out of the weft and warp, playing with them pensively.

The oppressive air—warm, thick, and sterile—pressed down on her, reminding her that she was trapped. Her entire life, at least what she could remember, had been lived under the weight of unseen chains. Her best was never good enough for Omega—was now, she understood, never going to be enough—and she couldn't escape. They always found her, brought her back, and punished her for her disobedience.

Except, what had Andrew Mosby said to her before he left? Ray was dead, and they had removed the tracker? She felt her head again, aware of the thin scar that had formed after her encounter with Theo that required stitches. Or had it been Ray that had made the stitches necessary? The pool? The last time she had seen him, he had tried to kill her. Unable to fulfill her designed purpose, she had become expendable to the one group of people she'd done everything in her power to please, and yet she had still failed.

She had failed Omega, but more than that, she had failed herself, and not in the way she would have thought. She held to the dream, the dream that Andrew had helped her unlock, the dream of parents that loved her. She held to the knowledge that someone out there had loved her and the coming realization that a history of failures didn't mean a life of failures. It meant a life of tries. It meant a life of individual moments in time that would keep evolving until she got more tries right than wrong. It meant that she was evolving.

She was becoming, not the woman she had been designed to be and told to be, but the woman she believed she could be. It meant that she would do whatever it took to keep moving forward until the bed she slept in didn't belong to Omega or Sojourner. She would keep moving forward until it belonged to her.

Even here, in the lowest of places, she found something within her that she had forgotten existed, and as she contemplated it, it grew. After years of pain and torturous survival, she realized she had finally found hope. If Andrew was right and Ray and the way he tracked her were really gone, what did that mean for her? What if freedom was really in her grasp now, and she was too afraid to reach for it?

Everything she had learned from Omega—and Andrew—was acquired skills she could use to follow her own path. Andrew had been there in her dreams. She knew this now. She knew it like she knew she was more than what others told her she was. She knew what she knew, and she would never, not for anyone, unknow it again.

She pulled a long piece of thread from the pillowcase and wrapped it around her finger loosely. She wasn't helpless. She didn't owe Omega or Sojourner anything. Andrew had helped her see that.

49

A IS FOR ALPHA

Andrew's alarm woke him all too soon. He was exhausted. The night's activities left him no time for the deep sleep he needed, but that would be ok. He didn't plan on staying awake long. Andrew would give this new information to Theo and Payne and then dream walk again in search of the hotel bartender. Surely the man had to sleep sometime. The need for sleep, like food and water, would eventually overwhelm everything else, drawing him into the shadowy dream realm. Then Andrew would catch him.

Eager to share all he had learned, Andrew phoned Theo and asked him to meet for breakfast in the restaurant beside the bar downstairs. Theo and Payne were waiting for him in the lobby when he got off the elevator.

"You look like crap," Payne said.

"Thanks. I feel like crap," Andrew said grinning. "That's why we're going to talk while we eat, and then I'm going back to bed while you guys work."

Payne rubbed the palms of his hands together. "Work," Payne said with a twinkle in his eye that made Andrew shiver. "I like the sound of that."

"Let's eat," Theo said, motioning toward the entrance to the restaurant. The lobby was too open, with too great a chance of being overheard.

After they gave their orders to the server and she'd disappeared into the kitchen, Andrew described everything he learned about the genomatrix Beta. He started with Doug, the sandy-haired bellhop who carried her bags to her room and then the vacuous redhead Paula who worked the front desk. "Either they're good at lying, or they are good at forgetting. I need to know which. And I couldn't find the bartender. Paula saw Beta go to the bar quite often during her week here. He must not have gone to bed last night, or else I didn't get a good enough bond with him to find his dreams. Either way, I need to locate him today, or you do."

The server brought their food, and they were quiet for a short time while they ate. "She was here the same time my father was. That can't be a coincidence," Andrew said.

"Didn't think it was," Theo said. He turned to Payne, "Doesn't sound like your *particular* talents are needed with the two he found. I'll take them. You concentrate on finding the bartender."

Payne nodded, his mouth full of food, but still grinning. His morbid enthusiasm both amused Andrew and made him nervous. He made a mental note never to get on Payne's client list.

"Lying verses forgetting—you're thinking it may be the same as Hector's memory after encountering Omega?" Theo asked.

"I keep thinking about what Hector said about hypnotism tapping the subconscious. What if our subconscious has a subconscious?"

"That's a little too deep for me," Theo said as he spread lavish amounts of butter on his toast. "But I trust you'll figure it out."

Andrew stabbed a hunk of scrambled eggs and shoved it in his mouth. The government's policy of keeping the dream walkers separated handicapped them. Faeder knew how to follow orders, but he didn't know beans about dream walkers or how to best utilize their capabilities. Who would truly understand and be able to discuss dream walking specifics with him on the level he needed? Andrew missed his father.

Also, he realized as his mind drifted to sweet smelling hair and fuzzy slippers, he missed Lexie. Andrew kept his encounter with Lexie to himself, preferring not to discuss his weakness for her. At least that was how he saw it. Her insecurity and desire, coupled with her ferocity, was intoxicating. She was like a beautiful tapestry made of fire and ice. He marveled that the two extremes could coexist.

Theo cleared his throat, bringing Andrew's attention back to the table. Theo and Payne were both looking at him, waiting.

"What?" Andrew asked.

"It's not like you to get distracted," Theo said, his voice tinged with concern.

"Yeah. What's up?" Payne asked. He bobbed his eyebrows. "Where else did you go last night?"

"Just thinking how good that bed would feel right about now," Andrew said, which wasn't too far off from what he was thinking. But not for sleep, for taking a walk, for the small chance that she might be asleep.

Theo picked up his coffee and took a sip, watching Andrew closely as he did. His gaze made Andrew nervous. Andrew cleared his throat and stuffed a forkful of eggs into his mouth.

"That cue ball head Faeder called," Theo said, breaking the silence. "He wants an update."

Payne did his best impression of Faeder, putting his hand on the back of his head and rubbing with a confused look on his face. Their disdain for the director of Sojourner was more than evident and Andrew couldn't help laughing at Payne's antics. Faeder had a very different relationship with Andrew as a dream walker. Unable to enter the dream world, Faeder was at the mercy of the dream walkers to gain their cooperation.

When Andrew refused to join Sojourner unless Theo and his men were assigned to him, Faeder's face contorted in a marathon of disbelief and frustration. Faeder openly resented the Mongrel's lack of discipline and abuse of the freedom that working for Andrew gave them. They were like wolves, circling one another. Andrew wondered how much longer Faeder would put up with his Mongrels. Being out from underfoot had its advantages. He needed Theo and Payne's help, but he couldn't help wondering if Lexie had been right. How long would Faeder respect Andrew's boundaries?

"Tell him it's too soon to know anything," Andrew said.

"You don't want me to tell him we've made some progress?" Theo asked, though there was something about his tone that said he approved.

"No. I'll call him later…after I sleep," Andrew said. "For now, let's just keep this to ourselves."

"Got it," Theo said smiling.

"Whatever you say," Payne seconded.

Back in his room, Andrew fought the urge to look for Lexie again. It was likely that she was awake already anyway. Instead, he focused on trying to find the bartender. This time he found him, and it was easy to suggest that the girl in his arms was Beta, the tall gorgeous red head with crystal blue eyes, instead of the shrill voiced, empty-headed Paula. Getting him to divulge additional information was more difficult as his current state of mind did not include talking.

Eventually Andrew pressed until the bartender gave up one more interesting piece of information and one more projection entered his dream. A few weeks after Beta disappeared, another dazzlingly attractive girl came looking for her. The bartender's memory of the events was clouded, but he remembered her name started with an A. Her topaz eyes were set in a wheat-complexioned, perfectly proportioned face. Framed by a rich milk chocolate tangle of soft curls, her face evidenced her intelligence and confidence.

Could she be the Alpha that they imagined came before Beta and Gamma? When he woke, Andrew would tell Theo to assign some of his men to find out what they could about her. Until then, he gave in to his exhaustion and sank deeply into dreamless sleep.

50

CONFIDENCE

As another day dawned over the air force station deep within Cheyenne Mountain, the sun pouring its heat out on the land above, Lexie woke with purpose flowing through her veins, her thoughts spinning like debris caught in a tornado. Part of her wanted to wait there in the heart of the mountain where four massive air conditioning units maintained a constant temperature. She longed for a constant, a known, a stability. She also longed for the possibility that Andrew would return.

Another part, an awakened spirit of strength and independence wanted to escape. The dream she'd had that night had been different—more substantial somehow—and the memory of it lingered as if it had happened. Had Andrew Mosby truly found her dreams even when he was away? And if he had, could he find her again? Yes. In fact, as she made her plans, she counted on it.

Days had passed since Andrew left. Andrew wasn't coming back to Colorado, not soon anyway. She knew that now. With Andrew gone, Faeder became a growing presence in her little world, a fact she loathed and, to a certain extent, feared. He came regularly with his bottle of antacids and questions.

What do you remember?

Besides Ray, who else do you know from Omega?

Why did they target Andrew?

What do you know about the mongrels?

Did you let yourself get caught?

Are there others like you?

She didn't answer his questions, though they made her think. *Were there others like her?* The session always ended with Faeder chewing a handful of antacids and tossing a few veiled threats her way. It was only a matter of time before he crossed the invisible line of Andrew's quasi protection.

Outside her prison, the sun burned hot in the sky, and Lexie longed to see it and feel a flower-scented breeze on her face again. Like every other day she'd spent in the cell, Lexie sat up and prepared for what lay ahead: more waiting, more watching, more questions. After bathing and washing her hair as best as she could in the sink, she dressed in her favorite clothes, a scoop-neck lavender t-shirt and blue jean shorts that Andrew brought to her on one of his visits.

A shower, she thought longingly. That was one of the first things she looked forward to if she could ever get outside of the mountain. But for now, she dried her hair, and taking a tiny lock of hair in her fingers, she made a braid about the thickness of cell phone charging cable, tying it off at both ends with thread she had pulled out of her ruined pillowcase. Then she broke one hair at a time until the braid lay loose in her hand, and she placed it inside the copy of Wuthering Heights that Andrew had given her.

She took the crayons that Andrew had given her and went to the small table that was bolted to the floor. She took out the black and white crayons and set to work drawing precise rectangles on the edge in a repeating pattern. She smiled. She would keep herself busy, and not allow herself to get bored.

The guards had been less than adequate since Theo and his team left with Andrew. She observed them cautiously, though always with a smile, as she carried out her preparations. The guards were young, and though they took their jobs very seriously, their inexperience made them easy prey for her wiles. She had, after all, been training for this ever since she could remember, both in physical prowess, as well as the gentler training like languages, cryptography, dance, music, repartee, and seduction. Still, they didn't know her, and these days had been refreshing.

Lexie spoke to the guards when they spoke to her, let them get to know the person she wanted them to believe she was. In truth, it was the person she wished she was and wished she could be that she showed to them—just a normal girl. She wanted to be the girl she was in her dream in the hospital, the one with friends and teachers who made her homemade cards and, most of all, parents who loved her. She wanted to be normal, but how could she go back to being normal after so much had happened?

She closed her eyes and let herself imagine a different life, one where she made her own choices, her own friends, and her own decisions about who she was and would be. It might not be what it could have been, but it would be better than what she had with Omega and Ray and everyone else who had made her decisions for her. It would be better because it would be her choice, not the choice Ray told her that she made. The choice she made was to live, not to sell herself as a slave to Omega.

Lexie wanted to make her own choices, and if one choice didn't work out, she would make another one. So, when the guard brought her dinner and lingered to talk to the normal girl behind the bars, she talked to him about her dreams of things she had never done, like going to the beach and wiggling her toes in the sand, riding a horse bareback and feeling the wind in her face, falling asleep in a hammock after finishing a satisfying book, playing a grand piano that she owned in a room flooded with sunlight from windows on all sides with no one listening or making judgements. She would be just herself with the freedom to choose who that was.

"You sound like you need a vacation," one guard said.

"A real vacation would be amazing," she answered with a sigh, remembering fresh guacamole on the River Walk in San Antonio. But she needed more than just time away. She needed freedom. "A vacation where I get to choose where I go, what I do, and when I do it."

The cell bars and the entire underground base still stood

between her and freedom. Escape seemed impossible, but she remembered one lesson in particular that Ray had drilled into her: sometimes the best offense was not a show of strength, but rather a show of weakness. *Don't show 'em all your cards, Darlin*, he would have said.

The person she was as a young girl—the person she wanted to be again—had not been weak as Ray had intimated. She had been a fighter. She had chosen life, despite the pain and difficulty that choice brought. She had survived, and that brave child still resided inside her, giving her strength.

51

SUN

With Andrew far away, Lexie felt her confidence returning. Without his daily visits, she felt a barrage of emotions, first anger and frustration, then fear and sadness. It wasn't necessarily that his presence robbed her of self-confidence, but rather that she found it difficult to focus on her situation with him there.

As the days passed, she felt awake, as if she could think clearly for the first time in a long time. It was as if her head cleared, and she could see herself outside of the expectations and desires of others. Then—then—she began to feel alive...for perhaps the first time in her memory. Her courage and determination had grown each day as she paced her cell waiting...and she was done waiting.

Andrew—Mr. Mosby—made two mistakes: one, he verified that Theo had removed the tracking device, and Ray was out of the picture, and two, he asked her what she wanted as if it mattered. As she paced in her cell waiting, she had had weeks to think about what she wanted.

For the first time in her memory, she knew she could leave captivity and not be found by anyone, except perhaps Andrew Mosby. From somewhere within her, she felt a calm she couldn't explain and a strength that she hoped would soon carry her out into the fresh air.

When she woke this morning, just like any other morning under the mountain, she felt just a little more alive. She found she knew things about the base and the people there that she hadn't before, as if she had walked the hallways and traversed the buildings as she slept. She wondered if Andrew had somehow placed these memories within her grasp. She held on to that thought—for who else could have known her location and cared about her freedom?

Just like every other morning, she prepared for the impossible. She thought about all the training she had been given at Omega in the history of warfare, for she was, as she saw it now, at war. Sun Tzu taught more than the art of physical warfare. Lexie had gleaned so much from her lessons in this regard. Know your opponent, their strengths, and their weaknesses. Know your options. Know your own skills and resources. Know your enemy's skills and resources and know how to exploit them to your benefit. Don't bring provisions for a long march when you can take them from your enemy.

If she could just get through the cell door, she could travel light and fast in unexpected ways. She took inventory of her current resources: crayons, paper, a couple of books, fuzzy slippers…. Those things would just slow her down or were simply useless to her. She chose her outfit carefully, something simple that would blend, but form fitting enough to fit under a uniform.

Lexie brushed her teeth, and then stuck her toothbrush in her back pocket. Somehow it seemed important, like this one thing might help her stay normal. Brush your teeth. Good girls brushed their teeth. She wanted to be normal. She wanted to be good. Finally, the ring that Andrew had given her she kept on her finger. Special, because it was a gift from him, she was still not above selling the ring if she got in a bind.

When the night guard walked in that evening, he didn't look at Lexie beyond a quick glance to see that she was still in her cell. He saluted the guard he had come to replace, placed a paper bag on the counter in the outer observation area, and looked at his watch.

What was he about, Lexie wondered.

The bag would be her evening meal. Since Andrew left, it usually consisted of a peanut butter sandwich and an apple. She expected the same. She'd seen this guard several times. *Efficient and unpliable*, she thought with a grimace.

This guard normally sat at the desk, reading a book, occasionally glancing at her through the monitors. He wouldn't even acknowledge her presence beyond the quick drop off of her sandwich and apple about 6:30, leaving it just within her reach outside the bars and quickly returning to the desk in the exterior observation room.

She looked back at the table where she amused herself playing piano in her mind. With her black and white crayons, she had colored piano keys onto the tabletop after Andrew left, and it seems to drive Faeder mad when she played during his questioning sessions. She smiled at the thought.

She played Gymnopédie No. 3 by Erik Satie to calm herself, Claude Debussy's Arabesque No. 1 to remind herself that beauty existed in the world, and Rachmaninoff's arrangement of Liebesleid if she wanted to block out the world with whimsy, the sound of the music calming and serene, playing nowhere but in her mind.

With her imagined piano, she drowned out Faeder's voice, the same questions, the same swearing, and she said nothing. She played a silent piano and made symphonies in her head. He didn't deserve her answers. He wouldn't believe her even if she told him the truth. She only had one desire. Escape.

Tonight, Faeder didn't come. Tonight, the guard paced, looked at his watch, glanced at her, and paced some more. Lexie watched him warily in her peripheral vision while she played Schubert's Serenade. Five minutes into his pacing, another young soldier entered the exterior observation room. After a quick exchange between the two, including pointing toward Lexie and the paper bag, the first guard departed, leaving the new guard staring through the bulletproof glass at Lexie. She finished her piece, looked up from her crayon keyboard, and smiled her most genuine smile.

The guard nodded, one quick nod of acknowledgement. Lexie looked back at her crayon keyboard, stretched her fingers, and began to play Beethoven's Moonlight Sonata. She felt his presence, even through the bars and the glass. He watched her with what she felt was fascination. She supposed she must seem odd, her fingers pounding out a silent sonata, her body reacting to the mood of the piece, each crescendo, each surprising shift of notes. It was the most peace she'd felt in ages as the notes waltzed in her mind.

When the guard brought her meal, she paused her playing, but didn't stand. He set the bag just inside the bars and stepped back.

"Thank you. I think sometimes they try to starve me with these paper sack meals, but I am grateful to you."

"Yes, ma'am," he said.

"What's your name?"

"Gabe, ma'am."

"Nice to meet you Gabe. I see your mama raised you well."

"Thank you, ma'am," he said. "I like to think so."

"What's the weather like outside today? It's been so long since I saw daylight or felt fresh air."

"It's calling for rain, ma'am."

Lexie smiled a wistful smile. "Even rain would be glorious compared to being locked in here."

He nodded, as if considering it.

She looked back at the crayon keyboard and laid her hands on the crayon keys. She began another piece, this time Alexander Scriabin.

"May I ask what you're doing?" Gabe said.

"Playing piano." Lexie shrugged. "They won't let me have a real one, so I play like this. It passes the time."

"How long have you been in here?"

"Oh…I've lost track of the days," Lexie said, and she knew it was true. In the heart of a mountain where the lights never went out in her little corner, day and night slid into each other. Her fingers stopped moving on the table. Then she set her hands in her lap and looked up at Gabe. "I'm really sorry your friend stuck you with watching me tonight. He seemed anxious to get out of here. I can't blame him."

"Nah," Gabe said. "I don't mind. He'll owe me one. So, what did you do to get locked up in here?"

"I'm not sure you'd believe me if I told you," Lexie said. She shrugged. "I'm not sure I believe it myself."

"Try me."

"I was kidnapped from a hospital when I was young, then genetically modified to be a genomatrix."

"What's a genomatrix?"

"An influencer."

"An influencer?"

"Of sorts. An influencer of one person in particular. If I understand it correctly, I was genetically engineered to influence Mr. Andrew Mosby. It turns out I'm harmless to everyone except Andrew Mosby. And to be honest, I don't think that worked either. I'm essentially a failure. But Faeder wants to know what I know about Omega, the group that kidnapped me from my hospital room and altered my genes. So, I'm here."

"Sounds like science fiction," Gabe said.

"Yeah. Funny thing about science fiction, wait a few years, and it becomes science fact. I failed my objective, so my handler from Omega tried to kill me. He would have succeeded if not for Mr. Mosby and his mongrels." Lexie sighed and spread her hands wide in a shrug. "Faeder won't believe that I don't know anything, so I'm here until they either finally believe me or decide to do something else with me. It's the something else that worries me."

"You're pulling my leg, right?"

Lexie stood and walked toward the bars, toward the paper sack that held her supper. "You might want to step back. I might grow tentacles from my head and attack you."

Gabe snorted. "You're funny."

"Faeder doesn't think so. He thinks I give him ulcers."

Gabe nodded. "I haven't been here long, but I'm pretty sure everything gives him ulcers."

Lexie laughed softly, picked up the paper sack, and opened it. A peanut butter sandwich and apple lay ingloriously at the bottom of the bag, just as she predicted. "You wouldn't happen to have a cell phone, would you? I'd love to hear some music. Just a few songs with my dinner?"

Gabe pursed his lips as if he were thinking, then gave a nod. He pulled out his cell phone. "What should I search?

"Something new. Something fresh."

"There's a brand-new Indy band everyone's talking about. The pianist is amazing." Gabe typed a moment, then the sweet, dulcet tones of piano filled the room and floated into her cell.

She took a deep breath and let it out slowly. It had been so long since she'd heard anything other than incessant questions, the shuffling feet of guards when they brought her meals, and her own breathing. "I've never heard anything quite like it. It's delightful."

"Good. I hoped you'd like it."

She took the sandwich out and took a bite in the luxury of sound. Then a haunting voice began to sing, the lyrics filling the space with hope-tinged sorrow.

Fulguration fills the night
With an earie, glowing light.
Fierce the wanton battle cry,
Pierce the night and crack the sky,

Still, I hear your tortured scream,
In the wakefulness of dream,
Liquid smoke drifts on the wind,
Another journey at an end.

Will you mind, Willow mine,
If I hold you one last time,
I'll search my dreams until I find,
My truest love, my Willow mine.

Sing the flight of fancy now,
For all the lost, I take this vow:
I'll search my dreams until I find,
The sisters of the willow mind.

So beat your earthbound tribal drum,
Until your bodies become numb,
Release your hold on Earth's delight,
And drift in seas of Willow night.

Will you mind, Willow mine,
As I twist the hands of time,
I'll search my dreams until I find
My truest love, my Willow mine.
I'll search my dreams until I find,
The sisters of the willow mind.

The song was haunting, the voice even more so. The song
ended and left Lexie with a awakening question. For her entire
memory, Lexie had been groomed for one thing, and one thing only.
What if that one thing didn't have to be her one thing anymore? How
would that feel?

Lexie's heart ached, and she found as she took the last bite of
her sandwich that the peanut butter stuck like a lump in her throat and
her eyes were moist. This woman's pain, and her own pain, poured into
one huge void, one need for connection, one need for freedom and
understanding.

She pulled the apple from the bag unconsciously and shined it
on her shorts. Every night an apple. Not a pear or banana or orange.
Not a guava or passion fruit or cherries. Not even a plum or a delicious
wedge of watermelon. Always an apple.

Lexie took a bite and chewed, lost in thought as the silent music
still played in her head, reverberating off her broken pieces, making
them thrum. Gabe watched as she tried to swallow the bite of apple
and force it beyond the lump in her throat, beyond the unbearable
peanut butter pain, and her body refused.

She felt the little girl in her, the one who languished in a
hospital room but knew she was loved, and the Omega operative in
her, the one who had failed to please and been discarded like tras. She

felt both parts of her struggle to make sense of the person she had been and the person she had become. She felt both parts struggle to force her body to take in air, to continue to fight to exist.

Here beneath a mountain of oppression, would it be a simple bite of apple that would end both fiery, determined parts of her? It had been a long time since she could breathe fresh air, could fully fill her lungs with the illusion of freedom. Now, her body refused to breathe. She stood, and her hand went to her throat, tapping out a desperate plea. Her eyes sought Gabe, the young man whose kindness had been like cool water and whose music had torn her soul.

She stumbled to the bars of her cell, her body refusing to take in air. The feral part of her fought her body, desperately trying to take a breath, the heaves of her diaphragm battling against the lack of air. The edges of her vision darkened, and she sank to her knees, the tears flowing down her cheeks. She collapsed on the floor. Her vision darkened at the edges narrowing to pinpoint focus as her brain tried to hold on to consciousness.

She couldn't find the way out for the broken, terrified girl dying in a hospital room, not even in hindsight with all she had learned from Omega. She couldn't find the way out for the trained killer choking on a slice of apple on the floor of a cell under an oppressive mountain. She wasn't breathing when the guard shouted. She wasn't breathing as he rattled keys in the lock and flung open the door. She wasn't breathing as he knelt over her body and shook her, prying open her mouth to fish out the piece of apple.

She stopped thinking when his hands roughly turned her on her side and his hand pounded her back. She didn't think as the panic spread. She spat out the apple and took Gabe down in one motion with one hit to his temple. She didn't hesitate as she tied his arms and legs with the strips of pillowcase and tucked his body under the blanket on her bed. She didn't waste a moment as she left her cell and locked the door behind her.

She couldn't save either girl, both suffocating with realization that death of one sort or another was coming for them both, alone with no one left to care, looking for hope, the smallest chance at life, and grasping for it. She couldn't save either girl, as both died on the floor of that cell. But, taking pieces of each of them, she thought she could salvage something worth saving.

The moment Gabe played the song, she knew that neither girl would rise again. Neither would find the strength on her own to fight for the life laid out for them, one endless doctors and pain, the other a lonely, empty life of causing pain. No, neither would rise from that moment. The girl who rose would choose her own path with all that she had learned. The girl who rose would belong to no one.

52

SUSPICION

Andrew had barely taken a disappointed sip of the pungent coffee he had brewed in his room when the news came in the form of a frantic phone call from Faeder. Lexie was gone. They had searched the whole base. It was as if she had help. She had just vanished.

Andrew closed his eyes and rubbed his face with the palm of his hand, silently cursing himself for leaving her and Faeder for losing her. Evidently, a base like the one in Cheyenne Mountain had tight security when it came to people getting in, but getting out seemed to be another matter.

With only a moment's hesitation, Andrew took another sip of the coffee and dumped the rest down the sink. Then he stuffed his clothes back in his suitcase. Theo and Payne had plenty of information to keep them busy for a while. In addition to the knowledge that Beta had been there at the same time as his father, the bartender, after his informative dream, was now missing.

After calling the airport, Andrew met briefly with Theo and Payne to discuss his alternatives and then returned to Colorado Springs, leaving Theo and Payne to deal with the bartender, and then catch up. Once on the plane, Andrew closed his eyes, blocking out the noises, and slept, looking for her, but she wasn't dreaming. She wasn't likely to come out of hiding, but he still tried. She would have to sleep sometime.

The flight back to Colorado Springs seemed shorter this time, between sleeping and his mind staying busy, trying to piece everything together, though without any luck. When Andrew arrived at Lexie's vacant cell, he took inventory of what she'd taken and what she left behind. Faeder, as usual, hadn't touched anything in hopes that it would help Andrew find her faster. Sometimes Faeder's predictable ignorance had its perks.

Lexie had taken the blue topaz set in white gold that Andrew had given her before he left. Andrew relaxed, if only minutely. Perhaps if she took the ring, she wasn't unreachable. Then again, she might have taken it to pawn. The next thing he noticed was the worn copy of Wuthering Heights, the book she had read so fastidiously. It had been new when he gave it to her. He picked it up and flipped through it, wondering what parts of the book had held her attention so unwaveringly.

As he flipped through the pages, a thin braid of her golden hair caught his attention. Coiled neatly between the pages, the hair that he had touched so many times over her weeks of captivity seemed like an invitation. Threads that looked to be from the pillowcase she'd destroyed kept the braid from unravelling at each end.

He ran his fingers over the soft braid, the feel of it like electricity flowing through his fingertips. In the margin of the marked page he read the words, written in red crayon, "Time and Nikki wait for no one." Andrew smiled at the taunt. He couldn't help but think of the little red dress she wore that first night at the club, hardly a dress at all.

Hearing Faeder's heavy feet approaching, Andrew shut the book and tucked it into his breast pocket. Faeder shuffled up to Andrew, his hand rubbing the back of his neck, as if trying to formulate his words.

"I didn't expect to be back so soon," Andrew said.

Faeder's eyes scanned the things on Lexie's bunk as if expecting an answer to appear. "You needn't bother with the accusations. I spent the whole morning having my ass chewed over this."

"I trusted you to keep her safe." Andrew was shocked by the

impudence in his own voice. He didn't envy Faeder, not that he ever had. Perhaps the Mongrel attitude was getting to him. Faeder may not like Theo and the other Mongrels, but there was no denying they were good at what they did. The fact that Lexie had only escaped after they left the base had to sting.

"You found her once. Find her again," Faeder said through gritted teeth.

"And if I can't? So far, I haven't had any luck. It's like she's vanished from the dream realm, too." Despite her taunt, her invitation to him to find her, he wondered.

"Don't worry," Faeder said, reading his meaning. "She's on the run. She's still out there, somewhere. She has to sleep, and when she does, we'll have her."

Andrew nodded slowly, trying to ignore Faeder's use of *we'll* and how it grated his patience. "What if Omega finds her first?" Perhaps Omega had found her already, or she went back willingly.

Faeder shook his head, "She's too smart for that. Ray tried to kill her, remember? She's not likely to go back willingly, at least not until she has something to offer them."

"By something, you mean me."

"You're sure you don't know anything about this?" Faeder asked. "It's kind of odd—Ray dies, and then she disappears right after you and your mongrel flunkies leave."

Andrew's angry gaze stopped Faeder's line of questioning. "We had nothing to do with Ray's death. He was in the hands of your doctors when he died. Maybe you should question them."

"Believe me, I have."

Andrew didn't doubt it. "And why would I help Lexie escape? Last time I checked, she still wants to kill me. Wouldn't it make more sense for me to know where she is?"

Faeder grunted, but his questions seemed to have run out for the moment.

"How did she escape?" Andrew asked.

"We've pieced together what we think happened, though we can't be sure," Faeder said. He picked up a fuzzy slipper and then tossed it back on the cot. "We traced her path until she got off the base anyway. After that, she just vanishes."

"Hitched a ride?"

"Could have been any number of vehicles out there, including the fuel trucks that supply the base. If she stowed away in one of the trucks, she could be anywhere by now."

"Was anything missing?"

"Nothing major. Just a duffle bag and a woman's uniform from a dryer in the laundry room. Dressed in that, she probably could have walked right out of here before we ever found Private Hill tied up and unconscious in her bed."

"There wasn't a Private Hill on the guard list I approved."

"No. There wasn't." Faeder pulled his pill fob from his pocket, opened it, and grimaced when he saw it was empty.

"If he wasn't on the list, then how did he end up guarding her?"

"A lot of odd little things added up to her escape. We think she had help, but no one will admit to it," Faeder glanced at Andrew. His suspicions were palpable, however unfounded and inane they might be. "No one even saw her including Private Hill who was supposedly guarding her. He's recovering from a concussion and a broken nose, not to mention a severely bruised ego. According to him, he doesn't remember anything from the last twenty-four hours."

Andrew looked once more at the things laid out in her bunk. "Nothing is missing here except the ring I gave her, some clothes, and her toothbrush." Andrew guessed that even on the run, there were some basic things that a woman couldn't do without. He imagined her in some gritty gas station bathroom brushing her teeth in the dingy sink. "Do you have any theories on how she got out?"

"The officer in charge of making the schedule said he wouldn't have assigned Private Hill, but somehow, he was on the schedule. We did a bunk check for all the people on your list that were approved to guard her. One was missing and still is. We have people looking for him."

"You said a lot of little things. What else?"

"There was a small fire, an unscheduled sexual harassment

meeting, laundry done a day early, and one person who has never been late for duty during his whole career overslept. None of these things would have been too out of the ordinary on any other day, but put together... It had to have been an inside job."

Andrew sighed heavily. He frowned, both at Faeder's implications that Andrew was involved and at the thought that someone else might have that much power over the people on the base, Lexie included.

"I talked to everyone, and no one knows anything." Faeder said.

Everyone and no one, Andrew thought. He'd heard those words before, the night Ray died. He had been afraid of Quin—everyone and no one. Could Quin be another dream walker? If there was someone helping her, were they even inside the base or simply inside people's heads?

"Talk to everyone again, including the other dream walkers you might have had work with Lexie—especially them; let me know anything that they can think of."

"Other dream walkers?" Faeder asked.

"I'm not naïve enough to think you didn't have other dream walkers working on this. Ask them. Something Ray said." Andrew started walking out of the cell. "I think Quin might be a dream walker."

Faeder grabbed Andrew's arm. "And you're just telling me this now?"

Andrew spun to face Faeder. "It was just conjecture before. You always want hard evidence. I didn't have any. I still don't."

"So, I'm supposed to re-vet all my dream walkers because you have a hunch?"

"Do you have any better ideas?"

"Do your voodoo. Find her. Bring her back."

"And how am I supposed to do that if another dream walker is helping her?"

"You, yourself, said that's just conjecture. And most of the dream walkers in our program have been working for Sojourner since before you were born."

"You wanted my conjecture. That's it. I don't have anything else." And even though he did have more, Faeder wouldn't get it until he was sure that anyone working for Faeder wouldn't benefit from the information and put Lexie in more danger.

"The base psychologists say your Lexie will probably sow some proverbial oats before making any rash decisions. She's been a prisoner for her entire memory. She'll want to find out who she is, and who she was. We still have time to find her before..."

"Before what? She escapes and has a normal life?"

"Before she kills you."

"My team caught her and brought her here. You're the one who lost her. Maybe you're the one we should be investigating."

"And you're the one who left her. Why did you leave when you were making progress? She was getting to you, wasn't she?"

"I thought you'd be glad that I got some of the mongrels out from under your feet."

Faeder tensed at the mention of Theo and his men. "Don't avoid the subject, and don't get attached. That girl's a genomatrix. She's a manufactured weapon. An Andrew-seeking missile."

Andrew flinched at his dispassionate portrayal of Lexie, as if she was an object. "Her genetic alterations don't change the fact that she's a human being. Omega wants her dead, and if Omega wants her dead, we should want her alive."

"Sure. Just as long as you remember which side you're on," Faeder warned. "If you're not with us, you're against us."

Andrew gritted his teeth. Working with Faeder these past several months, Andrew knew he was strictly a company man. For the most part, Faeder was a good guy. But if his superiors said jump, his feet were off the ground before he thought to ask how high. He would examine every possibility, including the possibility that Andrew helped her escape. But Faeder seemed to be hanging on to that idea a little too hard.

"Again," Andrew said, pausing for emphasis. His eyes flashed like steel daggers, cutting into Faeder's. "I'm the one that brought her here. Why would I bring her here just to help her escape?" Andrew paused to let his words settle into Faeder's thick skull. "I know my allegiance. I also know she's a person, not a weapon of mass destruction."

"No," Faeder said, placing his hand on Andrew's shoulder. "She's a human weapon of pinpoint destruction. And the bull's-eye is centered squarely on your back. You'll do well not to forget that."

"I'm sure you won't let me forget." Andrew shrugged off Faeder's hand, trying to contain the frustration in his voice.

Faeder let his hand fall to his side and his voice softened as if he'd suddenly remembered that Andrew wasn't military and couldn't be subdued by a loud voice and a superior rank. "Humans make mistakes. If she's human like you say, she will make a mistake, and when she does, you'll find her."

"And then what?" Andrew said.

"And when you find her, you can make sure she's brought back in one piece."

"One piece?" Andrew connected the dots. "Tell your men to handle her gently if they find her before I do."

"My men? You might want to have that talk with your mongrels. Regardless, whoever finds her first, she's not likely to handle *them* gently," Faeder said.

"She's alone and on the run; she's probably scared."

"Cornered animals are the most dangerous. And I'd lay odds that wherever she is, she's in control. She made it out of here, didn't she? Be careful. When she wants to be found, she'll be found. You just concentrate on finding her before then."

Andrew nodded, his thoughts returning to the book in his breast pocket with the tiny braid of Lexie's hair. Faeder was what his father would have called *Brownnose First Class*, and as such, there was no real reason for arguing with him. His views would always reflect the feelings of the organization that supplied his paycheck.

Regardless of Faeder's allegiances and allegations, one question ricocheted in Andrew's mind. *What had become of Lexie?*

EPILOGUE

RAIN

Rain thundered on the tarp covering the military equipment on the flatbed trailer, almost drowning out the rumble of the eighteen-wheeler's engine and the whine of the tires on the road. Fresh rain-soaked air had called to her spirit, drawing her through the tunnels under the mountain and out into freedom.

As she had darted from one pallet of supplies to another toward the truck, Lexie's hair and clothes had soaked up the rain as if they had been as exuberant as she for the feel of it on her face. She hadn't minded getting wet. She celebrated it. Still, she slid under the tarp unnoticed and stayed there.

As dawn crept across the land, the rain slowed and then ceased. She threw back the tarp that had covered her and let the fresh air tug at her clothes and hair, drying them. She took a deep breath, filling her lungs with air, and smiled up at the open sky.

For the first time in her memory, she belonged to no one, answered to no one, could become no one, a face in a crowd indistinguishable from any other. She would become the woman she dreamed of being—someone normal and good and loved.

She had plenty of time to figure out who that woman would be. For now, she relished the feeling of the wind on her face, the scent of rain-soaked earth on the air slightly tinged by diesel, and the unblemished view of the dawn-saturated sky as the eighteen-wheeler thundered down the empty highway.

Where? That didn't matter. What mattered at that moment was that she was free to choose.

ACKNOWLEDGMENTS

Evolving Lexie became more than a dream, in of all places, a Taco Bell in a small town in southwestern Virginia where my first writers group met. For students at Roanoke College, the food was cheap, the refills were free, and the corner booth might as well have had our names emblazoned on it. There, hope budded, and storylines etched their way into existence. I am forever grateful to Danny and Sondra for those days, a lucid dream all their own. I'm especially thankful to Danny whose vision of Theo Baily forever changed Lexie's course.

Thank you, Hollins University, for seeing potential and giving me courage in a safe space. Every precious moment there helped me blossom, and for every precious classmate, I am forever grateful. Words cannot convey the appreciation I have for all the people who have helped me on my journey. I want to thank all my many writer friends, groups, and poetry club. I am so grateful to and for my professors, beta readers, encouragers, and fans.

This is by no means an exhaustive list, but these dear people helped bring Evolving Lexie to actualization. Thank you so much for all you have done for me: Danny, Kathryn, Sondra, Lucy, Tony, Trena, Dan, Janine, Amanda, David, Asa, Mat, Cassie, Mary, Bobbie, Mike, Hillary, Robert, Dean, Tanya, Chris, Andrea, Kerigan, Renee, Gisela, Nic, Nancy Ruth, Cindy, Jim, Beth, Eddie, Enrique, Renae, Andrew, Zachary, Sarah, Katie, Ashton, Christina, and Stephanie. Thank you for being *just* what I needed when I needed it.

It is with deep humility that I thank my author and perfector, the writer and editor of creation, for the gift of creating, for the joy of the written word, and for loving this blessed mess that I am.

Finally, I especially want to thank all my children. You are the dawn breaking over the horizon in all its splendor. Remember, joy comes with the morning.

ABOUT THE AUTHOR

Just Kris grew up wandering the woods of western Virginia with her pony, at least in the seasons after mosquitoes went back into hibernation. During the summer she hunkered under the only window unit air conditioner in her home with a fantasy novel.

Kris didn't start out as a good student or an avid reader, though she turned out to be both eventually. Her love of fantasy books began when her brother tricked her into reading *The Hobbit*. Her love of science fiction came a little later when she found a stack of secondhand copies of *Isaac Asimov's Science Fiction Magazine* at a library book sale and her mother gave her the money to buy them.

Despite the odds, Kris earned her BA in English at Roanoke College and her MFA in Children's Literature, Creative Writing at Hollins University. While at HU, she maintained a 4.0 GPA, completed a thesis novel and critical thesis work, was a runner-up for the 2015 Houghton Mifflin Harcourt Award, and was a presenter at the 2015 Francelia Butler Conference. She is very grateful for her time in the protected space that is the Children's Literature Program at HU.

Just Kris is just that: Just Kris. After a lifetime of being who she was told to be, she has settled happily into being Just Kris. She hopes you can respect that. If not, she's ok with that, too. At present, she is blessed, safe, and on the loose in North Carolina with her Just Tony and her dogs.

Now, in one brief moment of bravery, she brings to you her debut novel, *Evolving Lexie: Awakening*. To learn more about Just Kris, visit www.KrisWritesBooks.com